About the Author

Jack Bright is a geographer and an English teacher from the UK, resident in the Czech Republic. He spends much of his spare time taking part in endurance sports such as winter swimming, running, cross country skiing and mountaineering. A keen traveller, he has been on expeditions to remote locations in Spitsbergen, Greenland, Kamchatka and Alaska in both winter and summer. He has a degree in geography and is a fellow of the Royal Geographical Society. He has made 3 films about his expeditions and gives talks about his experiences. He is also the co-founder and race director of the unique Kryathlon event.

www.extremewinterswimming.com
www.kryathlon.com

Dedication

To the memory of Dasha, she would have been pleased with the result of the Bering Strait crossing.

Jack Bright

THE BERING PAPERS: AN EXTREME WINTER SWIMMER'S STORY

AUSTIN MACAULEY
PUBLISHERS LTD.

A CIP catalogue record for this title is available from the British Library.

ISBN 9781785544682 (Paperback)
ISBN 9781785544699 (Hardback)

www.austinmacauley.com

First Published (2015)
Austin Macauley Publishers Ltd.
25 Canada Square
Canary Wharf
London
E14 5LQ

Printed and bound in Great Britain

Acknowledgments

Thanks to Alexandr Brylin, Oleg Dokuchaev, and everyone in Russia and around the world who was a part of this. Special thanks to my colleagues at 1.PKO winter swimming club in Prague and of course my parents Les and Jane who have always been there for me.

"Bering Strait is one of the most treacherous waters in the world, (gale follows gale, and in this part of Alaska there are practically no harbours in which one can seek refuge.)"

Knud Rasmussen (Danish polar explorer)

Lost in the Bering Strait!

We boarded the zodiac, our team of 4, accompanied by Vladimir Nefatov, Alexandr Jakovlev (Alex) and Oleg Ivanov. Our driver was the ever reliable Leonid. When we reached the swimming place Vladimir transferred to the other boat with Alex, acting as starter and navigator for us. Oleg Ivanov, himself a swimmer was with us as an assistant and cameraman on this occasion. I had no problem with this as I had got to know Oleg well and he was a strong and reliable man. The water was cold, around 5c, but we were already used to it and the only nagging concern I had was about visibility, which seems rather poignant given what we were about to face. I was swimming before James [*the blind swimmer*] which meant attention was taken from me and focussed on James as he prepared. I didn't like it when I was some 30m from the boat with nobody watching me. I was slightly worried by this as I calculated my own risk assessment and concluded that I was in a hazardous position during this swim and exposed to more danger than usual. Well, I couldn't say too much, after all someone had to take that dangerous position if James was to swim and why not me? Craig was doing his part by being James' buddy swimmer, Paolo took the perhaps more unpleasant first leg so now I had to be in the danger position. The only comment I made was a very subtle "Please keep an eye on me as I was a tiny bit worried last time that nobody was watching me." We noticed the fog but it didn't seem too bad and it was only when we were waiting at the swimming place, watching the Nuala, Anne-Marie and Toks team go through their rotation that we noticed a rapid and significant change in visibility. Still no problems and Paolo took over from Anne-Marie. I got a photo of this and you could clearly see how the conditions were changing. The air was heavy with moisture, maybe 100% humidity and the fog was now descending on us and was as thick as candy floss or so it seemed. I prepared for my swim and went in as usual, this time taking a tag from Paolo. The water was around 7c and the swells pretty big. I put my head down and got into a nice rhythm, every now and then rotating my head back a little more than usual in order to keep an eye on the boat, a technique I am used to adopting back in Prague when swimming in the Vltava river and keeping an eye out for lone rowers. The only difference this time was that I wanted to see a boat. I panicked just once when the boat was around 30m away and the fog was getting thicker but luckily I never needed to do more than panic and my swim passed without big incident. I was worried about getting lost but it hadn't happened so all was well. I tagged James, and wished the guys well. I slipped back onto the zodiac and proceeded to get my merino base layer and then my jacket on even if it was something of a fight. I kept my swim cap on and felt fine, leaving my bottom half exposed, just putting on my neoprene socks and shoes. I felt I didn't need my soft-shell trousers. As was par for the course Paolo was sitting next to me shivering away and probably wishing himself away somewhere on the Med! It didn't matter; he was swimming well and making a large amount of distance with his long and powerful stroke honed over many years of water polo, competitive and marathon swimming.

James swam well, only needing his special megaphone for guidance once or twice during the 10 minute swim. We got them back on board and soon we were in position and ready to get back to Irtysh. This meant Alex in front, Craig next to Leonid the driver, me, James and Paolo in the back with Oleg hanging around behind us. Now visibility was quite low, less than 100m and sometimes maybe only around 30 metres. The sun could be seen poking through and its diffused light cast a strange haze over the surrounding area. Oleg and I joked about going back to the ship for sauna, girls and tea. Our spirits were high after another successful swim with James behind us. However, after a few minutes it became apparent that there was a problem, with Craig simply turning round and quietly saying to me "They (Alex & Leonid) can't find the boat." This is an interesting situation and at first there was no big panic. It is amazing how time flies in these situations. Oleg commented to me about the thick fog and I agreed. We stayed rather passive at first because our job had been swimming, not transportation or navigation. Then gradually as time went on we became more active, keeping our eyes peeled for signs of Irtysh [*the Russian naval hospital ship which was serving as our support vessel*], in fact for signs of anything in that murky white wilderness. Here was nature again playing a trick on us, reminding us who was in charge and who had the most power. The next few minutes saw the anxiety rise gradually and I soon had my mittens on and was thinking about the soft shell pants and a lot more besides, such as whether this would be my final immersion not just in the Bering Strait but in any water. We had radio contact which was fine, but in this kind of situation with the strong fog it is very eerie and spooky. We listened for the fog horn of Irtysh but in the sea it is very difficult to pick up the direction of the sound. At this point I asked Alex about his GPS and it turned out he had left it on Irtysh. I handed him mine and I noticed the look of relief in more than one set of eyes when I did this. I kept this GPS in my pocket only for emergencies. As I had said before I was working as a swimmer and not a navigator therefore this was just my personal GPS but whatever the purpose of it, the main thing was that we had it. But still Irtysh proved difficult to find. Finally after much work with GPS, radar, compass and radio we took a course of w110 which led us to Irtysh. I heard Alex say to Leonid in Russian "Priama kurz na karebla", (go straight on this course there's the ship). Sure enough a few seconds later out of the white nothingness appeared a shape and that shape proved to be Irtysh, an amazing sight. I said out loud a few times, "Irtysh", and started to love that ship more than ever, it now took on a female form and at that moment I would go as far as to say it was like a goddess, saving us from the clutches of the Bering Sea. All of us were pretty shaken up by this. I went straight to find Alex who had run off to his cabin to get his GPS! We exchanged some words and I asked him why he didn't have his GPS with him. He replied that he had forgotten. That was fair enough of course because mistakes happen all the time in all walks of life in all situations. The only thing that got on my nerves was that he said he wanted to help James. My answer to this was that helping James would have been to have GPS, as our team had James under control, had a system for swimming with James. I was annoyed because my thoughts about safety when swimming with James were being proved right. So much attention on him and then you forgot about other things such as other swimmers or in this case navigation. James was a big strong man and a great swimmer, his only problem was that he couldn't see. He didn't need a fanfare he just needed to swim and some basic help with logistics which was taken care of mostly by Craig. This time we had gotten away with it. At this point it is worth me saying that Alexandr Jakovlev is a good friend of mine and a very capable sailor, navigator and swimmer. He fearlessly spent many hours in the water and I didn't in any way feel any real anger at him for this small error. As I said it is a fact of life that things go wrong, the important thing is to learn from experience and move on, which we did. We went to the bridge to speak with Oleg Dokuchaev and others about what had happened. If we thought that we had had an adrenaline filled trip, well there was more to come as the next boat also came back and a GPS mark had been made with the swim stopped by the starter and navigator Vladimir Nefatov. The reason was of course the thick fog but the story was more interesting than that. I got it from Zdeněk who had been on the boat behind us, indeed Zdeněk himself had taken the baton from James and Craig. After making his swim Zdeněk handed over to one of the Yakutians, Andrey Kuzmin. This man was not the best of swimmers and on finishing his leg he handed over to Toomas Haagi who is an excellent swimmer and very fast. Naturally Haagi powered off in the direction of the US coast leaving Kuzmin to clamber back onto the zodiac which he did rather cumbersomely needing a fair bit of help and thus taking the attention away from Toomas who was making rapid progress. By the time attention turned back to him he was out of sight and Vladimir and the driver, Yevgeny spent some time with the spotlight trying to locate Toomas. Luckily, Toomas was always able to see the ship and therefore didn't realize that he had been lost by the zodiac. That day Toomas Haagi swum a near 20 minute leg. On returning to Irtysh, Zdeněk and Toomas politely declined to swim again with Andrey. Quite simply, it was one thing being a danger to himself but now that he was endangering other swimmers it was time to pull the plug on him. I am still not sure how it was that he was still swimming as he was neither fast nor a freestyle swimmer. Obviously he had to be included for political reasons.

I relaxed a bit and spoke some more to Alex. I hadn't been really angry but I had been slightly annoyed with him. I decided that I must clear things up with him so that we had no bad feeling between us. I could see he was a little bit annoyed. It was a difficult situation and nobody was right or wrong. We agreed that everything was fine and that we could continue when the fog lifted. I spent the rest of the day in what I can only describe as a "very serious mood." I wasn't angry but I had been spooked by this episode and later I found myself frantically checking and repacking my bag and modifying my survival equipment and procedures if something untoward were to occur again on the open sea. Meanwhile, word was going round about what had happened, things such as "Jack saved them with his GPS" and it was very common to hear the mimicking of me with the phrase "It's simple! It's a GPS." Actually what I said word for word, which we have on video was "It's simple, it's simple, it's an 'etrex 20'."

The fog lifted after a few hours and the swim was able to start again with our next swim scheduled for 2am. The good thing about this was that I had time for both dinner and evening tea. This helped to calm me but I was still very serious about the next immersion and it was going to take a lot of bottle to get back in a zodiac and get out there in the water again. I was happy to do this but it was true to say that I had lost some confidence in the team and I was now concentrating on readying myself just in case I ended up on my own out there. The thing was that a swimmer would last I guess an absolute maximum of 15 hours in something like 8c, but maybe much less. 8c is fine for us ice and winter swimmers but that's when you have a support team and a mother ship not far away, getting lost while swimming would probably almost certainly mean death.

I thought again about our November 2011 swim in the icy Norton sound at Nome and the comments of Chuck Wheeler "This ain't the Hilton hotel you know, this is the Bering Sea." I understood more than ever what he meant and that he wasn't just a crazy old man.

The events that I have just described occurred during a world first attempt at crossing the Bering Strait by an international team of winter swimmers.

The preparation for this was long and complex and therefore before resuming the description of the epic crossing attempt it is necessary first to go back in time and explain a few things.

How did this all start?

I played rugby at an early age. This involved training on Sunday mornings from September until May. On the most freezing winter morning I can ever remember we were outside doing some drills which weren't the most energetic. I could see my breath in front of me and after an hour, my hands were going blue and had gone beyond painful. We had been wailing at our coach to let us go inside for some time, with no positive response until finally he said, " Ok, off you go to the changing rooms," and we scurried off whimpering like a bunch of girls! 30 minutes and a warm bath later my hands still felt a bit cold but there is no doubt that this experience was a good one for me as for the rest of my young life I never worried about the cold as I felt that Sunday morning was as cold as it could get!

It was about 3.30pm on Christmas Eve in the year 2000. I had just stumbled back into my small flat after several days and nights of partying and debauchery. I had just left the pub after my physical condition had worsened somewhat. Inside the flat there was a strange odour which wasn't coming from the flat itself but rather from me! The number one priority after shedding the stinking clothes was a damn good soak. I didn't have a shower so a bath it would have to be. At this moment my slow responding brain told me that here inside the flat it wasn't much warmer than outside. Then I remembered – the gas had run out some time ago. I had remembered to top up the pay as you go card but hadn't put it in the meter yet. I had an old immersion boiler which could just about get water to a reasonable heat when working well but having been off for days there was no chance of hot water now for at least 2 hours. I didn't have the time to wait as I was beginning to feel like a down and out wino and an immediate soak was all I could think about.

Within seconds the cold tap was running and the bath was filling up. I didn't bother heating any water, it was going to be cold so what did it matter. Soon I was lowering myself into the freezing water, gasping as I received the payback for my recent excesses. Minutes later I emerged shaking, but feeling cleansed and with a seemingly new burst of energy that saw me run to the nearby petrol station for some last minute Christmas presents.

Hours later, refreshed even more by a hot meal prepared by my mother I was back in the pub – the cold water hadn't stopped my thirst for a party but it had rejuvenated me somewhat and I will always remember this minor event.

I continued taking cold baths from time to time, including in 2007 while still living in England, when I had some technical problems with a new hot water system being fitted. At the time I didn't realize that in less than a year cold water would be an even more regular part of my life.

British people are quite tough, living on an island which is constantly ravaged by wind and rain. The climate is more humid than on the European continent and although there is little snowfall and minus temperatures, the wet nature of the winters can make them rather unpleasant. Taking into account the British love of going out in the cold wearing nothing more than jeans and a T shirt and you start to see why we could call ourselves a hardy bunch. On the continent thermal underwear is seen as a necessity during the colder months whereas the average British male would probably not admit to wearing Long Johns even if he did.

At the end of November 2008, by now a resident of Prague, I entered the 1.5c water of the Bolevecký rybník (pond) on the outskirts of Plzeňin the Czech Republic. It was my second winter swimming contest and although I had been training (hardening) for 2 months the lowest temperature I had experienced so far was 5c. Adrenaline took over and I swam as fast as possible from the start, after about 30 seconds I was right up with the leaders but unfortunately I seemed to have lost all feeling in my limbs. A few seconds later and I gagged as I swallowed some of the icy water, momentarily I stopped swimming and for a split second I could see the safety boat bobbing some 50m ahead of me. For that split second I thought about giving up as I felt as though I had been immobilized by the icy water and that maybe I wasn't really a winter swimmer; I had tried, I had done it, but it wasn't for me. These negative thoughts lasted just that split second and after that I told myself to keep going and not to be so bloody weak! Somehow my body responded and I made it to the turn buoy. Many swimmers overtook me but at this point I only cared about finishing. At the finish my friend Matěj Červený was ecstatic, he had finished second. I didn't really care where I had finished and for a while I had nothing much to say. I was pretty stunned by the experience and I really was glad just to have made it to the finish. Minutes later I was experiencing a feeling which I don't think I had felt since that day on the rugby pitch some 20 years earlier as I tried to encourage the blood back into my pale blue hands. An hour later and I was eating gulas in the pub and I felt much better, to the extent that when my phone rang I simply told the caller "I have just swam 250m in 1.5c water." Nothing else seemed to matter. In fact this continued on to the evening. I ordered a Pilsner beer in the local pub and told the barmaid how I had been swimming there earlier on in the freezing lake. She didn't seem too bothered, either she wasn't a winter swimming fan or she didn't understand my broken Czech. To be honest it was probably a bit of both!

A precedent had undoubtedly been set as I now knew that winter swimming was an activity that I simply had to pursue. I had broken through an important psychological barrier and I now felt like a bona fide winter swimmer rather than a wannabe or an imposter. Little did I know what was to come.

Fast forward a few years to 2011 and I was standing at a bus stop in Prague during a late May heat wave with an air temperature of 25c. It probably wasn't the best place to envisage the upcoming Bering Strait relay swim.

I was discussing it with my friend Zdeněk Tlamicha and although I felt slightly icy after a 2km swim in the 14.5c river Vltava I knew I needed to start finding colder water.

Even experienced winter swimmers forget what really cold water is like during the warm summer days. It is easy to stand there talking about swimming in 4c water and even outsiders can be quite taken by the idea, but when November draws to a close and both the air and water temperature falls below 4c, there are less jokes being made and the idea of swimming in such water isn't taken so lightly. Waiting for that 106 bus with Zdeněk I really sensed how ludicrous it was to try and imagine how the conditions would be in the Bering Strait. With most winter swimmers in the northern hemisphere experiencing a summer break I was now in the position of restarting my season or rather starting the new season a few months early. I knew I could keep swimming in water between 12c and 16c, twice a day at weekends. But for me Baikal was becoming the key to the Bering Strait. The evidence was pointing towards the possibility of 8c water. It would be perfect. Beautiful nature, I could swim in the morning, relax and then swim again in the evening, simulating the coming relay with the planned cold water swim every 10 hours for 2 or 3 days. If I could travel to the great lake early enough I would have enough time to acclimatize gradually rather than go straight from a central European summer and relatively warm water to a Chukchi summer and a potentially sub 4c Bering Strait.

Another morning, another cold shower and as the weather grew warmer the daily ritual seemed to be getting more difficult even though the water was undoubtedly getting a bit warmer. I was sure it was connected to the rise in temperature and therefore a slight decline in my "Otužilost" or hardiness.

Meeting with Tomáš Prokop

One of the good things about working for James Cook Languages was that it involved travelling all over Prague, meeting different people and teaching them English language.

Judr Tomáš Prokop was one of my students. About the same age as me, he was a high flying lawyer. Within a few weeks it became clear that he wasn't interested in having any structure to his lessons and he just wanted to talk. That was fine by me. His main interest was winter swimming and from the first time he mentioned it I was fascinated – even digging up information from the internet about it. When he found out that I liked swimming he asked me to join him at the club where he was president. I declined the offer, saying that I wasn't ready but that in a few months I might be.

It was early October and my outdoor swimming season had finished at the end of September. However, I had a new challenge now and at the pool where I was swimming there was an outdoor unheated pool. I started going once a week. The first time I managed just 100m in the cold pool. The water was about 13c but it really burned. I added a bit more each week until I was eventually swimming 800m. The water was about 7c and although it always burned at first I was getting used to it and I could easily endure the first few minutes after which it wasn't too bad. By the 20th of

November I agreed to Join Tomášat his club the following Wednesday at 4pm. I swam with Tomáš and Matěj who was also to become a good friend of mine. The Vltava river was 7c and in the darkness we swam 500m with Tomas having to call me back as I was about to go further. Once back in the changing rooms and I was barely dressed before I was signing the membership forms and running off to try and make my next English lesson feeling pretty fresh and revitalized by my first winter swimming experience in twilight of a late autumn afternoon in Prague.

3 days later and I was at Hradec Králové swimming 250m in the 4.5c River Labe (Elbe) before again visiting the club for training on Wednesday afternoon. After those Wednesday sessions I felt revitalized and ready for anything, although I just went off to teach another English lesson. By January I was swimming longer than anyone else on those Wednesday training sessions, always in the water for around 20 minutes and once or twice over the recommended limit of 22 minutes. I began to take it seriously and soon I was no longer teaching English lessons on Wednesday afternoons, rather taking the training session quite seriously, starting with preparation by way of a good lunch and then a short rest and followed by the swimming itself, some more exercise, plenty of hot tea and then plenty of food and relaxation in the evening and the luxury of a hot shower. I soon stopped with the hot showers as they are nothing but immediate gratification and once you understand the power of cold water they are really not that gratifying even in the very short term. The Finns have a far better idea by way of a sauna. A good, traditional Finnish sauna, which means very hot and very dry, is far better in my opinion than a hot shower.

That first season flew by quite nicely and I used only a silicon cap whereas many of the Czechs used the neoprene variety I was oblivious to the differences in conditions to a certain extent as I was operating on instinct and nerve. For me every time I got into cold water was the same regardless of the conditions. This meant that I knew it was initially painful but that I would withstand it, finish swimming and get out not just having survived but feeling even more alive than before. One day in Brno I swam 750m in still water with a temperature of 1.5c. Afterwards several people congratulated me and it was only later that I realized that I had obtained the coveted masters' degree in winter swimming. To me it seemed no big deal but not that many swimmers reach that goal in their first season. That spring I felt completely reborn and stronger than ever and I really believed then that winter swimming had had a positive impact on my life.

However, a wise old winter swimmer from the club, František Kosař said that it was the second season that was tricky and by January the next year I understood what he meant.

Second Season

I agree with what the wise František Kosař said; that the second season is pretty tough. The first season it is new, it's some kind of novelty in a way as you are doing something that is a little bit out of the ordinary and perhaps, well in fact definitely seen by most people as a little bit crazy. You enjoy it for what it is, a new experience and a rush.

However, by the second season you are already in some way a veteran and you know exactly what to expect. What's more you begin to pay far more attention to things like water temperature and conditions, meteorology, length of immersion, distance of the swim and nature of the course. The novelty has worn off and you remember that winter swimming hurts but then you also remember the old phrase "No pain, no gain." I think most people that start the second season carry on but those that don't press on are the ones that fall by the way side. My friend Matěj sums it up perfectly when he says "It's always a fight to get into the winter water." Each winter you have to go through that fight twice per week and for me I think it is much easier on the Saturday when we are racing. You hear the command to the water, or 30 seconds to the start and you know you must get in. At training on a cold dark Wednesday afternoon there are no referees or starters pushing you, it's just you and the river and it can be a struggle but so far I have never refused to go in and I think the day I do will be the day I stop winter swimming. Maybe that day will eventually come but I doubt it.

By the end of January in that second season I had started to experiment with using 2 silicon caps and I also now swore by earplugs, in fact I had been using them since summer. Forgetting the issue of caps for a moment I have to say that earplugs are essential for winter swimmer in my opinion. I have no problem wearing just 1 silicon cap but swimming without earplugs is a big no-no for me. Cold water can penetrate through the ear canal into the body and seeing how important the ears are for balance I think it is vital that they are protected. Given the choice I would probably take earplugs over a cap.

I also learnt in that second season that there was no need to overdo it in training. There was no need to always swim for around 20 minutes. It was more than enough to swim for 10 minutes, though I mostly swam for 15 minutes and upwards. Nowadays I like to be in the water for around 17 minutes with some longer swims and the occasional shorter swim although if I go as low as 10 minutes I want to be swimming 3 times per week in the winter water.

The Wednesday training was made all the more complex by the shooting of my documentary film "Winter Swimming." Cameraman Honza was with us all through that winter from January until March. I soon found that directing and producing was difficult enough without having to also worry about swimming too. Nevertheless I remained dedicated to the activity of winter swimming often staying at our Clubhouse by the river for around 4 hours in order to get a swim in and the shots I wanted. The snow was good that year and we got some wonderful material especially with cross country skiers and swimmers together in 1 shot and other such delights as people walking barefoot through thick crunching snow and the more comic slips on the ice when trying to get into the water.

Bled Endurance Swim

During that second season, in late 2009 I decided to enter for the endurance event at the world championships of winter swimming to be held in Lake Bled in Slovenia, scheduled for late January 2010. I asked my club colleagues in Prague if they were interested but nobody seemed too bothered. I remember one person summing up the mood by saying "So, you want me to travel all the way to Slovenia, pay 50 euros to swim 450m when I can enter a Czech domestic competition which is paid for by our club, swim 750m and receive a subsidized lunch?!" (Things have since changed and in 2014 the Czechs made their first foray into the world winter swimming championships, taking several medals including a gold for Magda Okurková who became the fastest female winter swimmer in the world over 450m, followed by Renata Nováková who took gold in the 1000m at the inaugural ice swimming world championships, not to mention Rostislav Vítek the fastest ice miler in the world)

I should note that there had been something going on between myself and Dasha for over a month and I saw the Bled trip as a chance to really cement that. It worked as we danced together by the lake on the first night and from then on we were really together. Bled will always remind me of her and when I returned in 2012 my only problem was that it was without her and I vowed that we would return again.

Sadly that won't happen but the lake is still a wonderful place even if I will probably never return there.

Back to 2010 and I was all set for the endurance race across the lake. The organisers were less happy and 5 minutes before the start I detected some anger in John Coningham Rolls as I yet again aimed my video camera in his direction as he explained something. I blame Honza Mika the cameraman for my documentary film "Winter Swimming" as I had spent a lot of time with him and his methods were rubbing off on me a little. For example the day before, at the opening ceremony I had somehow waltzed into a restricted VIP area to do a bit of filming and I simply looked at people who dared not challenge me as maybe I exuded the confident aura of someone who is supposed to there... Anyway I am not a natural behind the camera as the results of my labours show although I can direct a bit.

The build up to the endurance race started the night before at the technical meeting and as the organisers nervously went through everything I managed to add in the question "What about a longer endurance race?" which was met with a little disbelief and surprise with John Congingham Rolls quite rightly saying "Let's just get through this one first!" A bit forward of me but I wanted a bigger challenge. Little was I to know that the 450m would actually be more like 550m although even that wasn't enough for some of us, me included.

On the day of the swim me and Dasha went for a walk around the lake and I was satisfied with everything. We had ample changing facilities and there was time to meet other swimmers including Roman Karkachev of St Petersburg who was to become a good friend of mine. Eventually we got into the water ready for the start and it felt good, definitely around 4c and not 1c as someone had reported the day before. At least one guy pulled out due to nerves and uncertainties and this gave me the first hint that not everyone was so experienced. It was a great feeling as we set off and I went off way too quick in the first 50 – 100m right up with the leaders. However, I soon began dropping places although by the end I was making up ground again as I finished towards the back of the main group. On exiting the water someone handed me a blanket and hot tea and I saw Bojan the host at our pension who was keen to shake my hand before we were moved on. The crowd gave us a great reception and I am sure everyone felt like a winner. That's one of the great things about winter swimming, even when you are racing the best thing is finishing. I know it's the same in long distance but winter swimming is something different, a pretty short yet very intense feeling and on exiting the water there is added euphoria. The crowd that day at Bled were tremendous as we made our way to the sauna. Inside the packed sauna the scene was different as it became clear that some were used to this and others weren't. Personally I wanted to get dressed but I decided to stay put as it was what everyone else was doing and I wanted to enjoy the moment. Alexander Kirschner of Slovakia had other ideas and I heard him tell a Russian girl that it wasn't his habit to take a sauna after endurance winters swimming. He soon got dressed along with the other Slovaks who took part. My Czech friends would probably have been the same. The tradition in Russia and Scandinavia is sauna combined with winter swimming and I think it's a great combination but not if you swim around 20 minutes. In that case it is better to get into a warm room, then get dry and dressed, keep moving and take on warm fluids. Then when you are feeling better (and you will know when, maybe after 30 minutes or so) you can retire to the pub, ideally for a hearty gulas and a half litre of good beer.

One guy was struggling in the sauna but after sometime he recovered without problems while others sat and sat and sat in the sauna making their eventual exit ever the more difficult. I was soon out and got changed. Here I met Roman again and he presented me with a nesting doll (matrioshka) which his company had produced specially for the championships. The smallest doll was a real winter swimming walrus. I was thrilled as I had always wanted one of these and to receive a limited edition was fantastic. It still sits prominently on my desk and will continue to do so. In return I gave Roman the 2009/10 Czech winter swimming catalogue and he was also pleased as he liked the extensive rules. After more socializing all the endurance swimmers got onto the podium and we all received special awards which was nice. Dasha and I soon retired for a pizza and an early night, deciding to avoid the official reception at a posh hotel.

We left Bled on the Monday morning and it had been a good trip, mainly for the amount of people I had met. Little was I to realize that the contacts I had made would have yet more influence and bearing on my direction in future years.

Baikal

Throughout my life I have often been attracted to people for an unknown but seemingly innate reason and I am not talking about sexual liaisons now but rather simply a human connection!

I had one of those moments when I first came into contact with Alexandr Brylin. Physically big, the typical frame of a winter swimmer or walrus as they are commonly known in Russia, his features not those of a European.

I had already noticed him and his entourage and team as they were the biggest group and the most colourful with myriad tracksuits featuring the red white and blue of the Russian flag.

When we met, it was in the chaos of the sauna after the endurance race. Needless to say with my extremely limited Russian and Alexandr's non-existent English the conversation didn't flow.

Nevertheless, Alexandr's translator Irina Makarova (Irina/Ira) contacted me later that year to invite me to participate in the great Amur swim in the summer. Unfortunately I had to decline that invitation due to the fact that I had only just started a salaried job after having lived very much hand to mouth for almost a year. I had neither the money nor the time to take part.

However, I was content and had got through the second season of winter swimming without any problems and with the same thirst for the cold.

In spring 2010, just after the end of the winter swimming season I was in the Stanford's book shop in London in order to buy a travel guide for Lake Baikal in Siberia. I wasn't sure exactly when I would go but it had long been discussed as a destination by myself and a few friends. I was in the section for Russia and Asia and suddenly I noticed a map of Kamchatka with a magnificent volcano staring at me. It was a strange moment and I felt that Kamchatka would be the destination for me although at the time I only purchased the Baikal guidebook!

It was almost a year later in 2011when I received another invitation, this time to join them in relay to swim across the Bering Strait! This was the challenge and adventure I had been looking for and I was absolutely thrilled at the prospect of travelling to the remote region of Chukotka and finally swimming in the land of Eskimo, Walrus and polar bears. I had already been talking about trips to the arctic and the Bering Strait was an area I often lingered over whilst perusing my world atlas. I am not ashamed to say that for the next 2 months this trip was usually my final thought at night and always my first in the morning. In fact particularly in the mornings I was always extremely buoyant seeing it as another day closer to the departure date.

As the temperature rose with the days of May I needed to find colder water as the river was now at 14c and although I knew it wouldn't get above 16c until July this wasn't cold enough when I might be facing 4c water in the Bering Strait or even colder. Luckily 20km down the road is a big dam and I trained there where the water below the dam would hold 10c all summer as well as regularly swimming twice per day, usually in the mornings at the pool and in the evening in the river.

Although I was looking forward to the Bering Strait swim I, suspected that there might be problems and as I left home on the 1st of July I was prepared for problems. Many people wouldn't have risked it but I just couldn't resist it. At last I had the chance to be part of something big, something special and I felt I would just have to take my chance as it might not happen again. The added lure of the meeting place being Petropavlovsk Kamchatsky (main city of Kamchatka) was spellbinding for me as only 1 year before I had been in Stanford's map shop in Covent Garden looking at a map of Kamchatka – land of fire and ice – and wondering how I would get there!

But, that wasn't it; from being fairly good with a map and arranging travel I had managed to build a cold water training trip to Lake Baikal en route to the meeting place in Kamchatka. Somehow my plan of buses taxis and planes worked smoothly even with the first flight being delayed, some 17 hours after closing my front door I had made it to Irkutsk just 60km from Lake Baikal deep in Siberia. I was obliged to stay for 1 day in Irkutsk in order to obtain a stamp for my immigration card so I explored the city and tried out my Russian in the local market and mobile phone shop. Actually my Russian was holding up quite well and I even managed to find the obscure map shop where I was able to buy a 1:100,000 map of the area of the lake that I was to explore. This was the best map I could find. Russia is vast and no doubt there remain large areas that are not well mapped.

The next day, loaded up with enough supplies for 8 days I took a Marshrutka (minibus) to Listvyanka, the main settlement by the lake. I had taken it easy getting organised and I didn't reach Listvyanka until 3pm. The reason for my taking it easy was that although I was planning on trekking as well as swimming I didn't want to lose weight and become tired; easier said than done when you are carrying 30kg backpack. Consequently I planned meticulously for this trip so that although I was heading into semi wilderness I would not be without food or an alternative escape route if I had a problem with time. My flight was in 10 days and the trek was a maximum of 5 days according to my calculations which proved accurate. So it was mid-afternoon and I decided that the best thing to do would be to see if there was a cheap room available and stay in Listvyanka for a night before setting out the next morning. I headed for the tourist info and tried out my letter of introduction, and was promptly offered a room for 500 roubles. I took it and my hostess was no babushka but a 20 something blondie by the name of Masha, fine by me! I explained to her what I was doing here and that my first task would be to have a swim, this raised some eyebrows.

At this point I should say a little about the lake. On the approach to Baikal (Irkutsk – Listvyanka) you get a good view of the river Angara, which drains the lake. The Angara is big and as you reach the mouth, Baikal comes into view and it is quite a sight surrounded by mountains.

I made my way to what seemed to be the most popular public beach. Back in Irkutsk it was a stifling 33c but here in Listvyanka the temperature was about 22c with a gentle breeze. The reason for this big difference is that the lake is so big that it acts like small sea and takes the edge off the weather in both summer and winter. Conditions were great and the water looked clear and inviting. Nobody else was swimming or even paddling, or even dipping a toe in. As I got my kit out and started to get changed I had a little laugh to myself about what the other people might be thinking about me and my intentions of swimming. I noticed I had drawn some attention and a few people were staring at me. No doubt they thought that I didn't know how cold the water was and were waiting to see what my reaction would be to the icy water. Yes, the water, I was fairly certain that it would be below 8c but I had made the decision not to measure the temperature until after swimming. This is against normal protocol but I wanted to see how well I could guess it. I couldn't guess it but I knew it was really cold, several months since I had experienced anything this cold. It was a big shock but I continued on and had a nice 10 minute swim. After I got out I got the thermometer in before any shivering started. My watch was reading just under 6c. I took a few readings and the mercury was just above 5. The next day 300m down the shore it was the same. Water temperature of Lake Baikal in Listvyanka is definitely 5c– 5.5c. It took me a few hours to warm up and I knew I had done a cold swim as I could feel the tiredness that extremely cold water brings. Luckily my hostess was having a party and she invited me. My 3rd day in Russia and suddenly I was right in the middle of the people which was great. I was introduced to the omul fish and the preferred way of eating it; lightly cured in vinegar and onions. It was very good, especially washed down with vodka. I brought some Czech salami to the table as well as my English language. Without going into too many details this party confirmed stereotypes not only about hard drinking Russians but of the friendly people of the Irkutsk Oblast too.

Needless to say I only made 15 minutes the next morning and after a swim and a short trip to the Shaman stone I finally set off at around 4pm. The weather forecast was bad, rain was predicted, but with almost 7 hours of daylight left I decided that I must get on the trail. What's more, for the first section I was going into the interior with plenty of forest cover if it got too bad. The going was tough and I ascended to over 1000m before descending 500m to head back to the shore of the lake. The rain started falling as I reached a camp after a 3.5 hour continuous trek. It was a group of students and teachers from St Petersburg. They told me there was another good place for camping 1 hour further and that was where the rest of their group were. I had a look round and decided to stay as there was room for my one-man tent. I soon got the fire going and cooked pasta. Just as I was about to make tea I was invited for dinner with the Russians. I went on to have another 4 meals with them as it didn't stop raining for 16 hours. Air temperature at 11am the next morning was 12c, a pretty big drop from 22c in Listvyanka. I had another swim; this time 15 minutes and again I was getting a reading of about 5c.

After yet another helping of buckwheat porridge I was on my way. 4 days and many swims later I had made it to Bolshoie Goloustnoe the village at the Goloustnoe river delta, crucially with a road that led back to Irkutsk. It's worth pointing out that there aren't many roads in this part of Siberia. To travel on from Goloustnoe you must first go back to Irkutsk.

The trip along the shore of the lake was good, plenty of swimming and some beautiful views. There was even some tricky "Don't look down" scrambling along eroding cliffs to get the adrenaline up. I met a few more people but no one who would join me for a swim. I stayed in the village for a few days in order to explore the delta and the surrounding area. There was a great ridge at 800m altitude that gave a lovely view. Here I got even more of a feeling for the power and size of the lake. This delta hardly shows up on most maps but from where the terrain flattens and the river splits it's several kilometres to the lake and when comparing this physical feature with how it is displayed on a 1:100,000 map you get a real feel for the size of Baikal and the surrounding area even if its most impressive geographical feature is its huge 1,645m depth (deepest lake in the world) which isn't easily represented visually on tourist maps.

Again I swum in the lake and it was maybe up to 6c. By now I was used to it although usually I wasn't managing more than 1 swim per day due to the constant moving and tiredness this brought on. I got back to Irkutsk by bus on the only one of the day which left at 8am. I could have hitchhiked but there would be no guarantees that someone would be driving to Irkutsk that day and I was flying in less than 24 hours. Back in Irkutsk and I took a trip to the Angara river halfway back towards Baikal. This river is absolutely beautiful and clear with a sandy bed and beaches. The water was incredibly sweet just like Baikal and after swimming I sat there drinking the water straight from the river in the hot sun, watching a couple of wild horses, completely at peace with the world.

The Baikal trip had been a success. I hadn't swum as much as I had anticipated but nevertheless I had got plenty of cold water swimming in. It has to be said that the water in the lake was crystal clear and absolutely freezing. I will always remember that first swim in Listvyanka when the air was around 22C with bright sunshine but the water around 5C. My first thought was "F**k it's true this lake is absolutely freezing even in summer!" It was a beautiful experience and in the busy resort of Listvyanka I was the only swimmer apart from a few tourists who just jumped in and got straight back out again.

Soon I had made my way to the airport and I was on my way to Kamchatka via Khabarovsk. The flights were without incident but by the time I arrived I was completely confused regarding the time of day. I had flown at around 2am, so that meant a night without sleep and now it was 6pm local time.

Kamchatka

As the plane touched down at Yelizovo airport on the Kamchatka peninsula I glimpsed the spectacular volcanoes that little did I know were about to become an everyday sight for over a month.

Things went to plan as Viktor Godlevski was there to meet me. A big man with dark hair, a thick moustache and an impressive looking uniform marking him out as someone of at least some significance. Viktor had a few words of English but not as much as my Russian so we conversed in Russian. On the drive into town we stopped and Viktor ran out and bought me 2 large bottles, one of Kvas and 1 of the local beer as well as a dried fish. Although I was expecting to stay at his house he took me to a local hotel due to the need for foreigners to be registered. Frankly Viktor was happy to be my friend as we will find out but he probably didn't want the hassle of the paperwork he would have to fill in for me staying with him from the start. He agreed that he would pick me up the next day at 9.30am and left me to it. He agreed that the day after would be free and seeing as there was a tourist agency in the hotel it seemed that I would make it to at least 1 volcano. So once I had my room and had got into my tracksuit I went downstairs to arrange a trip to the Avacha volcano. Alonya, the travel agent said she would call me the next day. By coincidence this turned out to be the tourist agency that I had already been in touch with. I told Alonya that I would have a quick walk round the city and get some food but she said to me "don't go walking in the city it really isn't very nice." I soon understood. PK (Petropavlovsk Kamchatsky) isn't a pleasant city. It's just built along a main road next to the bay. The bay is pretty with great views when the weather is good but the city is a dusty, messy collection of buildings. In fact the bay is not just pretty but rather spectacular and it is obvious why Petropavlovsk Kamchatskiy was founded as a port city and a base for further exploration with its well sheltered natural harbour. The bay is rich in wildlife including seals, sea lions and fish. The presence of seas urchins and sea weed points to a rich ecosystem, meanwhile ships ply the trade on the way to the open pacific ocean and on the other side of the bay military submarines can sometime be seen emerging from the water for a short time. It really is a case of an ugly city placed in a beautiful location.

A visit to the local minimarket confirmed that prices were expensive in miles-from-anywhere-Kamchatka. Next day I breakfasted on porridge in the hotel and almost as soon as I got back to my room Viktor was knocking on the door; "Jack! Dobry Utra, davej, bystra, pasli!" (Morning jack, come on let's go quickly we've got to go!) Viktor had an action packed day lined up for us but first he had to check that the Hotel chef had given me breakfast! Then we drove to a few places as Viktor had a few errands to run before he took me to the bay to go swimming. I was happy with this and the 10c water felt almost tropical after Baikal, even in the overcast, heavy Petropavlovsk Kamchatsky. I made a circuit around the bay. (Actually I say the bay but it's one of many bays in the gulf of Avachinsky. The water wasn't very clear but it was almost fresh, not at all salty and it felt good. I made another lap and got out after 50 minutes. Viktor filmed the whole thing which was pretty amusing especially when he asked me to say hi to my mum. After getting dressed, the next stop was the local cafe run by Viktor's friend for Shashlik (kebab) and hot tea. After this pleasant sustenance it was time to go again (Jack! Davej! Bystra!) and things started to get interesting. Viktor explained that now we were on our way to do some media interviews. Fine, I replied. Before we got out at the first place Viktor asked me if I had swum the English Channel to which I replied no. He said, "Oh, no you have swum the English Channel." To which I replied again, "No, Viktor I haven't". This continued for a minute or 2 with Viktor quite insistent that I had swum the English Channel. Now I realized that I was possibly a big attraction for them. I was in a tight position and with no translator as Irina and the others were due to arrive in 2 days. I really am a modest person and saying that I have done something when I haven't is definitely not me. However, reluctantly on this occasion when assured that this was only local media in Kamchatka I agreed to the white lie that to me was more of a betrayal. It was a bizarre situation carrying this lie off as I didn't feel like myself. I felt like I was me, Jack Bright, but playing the role of someone else who had swum the English Channel. Never mind, it was for the best to help our expedition get some local publicity. Then we went to the local radio station. This was much more fun, but again I was obliged to lie. After this, the days lying was done (thank god) and it was time that I was invited to as Viktor liked to say "my house" in his heavily accented English. He picked up a large amount of Fresh salmon and a bottle of vodka. In the meantime I got a call from Alonya telling me to be ready at 7am to visit Avacha volcano. This cheered me up after the lying. Then Viktor tried to kill me with fresh Kamchatka salmon from the pacific. He filleted three large salmon and fried them in breadcrumbs. "Kushet, kushet" (eat, eat!) came the command from Viktor as I set what must be a British record for eating salmon. Viktor also took great pride in showing me how to prepare caviar with the main gadget for this a tennis racket. I have to say this was very useful. Needless to say Viktor forced me to eat huge amounts of caviar along with plenty of vodka and as always he was on hand to document it. Viktor's small kitchen smelt like a greasy spoon cafe back home in the UK and I was keen to get some fresh air, however I couldn't really move after all the food. Almost immediately after finishing eating as if reading my thoughts Viktor shouted "Davej bystra, bystra, bystra, pasli." (Come on quick, quick, quick, let's go). Now I don't want to seem like a moaner and as I said I wanted to leave, but as I also said he had forced a ridiculous amount of fried food on me (I forgot to mention the 2 chicken schnitzels that were a starter) and I had only just finished eating. The rest of the evening was spent with a stomach ache from the excesses although I did get my head down for a few hours before rising at 6 for the volcano trip. I got to the meeting place and met up with 3 other guys who were also going. We travelled 10km out of town before turning down a dirt road in the national park. 30 minutes and 5km later we met the Bolshoie mashin (literally big car, actually a 6 wheel ATV) that would take us to base camp. Another 30 minutes and we reached base camp Avacha, and I was happy that I was starting to see the Kamchatka that I envisioned in Stanford's Map Shop 2 years earlier. I confirmed with our guide that we were 800m above sea level which meant we needed to ascend another ~1941m to reach the summit. That's enough ascent for a day but it didn't bother me as just over 1 month ago I had finished the 100km 3800m ascent of Krakonosova stovka in 16h56mins and of course I had just been trekking with a big backpack at Lake Baikal. One of our companions, however, looked the wrong side of 60 so I kept a close eye on him. All morning we made slow but steady progress and once I had warmed up it was little more than a stroll for me. I didn't mind as I stopped to admire the amazing volcanic landscapes and particularly the spectacular sight of the adjacent Korayaksky volcano. Sergey (the older guy) was starting to slow before lunch so I gave him my poles, a couple of energy sweets and even breaking one of my own rules I resorted to giving him sips from my water bottle. We continued on and were 600m from the summit when Sergey keeled over. Our guide said he had acute mountain sickness and I wasn't going to argue judging by Sergey's condition, he had to descend. However, I could see the summit and that's where I was going and this is where there was a disagreement. I was prepared to go alone to the summit, using my Austrian mountain club insurance as a reason to do so but in the end I reluctantly agreed to go down with the others. It was of course the right decision. I got some special certificate for facing a problem on Avacha but it irked me that I didn't summit when I could see it and the weather was so good. Back in town I spoke to Viktor who agreed that seeing as the others weren't arriving until the evening of the next day I had another free day. I went straight to see Alonya in the office and we thrashed out a deal where I would only pay for the transport the next day and if I wanted I could follow their guide. This proved to be a very interesting day. The weather wasn't good and base camp was shrouded in fog. Eyebrows were raised by the bosses of base camp when they saw me return. I set out trying to retrace the steps to find the ridge (I had been careful to visualise and go through this with our guide the previous day) that would lead me to the main trail. After less than 500m I became lost in the fog. I had a compass but no map or GPS and was scared to follow a bearing that I wasn't certain of. I paced around for several minutes in circles. It was infuriating as I knew that I was close but I just couldn't find the path. There had been heavy snow this year and it didn't help the navigation. Reluctantly I turned and headed back to base camp. I saw the guide Dima leading his group in the other direction towards Camel mountain and Avachinsky pass. "Come with us" he said, and so I agreed. What followed was another adventure as I effectively played second guide to a young family and an experienced group of hikers. Dima chose a very interesting route over snowfields, small valleys, and the moraine like features of this side of Avacha. It was foggy, there was a lot of snow and quite frankly it was other worldly. Dima took us onto the saddle of Camel Mountain and another small peak before we continued on. Late morning and I had a distinct feeling that we were in trouble. I asked Dima, will you take these people to the summit? He answered "I want to." I asked him where Avacha was as I didn't know. He hesitated and consulted the GPS on his phone at which point I really knew we were in trouble. Over there he pointed, you can go if you want. I decided not to go it alone and I didn't blame Dima for being lost, this area was as I said other worldly. I did, however, continue on ahead like a scout ascending a steep snow covered peak where there was less snow. To my surprise Dima preferred the snow but I really wasn't sure what would be at the top where the snow was. Sure enough it was a sheer drop and Dima traversed to join me on the summit. Bizarrely by this stage the group were following me more than Dima. We were following cairns and on this peak there was a cairn but I couldn't see the way. We descended and traversed more snowfields with conditions at times almost whiteout. I was by now really enjoying myself even though I knew we would never make the summit, in fact we still couldn't see Avacha though the visibility was very low. I was later to find that we were in the area of Avachinsky pass. By this time Dima had left the family waiting in a sheltered place and with my support he told the others that the trip was at an end, it was time to go back. Several hours later we were back at base camp and I still hadn't been on the top of Avacha but I didn't care as it had been a very interesting trip.

I didn't want to return to town that night but it was time to let the volcanoes take a back seat in favour of swimming. The next day the others arrived and it was confirmed that aside from the 5 Chinese swimmers I was the only foreign swimmer who had decided to participate. First stop was a bizarre swimming pool, heated to about 32c very crowded and difficult to swim in. (later I found out that it was a thermal pool, heated by volcanism more for relaxation than sport and something I would get used to in Kamchatka) Never mind, after a short bus tour we went for a swim in the bay, water temp about 12c. We had been delayed a few days was the official line and I moved into an apartment with 6 of the Russians which was much better than the hotel. 3 days later, more swimming, more hot springs and another couple of media interviews and Alexandr Brylin called a team meeting to drop the bombshell that we had lost the ship. At this point everything fell into place and the potential problems that I had suspected began to unfold. I was powerless to do anything as our chance of swimming the Bering Strait seemed to be slipping away. Philosophically I thought what can I expect? Me, a normal guy without any big contacts let alone the breeding of the old school British adventurers and clearly the Russians were just the same, simple people with a great dream. They invited me and I had joined them without doing any organisational work myself. To everybody's credit there was no major split or fall out and I took it as a good introduction to Russian culture. "Anything can happen in Russia" was a phrase that I heard more than once. The other thing that struck me was how no problems fazed them. I deduced that they had all probably encountered various problems in their everyday life possibly quite regularly. For example, they live in a city of some 200,000 people but there is no swimming pool so during the winter they hire a minibus twice a week to make the 1 hour drive to the nearest pool for training. Although not extreme, it hints that life in the far east of Russia is nothing like in central or western Europe even though at first they seem the same as us. By Friday we'd had a big press conference and a mass visit to the senator's office. A boat was procured and we made a training relay swim from the Pacific Ocean back to PK. A nice event, it gave everyone renewed enthusiasm and hope. This event was dedicated to the 112 people who lost their lives on the Volga River in a sinking 2 weeks before and a priest was present to bless us before the swim. Ironically it was this tragedy that set the wheels in motion for our problems as all ships were recalled to port for inspection. As a result the governor of Sakhalin Island wouldn't release our ship from its duties and I suggested that he must be after a bribe. This comment of mine was even published in a Russian newspaper but I heard no more of it and no one tried to assassinate me! I was almost involved in another scandal though courtesy of my friend Viktor. When he found out that I hadn't been on the summit of Avacha he was livid and blamed the tour company. At one point a TV crew asked me on camera what I thought of the tour company. I was pretty angry and said I had no problems and I didn't want to hear any more about it. This led to a long overdue misunderstanding between me and Viktor although we remained friends and he redeemed himself in my eyes when he took us to some secluded hot springs and made a very good Ucha (fish soup). I was popular in PK and one day we were swimming in the gulf near the Pacific and a guy came bounding up to me as he had heard that I was famous. It was a bizarre situation. He was a policeman from Moscow working out in Kamchatka. He was with his friend and a Koryak man. (Koryaks are one of the native peoples of Kamchatka). They were fishing with nets, a privilege of the Koryak man. We drank vodka, ate ucha and laughed about life. They presented me with a fish and later on I was scaling, gutting and preparing it before making ucha. It's worth mentioning at this point that fish is a big staple for people in Kamchatka. As I was preparing the fish I realized that although I had done sports fishing in England this was the first time I had prepared a fish since 1997 when I worked on the fish counter in Sainsbury's supermarket. I had been in PK for almost 2 weeks and I was starting to be like one of the locals. I had seen fish being prepared on an almost daily basis and now here I was preparing ucha, just a pity that I didn't catch it myself.

As the meetings and waiting continued we got into a routine of swimming combined with a few trips. I was invited to the dacha (small weekend house) of Yevgeniy, the cousin of one of the swimmers, Anatoly from Khabarovsk. This was a pleasant trip with the chance to try a real authentic Russian banya for the first time complete with birch twigs for beating and beer to replace lost minerals. There were also several more bizarre trips to spa-like swimming pools, always full of people and always with a main pool in excess of 30c! It seemed like rather odd training to me. However, I experienced and witnessed perhaps for the first time the challenge of withstanding hot water. There was a small pool that nobody went into. The temperature was ~45c. Having put my hands in few times I confirmed that it was really hot, just like a bath run only with the hot tap. I decided to brave it and lasted 10 seconds and I certainly didn't submerge my head. A little later, one of the Russians, Alexandr Yurkov, a very strong, hardy man came to the pool. He had already been doing swim drills and various breath holding exercises in the other pool. Now he got into this one and stayed in for an incredible 10 minutes. This was a real feat and although many people say that if you are really hardened you should be able to withstand both cold and hot temperatures I can say that lasting 8 minutes in such water takes some doing and isn't for the faint hearted. I gained quite a lot of confidence from this episode as it cemented the belief in my mind that hot water is more dangerous than cold, pretty poignant as we were in the land of fire and ice.

Perhaps the best of these visits was to a place called ozerki (little lake). As I walked in I started laughing as it appeared to be another swimming pool spa, except with no large pool only several small ones. However, after getting changed and going outside there was indeed an ozerki on the other side of the pools. It was a strange little place. Only just over 1 metre deep it was just about okay for swimming in. It was about 10m wide and 30m long and there was a lot of vegetation. A wooden jetty had been built to ease access into the water. I decided that I wanted to know the temperature before I swam so I waited for my watch to acclimatize before measuring. One Russian guy came in and made a big show of going in for about 10 seconds or so. On exiting he asked me what I was waiting for, why don't you get in, are you scared etc. etc. In our short meeting I found him a rather boorish man and luckily he avoided speaking to me after I had completed my 15 minute swim in the shallow and somewhat confined little lake. The water was around 5c so I was satisfied with this as of course there was still a chance that we would face the icy waters of the Bering Strait. After this swim I decided to try the hot baths immediately after. I went to the hottest bath first and then after 5 minutes or so I retreated to the slightly less warm. It was pleasant after the cold swim, but rather addictive a little like standing next to the stove to warm up after a winter swim. I am sure the best thing in the long run is getting dry and dressed and moving about. This is a complicated topic as a trip to the sauna clearly works for many people. Personally I think it varies on how long you swim for, the water temperature, and also the air temperature and how long you are exposed for. 10 minutes or under and a sauna is a good option. At around the 20 minute mark I am really not sure that a sauna is a good idea as the body is so cold but I can't back it up with scientific info. One thing is certain and that is that attention must be paid to the air temperature. Generally in the UK and Europe it's not a problem but in the middle of winter if temperatures get below about -8c then take care how long you are exposed for. The human body's internal temperature is ~38c and it can maintain this indefinitely when the air temperature is above 16 or 17c. So you can walk around without clothes on and you won't get cold as long as there is no wind! Under this is the danger zone so you can see that minus temperatures represent a potential problem for swimmers, particularly the case when there is no immediate shelter available, and here we are only talking about the effect of air temperature, exposure to water has a far greater effect (It's worth reading the Jack London short story "To Build a Fire" which will give a grounding on the concept of cold and it's danger).

We also managed to make an extended swim in the bay of around 4km and we were joined by a seal and a jet skier. There was also a longer relay swim which we undertook from the Pacific Ocean at the mouth of the bay back to the port at PK. It was a nice swim but we were just killing time waiting to go north to the Bering Strait.

During this time I managed to make 2 more trips to the volcanoes. Gorely was a fantastic experience, seeing a huge caldera and an acid lake as well as several craters. I also eventually reached the summit and crater of Avacha in absolutely awful conditions. Visibility was almost zero, air temp also around zero and relative humidity around 100% so plenty of precipitation. Content, I returned to the city to be greeted by the news that we had found a new ship and that we would leave on Monday or Tuesday. Excellent news allowing us to enjoy the following day a prazdnik (public holiday) dedicated to the navy and seeing as we were in the biggest naval port of the far east there would be a big show. Plenty of free kasha (porridge) and macaroni was dispensed by military kitchen and there were parades as well as old fashioned competitions such as tug of war and other shows of strength.

Unfortunately, late that night news came in that finally our expedition would be cancelled. The US coastguard had called to say that our new ship the Georg Steller didn't meet the regulations for entrance to US waters. The news was short and definite, there was to be no discussion, although for now it was unofficial and a meeting was called for 10.00 the next morning and an official announcement would be made by Alexandr Brylin.

Now it was over. We commiserated in a local disco and the next day we assembled down by the beach where we had often gone swimming in Avacha Bay. I was angry but quiet as I had nothing to say. I made arrangements to head into the back country with a local guide who I had met on a previous trip. We had a final barbecue with the presentation of certificates for our training swim from the Ocean through the bay to PK. I said my goodbyes to the other swimmers and left for the Nalychevo nature park. We were to follow the valley and trek for 4 days to reach the ancient volcano Dhenzur. Along the way we crossed, rivers, mountain passes and rested at hot springs. We also had a close encounter with a bear, which ran away as soon as he saw us. 8 days later and I was back in PK again greeted by Viktor. This time he invited me to his house and to a banya which was interesting. He absolutely destroyed my back with the birch twigs. It was actually quite funny as he made grunting sounds while doing it and at first I burst out laughing. After more food and a good night's sleep the next day he took me to the airport and I was on the way back to Europe.

More drama was in store though at Khabarovsk airport. I was due to change there in order to board a flight to Moscow. However, due to weather conditions my Vladivostok air flight was delayed by 8 hours. This meant that I wouldn't make my flight out of Moscow at 11pm Moscow time. I was already on a visa extension and this was my final day, so there was a small problem. I simply had to get stamped out of Russia today. I went to the Vlad air window and asked what could be done. They gave me a phone number and I spoke to someone in English who referred me back to Vlad air in the airport. At this point I started to get a little worried and this galvanised me into action. I noticed that there was a Transaero flight to Moscow leaving in an hour or two. I decided that first priority was to get on this flight. I pulled out all my documents, including my letter of introduction and with my best Russian I told the girls at Vlad air that they must help me. Then the pantomime started as they referred me to the Transaero window next door. The rep spoke a little English which helped. The price for the ticket was about 27,000 roubles although that didn't bother me as I had no intention of paying but every intention of getting on the flight. I gave her my documents and told her that Alexandr Brylin would pay. Things started to get difficult and time was running out but still I sensed I could get on this flight. My message was simple either Vlad air were paying or if not Alexandr Brylin. At this point the Vlad air rep appeared and things started to look up. He saw the documents and I am pretty sure that the letter of introduction had him bamboozled. With less than 5 minutes to take off, me and my luggage were whisked through the now empty security and transported by quadbike onto the plane and I made it to Moscow with time to spare. I got stamped out and arrived back home in Prague after about a 40 hour trip, but at least I arrived back without an altercation with Russian immigration or police.

No doubt this Russian trip taught me a few things – the main ones being that anything can happen in Russia and that some things happen simply because this is Russia. There is in my opinion some wisdom in the words of Churchill when speaking of Russia: "It is a riddle wrapped in a mystery inside an enigma" Although he was talking about the state it is a fairly good metaphor for the nation too.

Something about the Bering Strait Region

As I was reading the third in a series of emails from a guy who wanted to kayak across the Bering Strait it dawned on me that I was maybe becoming rather knowledgeable about the area. How many people have actually been to Wales Alaska? I guess that the number isn't particularly high. I had also been studying various data including maps from National aeronautics and space administration NASA, National oceanic and atmospheric administration NOAA as well as scientific papers and historical information concerning the Bering land bridge. I had been fortunate enough to visit the national park service in Nome and Anchorage, speaking with workers from the Beringia shared heritage project and picking up reading material. I still hadn't been to Chukotka but I had started to delve further into the history of Vitus Bering and particularly Semyon Dezhnev the Russian explorer who probably found the Bering strait during his 1648 expedition where he sailed down the Kolyma river to the arctic ocean before rounding the eastern cape (later named Cape Dezhnev by James Cook) and sailing through the Bering Strait to make landfall somewhere around the mouth of the Anadyr river in the area which is now known as the Chukotka Autonomous Okrug.

The vastness of Siberia and the Russian Far East including the Kamchatka peninsula were areas discovered and mapped for the first time during the age of discovery in the 17th and 18th centuries. By 1741 Alaska had also been found during Vitus Bering's 10 year great northern expedition. Bering himself died of scurvy on the island which took his name – Bering Island, off the coast of Kamchatka and of course there is also the Bering Sea and Bering glacier.

But after reading up on this history it was Cape Dezhnev that I most wanted to visit, the most eastern point of the Eurasian continent a rocky cape with a monument and a few ruined buildings of a village called Naukan which was deserted following Soviet collectivization in the period between the end of World War 2 and the start of the period of Perestroika. I made up my mind that if there was any chance of getting onto the cape itself that I would be there. Cape Dezhnev had become a big geographical goal for me, more so perhaps than any other location including the finishing point Cape Prince of Wales, probably because as I have already pointed out I had already been to Wales and looked out to the Diomede islands and the Russian mainland and now I wanted to see it from the other side before actually making the crossing.

I still had doubts about the validity of what we were doing but I could see good in the number of nationalities that were taking part, surely it would be a fantastic advertisement for international cooperation. My main fears were that swimming in memory of some explorers wasn't a strong enough motive. I had thought the same about the lend lease act but now I was mellowing on that one. It was actually an excellent example of cooperation between The USA and Russia during the Second World War even if just a few years later these two nations were in opposition during the cold war which lasted until almost the final decade of the 20th century. During the cold war, the Bering

Strait region became something of a no-go zone with a heavy military presence on both sides but particularly the Russian side with a base on Ratmanov (big Diomede) Island just 4.2km from the American Little Diomede Island. Ratmanov was strictly for military personnel and all inhabitants were moved to the mainland following World War 2. In 1983 after the period of detente and at a time of high tension known as the second cold war a Korean passenger jet flying from Anchorage, USA veered quite clearly into Russian airspace, flew over Kamchatka and was subsequently shot down. Almost 300 people lost their lives including a member of the US congress. However in 1987 as Gorbachev was implementing his policies of Glasnost and Perestroika the American marathon swimmer Lynne Cox made her amazing swim from little Diomede to Ratmanov (Big Diomede). 4.2km across the frigid Bering Strait and the ice curtain she succeeded in making it to Russia. Her feat received more press in Russia and even though it is said that both Reagan and Gorbachev congratulated her it was the Russian that instigated this and he mentioned her when he was at an important conference in Washington later that year. It may be one of the most remote areas of the world but the Bering Strait region can both unite and alienate people, I hoped our relay would do the former just as Lynne Cox's great swim had done 25 years before.

Back to the Bering?!

(Or rather back to the Russian Far East and eventually to
the Bering for the first time!)

I was pretty disappointed that the swim didn't happen but I
was philosophical enough about it. I had my health and
Dasha had returned from Altai. After 6 weeks among
Russians I was struggling to let go of certain Russian words
particularly, Kharoso, Davej and da. I was also in the habit
of drinking more black tea and eating more biscuits. The
Russian language really got on Dasha's nerves in a funny
kind of way and eventually I managed to lose these habits
although it was strange as I had obviously become partly
Russian. There were still a few more weeks of summer left
and I managed to squeeze in a bit more adventure before
the autumn beckoned and with it the new winter swimming
season.

Before this, sometime in early September I managed to
get my thoughts down about the failed Bering swim and
send them to Alexandr Brylin via Irina. I was as positive
and constructive as I could be and to be fair I found a lot of
very good points. If it was glaringly obvious that the event
had been a bit of a mess then it was also glaringly obvious
that these guys stuck together whatever happened which
impressed me. There had been no major arguments and

everyone had been on good terms with each other which, all things considered, was quite something. I admit that Viktor's antics had got up my nose and I think he knew it but even he redeemed himself in the final few days when he met me after I had been trekking, accommodated me and took me to the airport. He didn't need to do that but he did, so I was very grateful. When we parted I felt he was an ok guy. The truth is that people are just people and we are all different, we just do what we do. We can't all be supermen/women and we can't all be winners just like we can't all be losers and we can't all be winter swimmers.

Overall, my friends from the Russian Far East have shown themselves to be great people and their actions pointed to what was important in life, the fact that we have it, not that we failed to make a complex crossing of the Bering Strait. Many people impressed me, including Irina Makarova, (Irina/Ira) the Russian/English translator with her knowledge of English and in the future she was to become a key figure in communications between people all over the world. It was true that I had come further from home than the others, but there were 2 Muscovites who had also travelled a long way and quite frankly Kamchatka is not really on the doorstep of anywhere.

Soon news came through from Russia and it seemed that Alexandr was adamant that he would not give up on this dream to swim across the Bering Strait. Originally I said I didn't want to be involved in the organisation for next year but that I would be happy to participate. However, I soon reconsidered that position that I had taken. How could I criticise and put down something and still want to be involved. It was a case of money where your mouth is which has always been my style. I hate to be thought of as the sort of guy in the words of a character from the favourite movie of my teenage years 'Dazed and Confused' "Whose mouth writes a cheque that his butt can't cash." I also knew that as much as I had my faults and limitations I maybe had something to offer this project. Perhaps in fact we were a match made in heaven. Let's face it they had reached out to people across the world and I was the only one who had taken the bait. I won't make myself out to be too silly as it was a calculated decision to go on that trip and I made sure that if it went wrong I would still have a good time and I did because it did go wrong. So those who didn't take the bait were justified. Beggars can't be choosers and I decided that there was nothing wrong in failing and that just maybe I could help to make it a success the next year.

I knew when I made this decision that I was, metaphorically speaking, in for some kind of ride so likewise I metaphorically buckled up my seatbelt and sat tight. How right I was; as October came and my movie "Winter Swimming" premiered at the Czech adventure film festival MFOF and I held up a train to let Dasha (who was as usual running late) join me, when she was in fact already on board. I felt like I didn't have time to breathe after that weekend as Alexandr Brylin was soon planning a trip to Alaska, there were more showings of the movie, an invitation to China, a possible trip to New Zealand, not to mention, winter swimming events, my studies and a full time job that required my presence. Something had to give and it was the full time job that I ditched at Christmas time, mainly so that I could concentrate on my studies. My studies were leading to 5 exams in May and required a great deal of reading of large, heavy textbooks. It was for this reason that I didn't go to New Zealand with Dasha. We consoled ourselves by looking on the bright side that the brief period apart would give me the crucial time I needed to concentrate on my studies and any organisational activities regarding the Bering Strait swim. Ironically it was Dasha who convinced me that I should study although it didn't happen immediately but rather had a knock on effect as she had suggested it some 6 months prior to me actually applying.

As for winter swimming, by the end of September the season was getting ready to start. In the final week of September Jiří Kuřina invited me to swim the Labe (Elbe) from Hradec Králové to Pardubice with himself and Jirka Beneš from Studenka. We set off at around 8.30am and swum for 2 hours in water that was about 13.8C. We had to get out as there was a weir. We were all shivering uncontrollably as we had a banana and some tea and then jumped back in. That day I spent 5 and a half hours in the water but I had to get out before the finish having swum some 18km. Kuřina was the only one to finish, a very tough man. It was a tough day in cold water and shows you that you can still harden to the cold in higher temperatures although when it comes to swimming in zero it is good to get some experience before you try it in a race or event because otherwise you may panic as you start to wonder why you cannot feel your limbs at all!

Beringia, the Pleistocene....Dezhnev, Bering, Chirikov & Cook

Due to its geographical location between Russia and America, not to mention the fact that it lies just south of the Arctic Circle and is covered by ice for most of the year the Bering Strait is both feared and revered. There are countless expeditions to undertake crossings by a variety of means and inevitably there are far more failures than successes.

It is necessary to go back in time several hundred years to the age of discovery in order chart the modern history of Bering Strait crossings.

However, going back even further to the Pleistocene epoch of pre 10,000 years bp (BP = before present, taken as 1960) to 2million bp and the last ice ages, the Bering Strait was an important crossing point. Due to the low temperatures, much more water was locked up in the great ice sheets that covered large parts of the northern hemisphere, combining this with the fact that colder water contracts as opposed to warmer water which expands meant that sea levels were much lower. The Bering Strait at the current time (2013) is only 30 -50m deep and during the last ice age, the sea was around 120m lower meaning that the Bering strait was actually the Bering land bridge, joining the Eurasian and American continents and spanning some 1000km from the Kamchatka peninsula, across the Aleutian islands and in the north as far as the northern tip of both Chukotka and Alaska. The area was unglaciated and instead was a great plain. It provided the perfect corridor for the movement of flora and fauna from the old world to the new. The exact reasons and the exact timing of the migration of people across the land bridge are unknown and more than likely happened on several occasions during the Pleistocene period with the last migration perhaps around 12,000 years ago when the world was still in the grip of an ice age.

The peoples of Western Alaska and Chukotka share a common ancestry and here on the shores of the Bering Strait many people are Siberian Yupik Eskimo by ethnic origin but Russian or American by nationality and citizenship. Not surprisingly St Lawrence Island being closer to the mainland of Russia than to that of the USA even though it is US territory consists of mainly Siberian Yupik people. In fact it is widely believed that all Native Americans are descendants of people who crossed the Bering land bridge during previous ice ages. It was the land bridge that was responsible for the peopling of the Americas. These original settlers who hailed from Eastern Siberia were themselves migrants who had continually moved up the Pacific coast from China. Biogeography tells a fantastic story and no more so than in the Bering strait region, a place where east meets west and where the cold north wind and ocean currents keep the climate cold and icebound preserving many more secrets from the past under vast areas of permafrost.

10,000 years ago the warm period we are now in known as the Holocene started. As the earth warmed, the ice sheets retreated and oceans experienced thermal expansion. A reverse of the previous situation as once again ocean levels rose and the Bering Strait was now under water with the land bridge disappearing. Interestingly during the colder Pleistocene period the Bering land bridge wasn't glaciated due to low snow levels and the landscape resembled a steppe. Conversely, during the warmer Holocene epoch the Bering Strait region experiences something of a thermal anomaly with the 10c isotherm moving quite far south, as far as the treeless Aleutian islands on the US side and the top half of the Kamchatka peninsula on the Russian side. The reason for this is the cold ocean current called the Oyashio which originates in the arctic and brings cold water south through the Bering Strait. Kamchatka is at a similar latitude to the UK but the climates are totally different due to the differing ocean currents. During the Pleistocene the land bridge acted as a physical barrier to the Oyashio current and therefore the climate in Beringia was less harsh even though it was an ice age and a large part of the northern hemisphere was glaciated.

With water separating the 2 continents the attention turned to sea travel and in the modern age of exploration it was the Spanish and English who ruled the seas and explored the world. At least this was the case in the west. In the north East by the 17th century the Russians were busy conquering Siberia and the northern coast of Russia. In 1648 the Cossack, Semyon Dezhnev led an expedition in wooden boats known as Koches down the Kolyma to the Arctic Ocean. From here they sailed on in an easterly direction before rounding the eastern tip of Russia and making landfall somewhere around the mouth of the Anadyr River, founding the Anadyr settlement in the process. They had found a good source of furs, but lost many men in the process. Dezhnev didn't receive much credit for his ground-breaking descent of the Kolyma River and his first rounding of the far eastern tip of Asia and it would be over 70 years before more headway was made in exploring this remote area of the globe. Although Dezhnev married a Yakutian girl and settled in Jakutsk he was actually of Pomor origin and thus perhaps it was no surprise that he should travel so bravely in the icy northern waters. Pomor people were from the Kara Sea/White Sea area of north western Russia. They were excellent seamen akin to the Norse and they had almost certainly discovered and settled Spitsbergen before William Barents officially discovered the island in 1596.

A Danish sailor, serving in the Russian navy, Vitus Bering, entered the fray in the 18th century. He was instructed by Peter The Great to explore the coast line of the Far East as Dezhnev had done and finally solve the mystery of where the end of the world was and where America started. Bering's first Kamchatka expedition, which started in Okhotsk before sailing around the Kamchatka peninsula and north to Chukotka started in 1725 and ended in 1728 by which time he had corroborated Dezhnev's tale but had no real proof. Although seen as just a minor success Bering was granted permission to continue and by 1741 he was mounting his second Kamchatka expedition. His ships the St Peter (captained by him) and the St Paul (captained by Alexei Chirikov) both reached the American coast in July of 1741. Bering is credited with the discovery of America but it was the German naturalist Georg Steller who went ashore with a watering party and documented, first identifying the Stellers Jay which being different from the European Jay was proof that the expedition had reached America. Bering was undoubtedly a skilled navigator but he was already becoming weary and starting to suffer from scurvy.

Chirikov, meanwhile, took his vessel back to Russia having made landfall further south. He reached Kamchatka by October whereas Bering and the St Peter ran into storms somewhere near the treacherous and rocky Aleutian Islands. They tacked along this island chain and finally made landfall in the Commander islands in December

1741. Here they spent a wretched winter on the treeless island and Bering perished sometime in early December, severely weakened by scurvy he died knowing that they had finally succeeded in reaching America. The following spring the 46 survivors built a new boat and set sail for Kamchatka with news of the expedition. Bering perished but his name lives on in the form of the Bering Strait, sea, island and glacier.

James Cook the famous English seaman and explorer is perhaps most well-known for his travels in the South Pacific, but he was also responsible for mapping much of the Alaskan coast and confirming the work of Bering some years before. In fact it was he who named the strait after Bering.

The link to these original explorers may seem tenuous but our own idiosyncratic expedition had the potential to turn into something akin to these original voyages.

As is customary for all Russian expeditions that try to reach Alaska, Petropavlovsk Kamchatsky is the starting point with the large natural harbour and the possibility to meet and stock up on supplies, indeed it is often said that PK possesses the best natural harbour in the world. So the scene was set but now as always we needed a ship that was suitable for the job.

Alaska trip 2011

It was about 11 days ago that I left for Alaska saying I don't really know what to expect. I was right. It was a business trip that turned out to be more of an adventure than I thought. I gained new knowledge and experience and came back with a good opinion of American people. I liked Anchorage – not a pretty town but the people seemed genuine and down to earth, I could see myself spending more time there.

Alexander Brylin since I first saw him has always struck me as being a big guy with big energy. More than ever now I'm certain that it's good energy. I have a huge amount of respect for him as a man and as a winter swimmer even if sometimes I find his ways strange. That is the beauty of meeting different people from different parts of the world. He has swum for 48 minutes in near freezing (0c) water which is pretty amazing. His exploits are not so well known in the western media as he is from the Russian Far East but his ability as a "walrus" is immense. I had wondered in the past if he was a bit of a prima donna but I don't think he is. He is a normal guy like me with a dream to make this relay swim across the Bering Strait. After his previous success with the great Amur swim he made the mistake of being a little complacent regarding the new project. I don't hold that against him, I probably couldn't have done any better. These kind of events are complex expeditions and as such take huge amounts of planning. We did great work in Alaska for 10 days but it was just a fraction of what we need to do.

Now I move to Jiang Liang Zhe and immediately I start to smile. Known to his friends in China as "teddy bear", well to be frank you can see why. And he is just as lovable, in fact it's a perfect nickname. Between us we know 5 or 10 words of each other's languages but it doesn't stop us communicating and being friends. Liang Zhe is a master of subtle sounds, gestures and facial expressions. In life you meet some special characters, special for a variety of reasons and Liang Zhe is one of those characters. His enthusiasm for photography and giving of gifts know no bounds. He bought a huge amount of electrical goods to take home and this shopping was an enjoyable and interesting experience as we helped him to decide what to buy. His funniest moment was surely when myself, Alexandr and Igor were sitting in the lounge of our hosts' home in Nome discussing the next morning's swim. We were using a mixture of Russian and English with Igor translating when needed. There was a bit to discuss as it was already extremely cold here in Nome and conditions were looking tricky. I was counting on a maximum immersion of 10 minutes with the air temperature possibly as low as -20c. I asked how long shall we swim? Alexandr and I agreed on around 10mins but Alexandr then added that Liang Zhe had said he would only swim for a max of 5mins. As we discussed more details such as the route Alexandr smiled and suggested running 5 or 600m up the beach with the flags and then swimming back. That way Liang Zhe would have no option but to swim back! At this point Liang Zhe (who was asleep and snoring his head off as usual) bolted upright, pointed his finger at Alexandr and shouted something in Chinese before going back to sleep. Needless to say we were pissing ourselves in fits of hysterics for a few minutes. It was a classic "Liang Zhe" moment of which there have been many, partly due to his amazing ability to convey emotions and opinions through body language, facial expression and even sounds! A truly unique character hard on the outside but soft on the inside. No matter how well you treat him at first you will be met with neutrality but slowly he will open up to you and show you his amazing personality. I am not sure how reliable he would be in a crisis situation but certainly as a human being his integrity and trustworthiness are top notch.

I already wrote about flying North-West to Wales over the frozen wastes of the early winter Tundra. What I didn't write about was the throbbing pain in both of my feet after I made a blunder in rewarming after the swim in Nome. Well that was the second blunder, the first came after I decided to go outside in -10c air with no shoes and then go for a swim. A stupid error caused by the fact that I was being complacent having 5 days previously been in the mild autumn of central Europe. The second mistake was a bigger 1 and involved me putting my socks on too quickly and then another pair of socks, my boots and my gators. Blood flow was restricted and it was 30-60 minutes before I realized but by then the damage had already be done – Frostnip! Although I should have known better and should have worn something on my feet on the way to the swim the final nail in the coffin was the fact that I was distracted after the swim first by photographers and then crucially in the changing room by the need to get to the airport and before that send a crucial email. Back to that flight over the frozen tundra and the throbbing pain in my feet while looking down at the beautiful white landscape was having a big effect on me. I could see ice, snow, water and it looked powerful and menacing; more than ever I knew that I must always respect nature. I already do but even so perhaps sometimes not enough.

As if to prove that, less than 24hrs later and I had made another blunder resulting in me slipping through the ice and getting saturated to my mid/upper thigh. It was something I knew could happen but the adventurer (and nature lover) in me had already taken over. I had spotted a colony of seals and couldn't resist trying to get as close as possible to them. It served as a warning to me and I thought carefully about my own ability as a risk assessor or on the short trip back to change my soaked and now-on-the-way-to-frozen trousers. It was my first visit to the arctic region and a winter swimmer, I might be a tough guy, hardened, fearless – all these things I might be, but it would only take one mistake and any man can be taken out by nature. I wasn't too worried as I saw this as part of my arctic learning curve. In fact a small part of me was already looking forward to another similar encounter, perhaps next time in an immersion suit on my way to the North Pole!

Within our group I achieved high status for this mishap especially with Liang Zhe as he stated that Alexandr only suggested a swim in the Bering Strait but Jack has actually done it. Well it may have been a mistake but perhaps it was a good omen that at least one of us went in.

At this point my feet were giving me some problems and had become uncomfortable, although I had another pair of trousers I didn't have any spare shoes! Eventually I got back to Meg's house in Eagle River near Anchorage and bathed my feet. Problematic and blistered but they were ok. In fact 3 days later and we made a short exhibition swim in the 6c Puget Sound in Seattle. 6c is cold but after Alaska it seemed rather temperate.

As for our meetings in Anchorage we were the definition of a motley crew. Representatives of the swim were me, Alexandr Brylin and Jiang Liang Zhe of China. Let me elaborate on this, so we have me – a Brit living in Prague who speaks a bit of Russian and a few words of Chinese; Alexandr, a Russian who speaks some Chinese and a few words of English. Then there is Liang Zhe, a Chinese man who speaks a few words of Russian and a few words of English. That said we managed to communicate between ourselves pretty well, especially with the addition of the Russian film maker Igor Dadashev who also speaks English. Leonid Kokaurov, fluent in both Russian and English was also present and added a wise head of experience to our group. However we were extremely colourful with Alexandr the leader, only able to communicate in Russian but Liang Zhe was the real joker in the pack. A short and stocky man with a long, thin beard he is extremely charismatic and seemed to take on the role of official mascot and photographer as he proceeded to snap away almost nonstop. However his battery ran out when he met Nicholas Cage in a lift which was amusing especially as I was in another lift and he was alone with Alexandr. In the governor's office we met with Patricia Eckert who deals with international trade. She was an interesting lady and although she was initially annoying by continually referring to me as Nick even after being corrected and not listening to me in the end I warmed to her. The reason was that it was highly amusing to see her perplexity at what exactly Liang Zhe was doing with us and what his role was. Liang Zhe was happily fulfilling his paparazzi role and Patricia took exception to this and asked him to stop. It was a bizarre scene and I managed to control my laughter. Patricia went on to say that she knew how things were different in China and she was very keen to know exactly who Liang Zhe was and who he was working for and who he was connected to. It smacked very much of fear that he was working for the Chinese state as some kind of spy.

Whether Liang Zhe had a spying mission I don't know but it soon became clear that one of his main tasks in the USA was to buy electronic equipment and other gadgets such as Casio sports watches! We had a few memorable shopping trips. I assisted Liang Zhe in the important task of spending his seemingly endless supply of dollars as he purchased camera after camera after watch after iPad and so on. Alexandr also got in on the action and the final shopping spree meant that we made check in by about 40 seconds for our flight to Seattle. The two of them were absolutely laden with electronics and I am sure that the three of us were quite a sight, me mainly by association!

Back in Prague, I got through the front door, dumped my stuff and went straight out to the diving shop. I bought some neoprene socks. I had decided that I would protect my feet for a couple of weeks. The next day I swam 1km in the Vltava River, water 6c. Then on the Saturday I was faced with a Stillwater 750m in the Czech Republic, water temperature 3.5c. I used the neoprene socks. They hampered me somewhat, making me even slower than before but they seemed to do the trick and I have to say it had a positive, comforting effect on the psyche. As we know the psyche plays a huge role in long distance winter swimming. The final time I used the neoprene socks was at training the following Wednesday. Then on the Saturday I had them in my kitbag at Hradec Králové but in the end I decided not to use them. At the registration desk I was deliberating over whether to swim the 1000m. I met Jan Novák who asked me what the problem was. I told him about my feet and he simply said use some cream and maybe a few plasters. I was glad I had met the no-nonsense English Channel veteran and now I was certain to swim the 1000m. Due to the low flow of the river for the first time here at Hradec the water conditions would be still. This meant a circuit in the river with us swimming both up and downstream, rather than a simple downstream point to point swim. Air temperature was ok, at about 5c above although there was a little wind to add to the mix. The water was just over 3c and this would take some swimming. There were well over 100 participants in the event but only 14 lined up for the 1000m. I knew I would be right at the back of the field but I didn't care. However, I surprised myself at how I was left for dead. I kept up for the first 100m but after the first buoy the entire rest of the field got away from me and I felt pretty much alone. It was a tricky swim but I got my head down and kept going. I saw my friend Jan Novák the referee standing by the steps as I started the second and final circuit and I pushed on to try and make some ground. It was a hopeless task but I made it to the finish in 20m 42s so I was happy with this. I was cold, but I had been colder. This was a tough swim but mostly they all are during the winter season.

After a quick goulash and beer I had to leave early so I missed the results and prize-giving. A pity, because actually I had been declared overall winner of the entire contest. The reason for this was because on the 40th anniversary of the event it was throwback to the old days of he who lasts longest is the winner, not the fastest. The time limit before disqualification is 22minutes and my 20m 42seconds was the slowest time of the day so I was the winner. I felt pleased with this although I don't agree with the idea of making a competition out of staying in the water as it's much better when based around distance and speed like any other sport. Still, it was a pity to miss the prize giving as one of my friends Jiří Kuřina was the main organiser.

Alaska, Seattle – going into Novikov

The trip to Alaska had been okay but we didn't achieve anything spectacular. Slowly we met various people in Anchorage and me Alexandr and Liang Zhe along with our translator, film maker Igor bonded well, especially on our trip to the remote native village of Wales, where standing next to me Alexandr looked through my binoculars past the Diomede islands to the faint and distant outline of the Russian coast. "My family, are from Chukotka he said." At this point I realized that for him it was something special as a Russian to cross the Bering strait to the USA just as those early pioneers of the Alaskan trading company had done when they took Alaska as a Russian colony several hundred years before, and of course going even further back in time to the last ice age some 17,000 years ago when the Bering Strait was actually the Bering land bridge. Sea levels were lower due to the cold period and people from Eurasia were able to populate the American continent by migrating east to what we now know as Alaska.

And in that final sentence the present day paradox begins. Yes we travel east from Chukotka, the furthest eastern point of the Asian continent, meeting two islands one Russian and one American which are just 4km apart, before we arrive at the native village of Wales the most western point on the American continent some 86km as the crow flies from the Russian mainland. So to sum that up we travelled as far east as we could in order to arrive in the extreme west. During this time we crossed the international dateline and gained a day, and at this point the old Slavonic name "Встречь Солнца" translated into English as "meeting of the sun" starts to seem a pretty fitting title.

Going back to the Alaska trip and we had made a good impression on people but it was soon clear that in general we were probably just seen as a group of fly by night crazies who wouldn't be back again.

Before returning home we stopped for a few days in Seattle where there were plenty of Russians and I had an audience of at least 200 as I proceeded to introduce our project at the traditional post service Sunday Luncheon at the Orthodox Church hall. The only thing was that I am pretty sure that only between 5 and 20 people were taking any notice whatsoever. Well, at least the priest laughed at my joke that why should I talk when we had such a great spread of food ready to be eaten. Like I said before we didn't have great financial backing and never look a gift horse in the mouth really applies here, free food is great, after all it's what keeps us going and sustains us and our passions and dreams. Therefore I really appreciate it when someone offers me food and I always feel at home when offered food. The weather in Seattle was positively temperate and this was very noticeable having just travelled from Alaska, no need for a hat here let alone a down jacket! However, the beautiful water of the Puget Sound was still only 6c and although this was a huge jump from negative 1.5c in the Bering Sea at Nome it was still cold enough. My feet were still recovering and I had been hoping that we wouldn't swim as I was already planning my comeback for the following Wednesday in the Vltava River back home in Prague. I quickly found a chemist and bought some sticking plaster to at least give the tender areas some protection. They weren't too bad but in an ideal world I wouldn't have swum. Needless to say the swim was good fun but as a marketing event it did very little as there were no media there though there were plenty of amateur videographers from the Russian community. Actually I was glad that I swam in the Puget Sound as it was absolutely beautiful. The water was crystal clear and not very saline at all. Considering that the Puget Sound is in the middle of a city as big as Seattle I thought the water quality at Alkai beach was excellent and I looked forward to another chance for a swim there. It wouldn't be on this trip though as I was soon flying back leaving Alexandr and Liang Zhe with a business card for a contact who might help find a ship. They didn't get much done after I had gone but they were left to their own devices by the Russian community until Sergey Novikov stepped in.

I never met Sergey Novikov and I hadn't even heard of him until 2 weeks later when I got an email from Steven Munatones asking me to politely tell Sergey to stop bugging him about various open water swimming issues. Little was I to realize that I was about to be hearing his voice a great deal over the coming months.

At first I was confused over the identity of Novikov believing him to be the young Sergey Gladysh president of a youth organisation who had been with us in Seattle. Novikov soon set me straight and explained that he was now working with us, a fact which was confirmed by Alexandr through Irina. I was happy with this. Now we had an American partner who wanted to push this event and was maybe capable of attracting some US investment for what was undoubtedly an expensive project even if attempted at a budget level. Some people were suggesting $2million, others $6-800,000. The latter figure especially was not fanciful and by my own estimates if we got a ship for free the other logistics would still run into the hundreds of thousands of dollars. Sasha was convinced that the cost should be divided between the participants, which in theory I had no problem with. However, in reality this would rely on money coming from around 30 different sources which would be tricky. I always liked a gamble and I likened this to trying to pull off an accumulator. Always very difficult to do even with just 4 horses. And here we were looking at 30! In my opinion we needed some base funds or at least some way of securing credit so that we could get the logistics in place to prove to the participants that their money was safe and that the event would actually happen.

Sergey Novikov immediately scored points with me as he agreed with my ideas. I wasn't totally convinced by him as he lacked knowledge about open water swimming, Alaska and also expeditions in such difficult environments. However, he was extremely enthusiastic. At the time I also thought it crucial that he was a Russian American who was aspiring to the American way whilst still understanding the Russian manifesto. I believed that this last fact could be the key factor in making this a true Russian/American project with me bringing in the international help in the form of swimmers from around the globe. Going in to the festive period in December I now felt much more comfortable and under less pressure as I could concentrate on doing a job which I could realistically do well which was to find those international swimmers.

I started to contact people around the world with the help of Steven Munatones and one of the swimmers from South Africa, Andrew Chin. The emails were flying through cyberspace thick and fast and I gave thanks for the wonders of the internet and pondered whether such a project would have been possible 20 or 30 years ago.

Soon the organisation seemed to be moving quite swiftly and with the help of Munatones and Chin and me word was spreading and the profile of the Bering Strait swim was being raised.

The next milestone would be the world winter swimming championships in Jurmala, Latvia at the end of January as this would be a good chance to meet winter swimming friends, old and new and of course catch up with the Russian organisers, namely Alexandr Brylin.

By early January Sergey Novikov was calling me regularly, always upbeat and positive about the project which was a great boost at first as I believed he would deliver the goods in the form of American support. He spoke a lot about being on the verge of government support but as yet he hadn't secured it, although according to him it was just around the corner. By the middle of January there were developments as Sergey had convinced his friend Marty, a marketing specialist to work with us. Marty talked a good game just like Sergey and he really seemed to know his stuff when it came to promotion and marketing as he produced a website that looked very impressive. Meanwhile Sasha had located a ship, the Russian icebreaker, Akademik Shokalskiy which would escort us across the Bering Strait. It had the credentials having been all over both the Arctic and the Antarctic oceans. There was just one small problem – due to it now being classed as a passenger vessel it couldn't take US citizens across the border which gave us a big headache as without US swimmers the project had far less scope within the USA. When I mentioned this to Sergey Novikov he became defensive for the first time and told me not to worry, that he was soon going to have government support and that this problem would be overridden by going to the top. As always I couldn't fault his enthusiasm but I started to question his integrity and his ability to physically deliver what his mouth was promising. This situation with the US citizens bothered me especially seeing as I was trying to recruit a team of 5 US swimmers and I already had at least one solid and extremely enthusiastic US participant in the form of Claudia Rose, the specialist long distance swimmer from San Diego. From the moment she agreed to take part Claudia began to post huge amounts of questions and I soon referred her to Irina as there were so many. She highlighted a great deal of relevant issues in meticulous detail but at times it was over the top. For example she was extremely concerned with swimming for long periods in the dark but had forgotten that we would only be facing a few hours of darkness at such northern latitudes in July. Her worries about the feasibility of the swim from Russia to America due to ocean currents were relevant but started to become obsessive. She stated that she was in touch with scientists at NOAA who told her it was impossible due to the general northerly flow of water from the pacific throughout the Bering Strait to the Arctic. I knew about this and of course the shallow depth of the Bering Strait wasn't going to help. However, I also knew that a prevailing north westerly could be of significant help, but obviously not too strong such as a Force 5 or above which would probably make the strait unnavigable to us swimmers. Claudia talked of ferry lines which was a job for the navigator and when she mentioned that a certain NOAA scientist had stated that we would get eaten by walrus I found my humour and took that as a positive. It was also another good reason against the use of wetsuits which would make us appear like sea mammals.

In the native village of Wales I had spoken to some of their hunters who had told me of the strong currents heading north and that it was between the Diomede islands where it was strongest. Gilbert, who was also the village preacher, had spoken about the great influence of the winds. He appeared to be a wise man and was well respected in the village. After our conversation he said to me "We better stop now or I am going to start bullshitting!" I thanked him for his time. Clearly these people from Wales, known as the Kingimuit tribe who had been in the region for centuries knew the forces of nature here better than anybody and also knew how fickle they could be. But as always it was a case of not putting all the eggs in one basket and I wasn't prepared to rubbish the data provided by experts from institutions such as NOAA any more than I would rubbish the views of the indigenous people of the region. Back in Anchorage when I was speaking with Karlin Itchouk from the Institute of the North, himself a native Alaskan he confirmed this, and I knew that I was approaching this project in the right way. Regarding the swim itself I was given confidence by 2 previous swims and that's without the most famous Lynne Cox swim. Back in 1999 the Russians had made a swim from the mainland to Ratmanov Island (big Diomede). It was a relay and they had managed it without problems. I knew one of the swimmers, Elena Guseva from Perm near the Ural Mountains and she was ready for the coming swim. Elena is a great ice swimmer and as a person she is calm, unassuming and modest. She simply said "It was cold but it was ok." That was good enough for me. All the data and opinions I had, convinced me that the great thing about our relay swim across the Bering Strait was that it was right on the borderline. It would be tricky but it was doable. Further north and probably it wouldn't be possible but here this short gap between the Eurasian and American continents just below the arctic circle would be a great test for the world's best ice swimmers – but not impossible. The second swim that gave me a bit more confidence was by Marcos Diaz who swam from Ratmanov (big Diomede) to little Diomede. Admittedly he was in a wetsuit but crucially he had swum to an extent in the direction we wanted to go and he had been successful. Many people had been saying that Lynne Cox swam the USA to Russia direction as it wasn't possible the other way so Diaz had disproved that theory. I have to say I was surprised that he made his swim at the end of August, well in to storm season and also with the water temperature dropping a little as the insolation decreased. I was happy with swimming at the end of July, weather permitting, although some Alaskans had been saying the earlier in July the better. I remembered the reactions of the guys in Wales, which was basically, "It's tricky, but you could pull it off."

Jurmala 2012

Meanwhile the winter swimming season continued and there was an important event about to take place. In 2012 the world winter swimming championships were to be held in Jurmala, Latvia, a small spa resort on the Baltic Sea just 20km from the capital city Riga.

Again I was going alone without any of my Czech friends. Zdeněk asked me about the trip far too late which was a pity as he had the chance of taking a medal in the endurance swim.

2012 was a year of serious economising for me so the route to Riga was 2 Wizz air flights coming to a grand total of 30 euros! I had 4 budget flights in a week and a large piece of luggage and the fun and games began as I made the first flight by the skin of my teeth as I was driven to board the plane by an emergency car at Prague airport. Good old laid back Prague, anywhere else and I would have been in real trouble. On arrival at Eindhoven I had to go out and go back through the security rigmarole again. But before I could do that I had to get to security which meant having my bag weighed and inspected. I tried my best to interfere with the scales but eventually the real weight of 19kilos was shown. Unfortunately the girl who was operating this did everything by the book and much as I tried I was sent back to check the bag in. Now most people would give up here and check the bag in but not me. As I said I was economising and there was no way I was paying to check a bag in. I still had 2 more budget flights to go so paying this early was not a smart move or a good omen. I hung back a bit and watched what was going on. There was a second line and this girl seemed slightly more lax in that she was checking most but not all bags. I picked my moment when she was on the phone and shielding my bag on the opposite shoulder I breezed past giving her a big smile as I went. On reaching security my small bottle of Czech rum (a present for my friend Roman) was taken from me. I hung around intent on taking out of the bin when I got the chance but wisely decided against it; after all I had got away without checking my bag in.

Finally, I arrived in Jurmala at the cheapest accommodation I could find. The room was adequate, the bathrooms bad but I took solace in the fact that although there was no kitchen there was a kettle – one of the most useful appliances for a winter swimmer!

I made it to the technical meeting for the endurance swim where I met with some old friends including Alexandr Brylin who appeared as his usual colourful self. A man of few words but he always sports bright Russian tracksuits and has a certain aura about him. There were quite a few people there but nothing out of the ordinary happened and in fact I needn't have bothered going. It was clear that the organisers were still very wary of this event and if the 25m and 50m were just a bit of fun, this was serious and they knew it. Let's face it the championships are a good business as the shorter races are just like having a dip after a sauna but this endurance race was more demanding. At 450m it represented a challenge even if many of us had more experience of longer distances, me included.

After a few brief chats I got some food and trudged 30mins back to my room at the other end of town for some comfort in the form of tea and biscuits.

The next day I got to the event and started meeting people including Anna Carin Nordin who proved to be a small person in stature but huge in both winter swimming ability and character. She easily took a gold medal in the endurance race and confirmed that she was looking forward to joining us for the Bering Strait relay. When I saw Alexandr Brylin he said to me "Robotit, robotit" (work, work). To his credit he handed me a new batch of leaflets which he had corrected after I had pointed out in Alaska the glaring error declaring that the Chinese swimmer Dr Wang had swum from the Arctic to the Antarctic! Actually it was a pretty low key day in terms of meeting people but of course the main event was the endurance race. I knew I didn't have a hope of getting a medal but I didn't care as I am committed to the sport win lose or draw. Considering how many races they had it was extremely well organised and smooth running but there was so little time that I failed to set up my video camera in time to film the swim!

The swim itself turned out to be a war of attrition. I never got going and I didn't swim straight in the tight 25m long ice hole, squirming like a snake there and back to make 18 laps and 450m in just over 10 minutes. I really felt I should have got just under 10 minutes but it isn't easy swimming in the ice hole having to turn but with nothing to push off. Water temperature was just above freezing and they did a good job of circulating the water to stop it icing over. Air temperature was between -2c and -5c. I would have been happy to swim longer but I still felt the chill minutes after getting out. I decided to do it the Scandinavian way and went into the sauna after a quick cold shower. The sauna was interesting as one guy was complaining of the pain in his hands. I told him "Don't worry it's good that your hands hurt, they will be ok in a few minutes." Of course I was right but what amused me were his theatrics. He had surely swum in this kind of water before and if he hadn't he shouldn't have been swimming. My suspicion was that he hadn't experienced water just above freezing and there is a big difference between 0.5c and 4c. 4c is very cold and you can't swim very long, it hurts. However, 0.5c is something else and the extremities are numb very, very quickly. Another guy came in who looked in quite a bad way but he was fine after some time, again I doubted his experience. Then there was another guy who was almost carried into the sauna and shower area. For me and many others we are used to the effects of extremely cold water but some of the endurance swimmers acted afterwards like they had never known anything like it and as I alluded to, maybe that hadn't. After all, even amongst the hardy there are few that will swim in the ice hole. I saw some sights that day but everyone was ok and the organisation was superb. Even after witnessing those scenes in the sauna the most bizarre scene is still when I saw a strong swimmer but first time winter swimmer Petr after a race in Choceň, Czech Republic, crouched in a ball on the floor hugging a radiator. I offered him some tea and told him to get up but he didn't listen. However, he soon learnt and stopped his love of radiators quite quickly.

Not much more happened in Jurmala but Paolo Chiarino and Alberto Salvi took silver and gold in their endurance races and Henri Kaarma gold in his. Jackie Cobell also took a gold while I was maybe one place off taking the wooden spoon in my category!

Later that night I attended the presentation ceremony which was nothing special. I managed to get a coffee and some biscuits before they ran out and congratulated various people before making a date with the Italians for a swim in the Baltic Sea next morning.

Air temperature that morning was -8c and the wind was blowing. It was more a symbolic dip than a swim but still it took me some time to get changed and thaw out my feet which were still a bit sensitive from the Alaska trip back in November. Back at the venue and I had more tea and biscuits along with the usual chat with Alexandr Brylin. Not much was happening so I made my way to Riga for a bit of sightseeing. On the way I was fortunate to bump into my friend Alexander Kirshner from Slovakia. We had a good chat and he informed me that the Baltic Sea was about

-2c that morning. I know he measured it himself and I trusted his measurements to be accurate. What's more Paolo's watch had gone to zero very quickly and mine had read 0.5c. The thermometers on sports watches are fairly reliable but due to the heat of the body they take at least 10 minutes to give an accurate reading.

Soon I was heading for my 3rd budget flight and this time I was forced to pay a 10 euro charge for airport tax, courtesy of the wonderful Ryanair. A pain but at least I did finally arrive in London and get my head down.

This part of the trip was centred around the Royal Geographical Society and in particular a lecture that would be given by Lewis Gordon Pugh, an old winter swimming companion of Alexandr's. In fact he actually mentioned Alexandr Brylin in his lecture. If the truth be told I had been inspired by reading a book about George Mallory and how he asked a question at The Explorers Club and I felt that I had to make myself known when the Q&A started. I picked the right moment, managing to get the last question and I drew attention to the Bering Strait swim. Lewis also spoke about it which pleased me. Afterwards I met a few people and even managed to more than hold my own in a very short debate with some rather well-spoken and well educated types who were probably earning more money in a month than I do in a year.

Lewis asked me to meet him the next day and we had a good chat, I couldn't get him to join us for the Bering Strait swim but he did speak well of Alexandr Brylin. His only negative comment was why the hell does he have to dedicate these swims to so many people with which I agreed entirely. In fact by June the Bering Strait swim was not only in memorial to Semyon Dezhnev, Vitus Bering and the Lend Lease Act but also to an obscure Russian poet. There was a problem with money and now an idea to align the swim with a dead poet, again the phrase "anything is possible in Russia" rings true.

I also got in a swim at the Serpentine Lido as a guest after I contacted Colin Hill. Bizarrely we had met in the changing rooms at Jurmala straight after he finished his swim where I gave him some ginger tea. He left his accreditation which I picked up but I didn't see him again to give it back. The Serpentine was fine at about 4c but I ended up ditching my down jacket and walking around London in a t shirt it was that warm.

Not much else swimming related happened and I was again fobbed off by Christine at Speedo, after a pleasant phone call. But what could I expect, some crazy winter swimmer who does a bit of this and that and goes here and there, when they are interested in elite athletes like Kerri Anne Payne. I had felt good in London and could see myself returning to live there sometime in the future but I needed more support from my home country I just didn't know exactly how and more importantly how to go about getting it.

The final aeronautical drama of the trip was the most farcical as I was stopped with my large pack by 2 eagle eyed and savvy Ryanair hostesses at the gate. My bag wouldn't go in the slot but I just walked towards the gate trying to ignore their cries. They made me go back but I remained calm and said that the bag would go in. I had no intention of giving them £40 which at that moment was almost my wages for a week as I was just teaching a little English while focussing on my studies.

I put the thermos and some other things in my pocket but still it wouldn't quite go in. Then their attention was distracted by another unlucky passenger with oversized luggage and I seized the chance to shove my laptop down my jacket. "Look, it goes in" I said and walked off to board the plane looking like a Michelin man. What a fiasco in the plane as I tried to find a place for my bag and my various bits and pieces in the overhead lockers. A steward tried to help me and nearly dropped the bag on feeling its weight.

"Is it really 10 kilos?" he said, "Oh yes" I lied without feeling in any way guilty!

Back in Seattle Novikov hadn't come up with anything concrete although after input from various people, Marty had produced a 5 minute promotional video. The quality wasn't great as the material had been ripped from various different sources but the message was clear – "Come and help us swim the Bering." Along with the website, the blogging and social media plan and a PDF brochure this side of the project looked good. My view was to let the guys roll with it for now as they were confident they could attract support with these materials. My reasons were simple – America barely existed until the 17th century at which point it was populated and exploited by Europeans who proceeded to turn it into the dominant world superpower by the end of the 20th century. Its power has faded somewhat in the first decade of the 21st century but it is still a force and a new country when you compare it with China. My opinion was that what might seem fanciful in Europe could be possible in the USA. I was also convinced that even in times of hardship there was still more wealth and freely available money in the USA.

Around this time I sensed some tension for the first time between Alexandr Brylin and Sergey Novikov. The latter was demanding money from the former in order to pay Marty for his work. As was his habit Alexandr sent less than what was agreed. This time he wired $5000 to Novikov instead of $20,000. Novikov already had an invoice from Marty for 10 or $12,000 which needed to be paid. Now the fun and games really started and just as the marketing materials were about to be released and the campaign started Novikov called a Skype conference between the two of us, Marty and the guy that he wanted to work on logistics, an ex US navy diver, Terry Beaver.

In a bizarre twist Novikov revealed that Alexandr was under investigation for fraud and that he had embezzled funds from the project! Sergey had been in touch with Oleg Dokuchaev, an aide to General Moisseev in the state Duma in Khabarovsk, Russian Far East who had informed him of this. My initial reaction was shock and whilst Alexandr was difficult to work with I didn't believe that he was a fraudster. He had an ego and he was maybe hungry for fame but I didn't believe that he was so desperate for money that he would resort to fraud.

So the project according to Novikov was put on hold, it was now with the Russian authorities who would make a decision on when and how it would go ahead.

In Russia, Irina had also been in contact with Novikov and was in the same situation as me although she had more allegiance to Alexandr than me. I wasn't making any judgements until I had the facts. Novikov continued to call me on an almost daily basis. He continually rambled on about what a crook Alexandr was and when I suggested that perhaps someone in Russia was trying to usurp Alexandr and take the project he dismissed that suggestion. It was now clear in his mind that he couldn't work with Alexandr. It was a very difficult time for me. I was caught in the middle of this and I sensed that I was a key figure in that I was holding control of the international swimmers, a crucial part of the project. I decided to remain impartial although at the same time I tried to convince Alexandr to postpone the swim until 2013 now that there was a split within the organisation. Alexandr was having none of it and reverted to his belief that the cost must be divided between the swimmers and that was the way we would realize our dream. He argued "What would be different next year?"

This puzzling situation continued and of course Alexandr was furious with Novikov but seemed to disregard him as a threat. He used the Latin phrase "divide et impera" to describe Novikov's actions. It was quite true but actually it could be true for Alexandr too if he felt under threat. People suggested that I should distance myself from the project but I wasn't prepared to do that while the facts weren't clear, not to mention that Alexandr was still pressing forward to do the swim this year 2012.

Novikov kept calling me and a pattern was starting to develop. Everything he said would happen was somehow delayed. This had started with his insistence that he would obtain government support back in December.

In April I needed to concentrate on other matters so I told Novikov not to contact me for a while unless it was something urgent. He stopped calling me. By early May things were looking up and I got a message from Alexandr who was asking me to finalize the international swimming team following commitment from a sponsor, namely Russian Railways. Things were looking up. Inevitably I heard again from Novikov and it was clear that he was annoyed by the fact that Alexandr seemed to have control of the situation. I relaxed and tried my best to maintain clear communications with the international swimmers who were still interested in being part of the team to swim across the Bering Strait for the first time in history.

Little did I know that my life was about to be turned upside down...

Death of Dasha

Our relationship wasn't perfect but it was certainly good enough and we were looking forward to seeing each other again soon. Dasha was away in New Zealand and we were due to be reunited either before or after the Bering Strait swim, either in New Zealand or the Czech Republic. Sadly that never happened and now begins a few words about the most dismal episode of my thirty something years.

Sitting in the kitchen on the 29th of May and Dasha's cousin Lukáš had just uttered the words "Dasha is probably dead." I can't begin to explain what a shock it was to hear such words and the feeling of nothingness that I got, I pictured her and then I had a moment of clarity as I understood dead to mean the end.

Moments later I received an email about the Bering Strait project and I simply replied "My girlfriend has been murdered, I can think of nothing else right now." So at that moment it was the finish of everything.

2 days later after some-how finding my way to the clubhouse I was back in the water and incredibly it helped and I seemed to gain some much needed strength. Zdeněk said "Somehow you will find a way to carry on" At first I didn't believe it but I soon came round and after a short 25 minute swim I genuinely felt better. The power of cold water was working its magic yet again.

Death of Dasha 2

Sometimes life is tricky, annoying, boring, and equally fun, rewarding and joyous. However, occasionally life can throw up bigger challenges and also give bigger rewards. Then just perhaps once in a lifetime and luckily even then to only an unlucky few, something truly horrible happens.

An example of this is the meeting with evil that leads to the assault and murder of a loved one. When this happens to you the feelings of shock, loss, devastation and anger are all consuming. Life has to go on even though it seems pointless. Time is suspended and the actions of eating, sleeping, sitting, going to the toilet, walking to another room, or any other simple thing all take on the same meaning in that they are pointless yet still they must be done.

There is no easy way to justify or explain the acts of evil. But certainly there is enough of it in this world. The human being is capable of many things to make itself feel good and extreme violence is a means to an end for some, with no regard for the victim, their family or the domino effect that such evil acts cause.

I decided after the murder of Dasha that from now on I would be firmer in my decision making, I would get what I wanted but without compromising my good principles. I acknowledged the existence of evil but I wasn't prepared to succumb to it.

Speaking to Leonid Kokaurov in Alaska and it became apparent that Alexandr Brylin wasn't much closer to getting the swim on even though he had crucially secured the ship by signing a contract. Money seemed to be lacking and I already knew that he wanted to take money from the international swimmers without using my suggestion of an ESCROW account. It didn't look good to me. Leonid was understanding but asked me if I had more info about the awful events in New Zealand and more precisely the demise of my beloved Dasha. I said we were waiting for the police to finish the investigation. Of course it was clear to all of us what had happened although it was a case of was she chased, or was she forced. I personally needed to know these details and more in order to get through the emotional ordeal and carry on.

Death of Dasha 3

Two and a half weeks after the death of Dasha I managed to decide that I was back in with regards to the Bering. I had received many messages of support from Alexandr Brylin through to the international swimmers and others associated with the project. Of course not much had changed in those weeks and I was soon sifting through emails trying to work out exactly what was going on. Luckily I spoke to Leonid Kokaurov, always the voice of calm and reason and he seemed upbeat. In fact, interestingly Leonid was becoming more and more confident and ever since I first met him I trusted him and his experience 100%. I was a novice, so too were others on this project but Leonid had a quiet but clear and firm manner. I believed that if he thought things were looking up then that was probably the case whereas if Alexandr had told me the same thing I would be seriously wondering. I felt for Alexandr – although he has a big ego he wanted to do the Bering as a team event and I felt he deserved support. I didn't agree with many of his working practices but I respected him as a man and a swimmer. He was also teetotal and although I like the occasional drink myself I saw this as an excellent quality. Alcohol is ok in moderation but in larger quantities it can be a very dangerous drug.

I hoped that we could at least get to the starting point this year after the disappointment of 2011. The truth was we were just a bunch of normal guys, between me, Liang Zhe and Alexandr there wasn't much difference really. I had read and seen so much of the well-connected and well-bred British adventurers and knowing I didn't quite fit the mould was always playing in the back of my mind. Polar travel in particular seemed to be the preserve of the blue-blooded. However what we were doing was something totally different and I had a hunch that if we could get some media attention we could really put extreme cold water swimming in the spotlight. The general public simply didn't understand our sport and how extreme it was. Not only that but also they couldn't understand how we were used to the cold water and that there was scientific evidence to back up the idea that the human body can adapt to such conditions.

Increasingly it seemed that the role of promoting the swim in the western media would fall to me and that it (the role) would fall late and be important. My potential trip to Alaska could even be make or break in some way…

Death of Dasha 4

Although I was carrying on it wasn't easy. I had come to the conclusion that there were 3 options and the first 2 (commit suicide and live sadly) simply weren't options therefore I was going for the third which was to summon all will and strength in order to live on. At first it seemed easy, but then in the unreal world of the first few weeks life is rather strange – money seems to have no value and all activities from going to the toilet, eating a meal, to swimming a 10km or sitting in the pub seemed the same, in that they had limited value and were just a means to an end.

Between the 3 and 4 week mark I noticed things started to change. I had a few busy days and it tired me out mentally. I concluded what I had already suspected and that was that I needed to have activities everyday but not too many. I needed to be busy but at a leisurely pace and it was clearly a mental rather than physical issue.

As I said I had a problem in the pool on Friday, albeit a minor one. The thing was that even though I had shied away from swimming underwater I didn't believe that it would be a problem. It was just at that moment in the pool I didn't want to struggle for air. I didn't want to push myself in that way – being starved of oxygen even if it was only a matter of seconds. I contemplated how I felt about winter swimming but I was pretty sure that it would be no problem in fact I was looking forward to the buzz and adrenaline rush of extreme winter swimming especially if the next such swim was to be in Alaska.

Would I get the luck I so desperately needed? If I didn't then what did it matter, for the Bering strait had as much value to me now as eating a meal or going to the toilet except that it was a longer distraction. Crucially it would also give me something big and different to talk about in future rather than how the love of my life had been cruelly taken by the hand of evil.

Talking to my mum on the phone I touched on how I felt that now I had nothing. It was true that I had limited economic power in the work place although I was working on it. With Dasha in my life this didn't seem to matter but with her gone I felt more vulnerable and that my weaknesses were exposed for I would have to start again. I saw a picture of a new baby on Facebook and it really hit me how I was now, way behind most of my peers. Most of them now were finding the joys of starting a family but at 33 my chance at that had been taken and I would have to start again from scratch. The Bering Strait beckoned and I felt like it might be my first foot back on the first rung of the ladder of life.

Death of Dasha 5

As I said Leonid Kokaurov was getting more and more confident which was quite bizarre given that Alexandr Brylin had failed to attract a headline sponsor in Moscow despite all his efforts. Since April he had spent more time in Moscow than his home in the Far East.

However, a contract had been signed and permits were in place and without those things no amount of money could get us across the Bering Strait in a non-stop swim relay.

He didn't have a sponsor but he did have support from the Russian Geographic Society and a certain General Arthur Chillingarov. This gave the project some credibility in Russia but as yet no big sponsor. I wasn't too concerned as it isn't unusual for this to happen with such big projects.

I was thinking ahead to my Alaska trip and how probably all those people who had humoured us in November would probably really want to be on board now that we had everything in place in July. The trouble was none of those people had the money although maybe they could lead us in the right direction. I was thinking about sales – I had sold enough things in the past to know how it worked from 25p games of bingo to expensive watches, meetings, shoe soles and even my own skills as an English teacher. I knew that if you knock on enough doors, follow enough leads and eventually you get a sale. So surely someone would have the money for us?

On the 21st of June just before 5pm Central European time as I was about to leave to teach an English lesson Leonid Kokaurov called me. More good news, he was expecting Alexandr to send the rest of the $110,000 for the Alaskan side of the project. "You should come on the 5th of July" was his advice. We talked briefly about goals and then I broached the subject of money, "How much do you want to obtain from the oil company? 100, 200,000?" I asked. "1.5million" came the reply, calm, serious and matter of fact, typical Leonid. "Ok" I said, trying to emulate his manner but inside my head it seemed crazy that potentially I was seen as the person who could clinch a 1.5million dollar sponsorship deal! I was happy to try and since Dasha was now dead I didn't really care about failing as I couldn't get any lower than I had been in the weeks since her death.

Now, if we could achieve that level of sponsorship then this project would certainly become interesting as it could surely be done for under 1million so what would we do with the rest of the money? I didn't know but I believed that anything was possible in the USA mostly in a good way and also that this phrase was true with regards to Russia so I felt to some extent like a backseat passenger in a car with a fast, erratic and unpredictable driver. In fact that was probably a way to sum things up. The project, the Bering Strait was so big that it just took on a life of its own and headed onwards for good or for bad, at times I was being asked several questions that I didn't know the answers to and I myself was asking several different questions that it seemed there were no answers for. It was almost at times as if none of us knew everything but we all knew a bit and the project somehow kept moving towards its goal.

Hilariously I found myself starting to get annoyed with the lovely Nuala Moore; although I knew this was because I didn't really care about things like safety following Dasha's death. My attitude was that whatever happened in the cold and dangerous Bering Strait was unlikely to be as bad as what my poor Dasha had faced in her final moments. I told Nuala, that "Ideally we want a north westerly blowing for a while which should help us at the start." I went on to say that "At first I was worried about being pushed north but I don't think that matters as we can land anywhere on the US coast and there shouldn't be a problem with sea ice at this time of year as the ice has retreated far away to the high arctic by now."

Interestingly, although I gave the impression that I couldn't care less it was in the pool in training that I had a psychological problem. At the end of the session Dita asked me to swim 4 x 50m with the first 25m of each 50 underwater. I usually like the challenge of swimming 25m under water but I suddenly had a mental block about it due to the death of Dasha. My reasoning was that it was close to death. What I meant was that I would have unpleasant thoughts as I struggled for breath thinking about Dasha and her last moments. Later on I realized that I must go through this so I vowed to myself to swim a 25m underwater at the next session.

I wasn't overly concerned about my psyche and this was just a blip. However, I was more worried about the cold water. Up until the middle of July the Vltava had stayed at 12 -14c and I had managed a 1 hour swim at 13.8c on the 14th of June. But now by the 26th of June the water was at 15 and that without exaggerating, as some winter swimmers are prone to do, I would describe it as lukewarm. Many go over the top and say it's like coffee but often these are the swimmers who are immersed for around 20mins per swim all year round so they have no experience of an hour at 12c or even 14c. No doubt I will find some suitable training in Alaska.

Luckily due to some rain and the opening of a few dams there was a negative flux in temperature which saw the Vltava river back down to below 14c on the 23rd and 24th of June. I was happy with this but after 30 minutes I was starting to feel a little numbness although this was after a second immersion. I knew only too well following my experiences last year that it's easy to be complacent about cold water during the summer. Having said that I did well in Baikal last year as I faced a 10c negative fluctuation in temperature. As far as the Bering Strait relay goes, a 5 hour break between swims would be too little in such cold water whereas a 10 hour break is pushing it but is probably just long enough. Of course the Bering Strait is sea water, saline and therefore gives more buoyancy and makes swimming a little easier. Many people also say that cold sea water somehow has less bite than fresh water at the same temperature. It may be true in the temperate seas but at 66 degrees north things could be a little different. A few years ago Lewis Gordon Pugh took an icebreaker to the North Pole and found a spot that was relatively safe and ice free and made a 1km swim. This was a pretty ground-breaking swim as he recorded a water temperature of -1.5c.He talked about having problems with his fingers for some time afterwards and I really understand that after my experience in the Norton Sound in November as well as my general experience of extremely cold water. Lynne Cox famously swam the 4.1km between the Diomede islands in the middle of the Bering Strait in 1987 and she also made an amazing 1 mile swim in Antarctica although the water wasn't as cold as for Pugh's swim at the North Pole. Aside from these few there haven't been many swims at such northerly latitudes and nothing of such magnitude. We may be team of 30 but we have a big distance to cover and it will be the length of time at sea and particularly the multiple immersions which will make this an interesting swim.

Saturday 23rd of June

Saturday 23rd of June was 4 weeks after the death of Dasha and it was an interesting day for me. I already felt strange but that was normal. I had slept well and made my way to the river. I met 2 of the guys at the clubhouse and one of them, Vladimír Kolář said "Let's swim downstream today as there's a strong flow and it's a bit dirty." I agreed and we ran 2.5km upstream to the weir at Modřany. The water was about 12c which made a nice change from the 25c air and bright sunshine. Although I was struggling for fluency and was changing strokes a lot all went ok until the final 500m when I came within 20cm of a 4 man rowing boat and only 5cm between my head and 2 oars. It was the closest call I have ever had and I was furious. I let my feelings be known to the driver of the speedboat that was following them. It is true that I had been testing out a new swimming hat and it had just come off so I wasn't too visible. 10 minutes later there was a confrontation. Luckily I managed to control myself even though I was so angry I could only speak in English! I got back to the changing rooms and realized that it was of course my situation – meaning the death of Dasha – that had caused my anger more than anything. I felt alone and frustrated –how could anyone understand what was going through my head right now? And the other thing – how long would this continue, meaning my feelings and potentially erratic behaviour? This was the first strange act that I had instigated but I knew that I didn't care about too much now and that more could be possible. A few hours later and I had been proved right! I saw Lada (female) for the first time in a while as she came into the mens' changing rooms to offer condolences and tell me "If there is anything I can do...." I immediately thought, well I would like to have sex, but I was in no frame of mind to pursue that. However, 30 minutes later I had calmed down and I went to sit by the river to relax by reading and enjoying the nice weather. I saw Lada lying down and after finishing the sausage I had bought. I made my way over to her. 2 hours later we were back at her flat having sex. I didn't feel guilty as for me it was just sex and nothing more, like eating a meal or having a rest, it was just an action for me and therefore devoid of any meaning or emotion. I left Lada making it clear that we could maybe do this again but that it was only sex and nothing more. She agreed and although I was sceptical I didn't care because as I already mentioned I didn't care about anything anymore. I knew the only way I would ever change after what had happened would be if I could live on and find new happiness which meant a new woman. Lada wasn't that woman and anyway it was much too early to be even contemplating that. I had simply fulfilled an urge. Back at home and I received a message from Dasha's mum saying that they would probably be coming for her things the next day. This meant more sadness but after such a horrible thing had happened we had all got used to this.

I was already looking forward to the Bering Strait swim and somehow it represented a chance for me to get away and get a break.

After such a day I decided that it would be a good idea to relax at home rather than going to the pub to watch the football and drink a few beers.

Next day I woke up after a good sleep and immediately attention was drawn to my left eye. Something was wrong and after a while I concluded that there was something in my eye. No problem, I will just wash it out, but 2 hours later and it was still a problem. Never one for the doctors I trusted my eyelashes to wash it out over the next day or so. Before I left the flat to go swimming I looked in the mirror and as suspected I looked an absolute state. In fact I looked how I felt to a certain extent – which was sad. My left eye was swollen and red and it looked like I had been crying for some time. After what happened to Dasha all other problems seem irrelevant if annoying and I was starting to get a little annoyed. All the work going on at the flats, no internet connection, the uncertainty of the Bering project and now this problem with my eye, not to mention financial issues. I just hoped that within a few days my eye would improve and that the internet connection would be restored.

Bad luck, health problems, 6 weeks on

When I reached down to scratch a delicate place I felt something strange and sure enough there was a tick firmly attached to my scrotum! Physically I believed that I was going to pieces. First the conjunctivitis, then an ear infection and now a parasite trying to make a meal of my genitals! It was a pretty good metaphor for my life in the last 6 weeks.

I had always had a little joke with myself that even when you think that you are settled and everything is ok you really never know what you will be doing this time next year. It has certainly been true in my life for many years, including those years in which not much seemed to be happening.

As I received Dasha's mini-computer with a view to borrowing it for my upcoming trip I wasn't really looking forward to opening it again. I had managed 5 minutes last time but the photos were just too fresh and combined with her comments on them it was simply too much. Luckily the computer solved this problem by the screen refusing to work. Again something not going well for me. Amongst other things I was still convinced that I was swimming slower than 2 years ago even though I was now training in a group with a trainer doing intervals and drills rather than alone just simply swimming with the odd change of stroke and the odd interval. Then there was the matter of what I would do for work in the future. The obvious answer was to teach English starting in September which is what I told everyone I would do. I had a verbal agreement but I wanted to make sure that was a bit more concrete. Quite frankly it was also bugging me that I had been living in the Czech Republic for almost 4 years yet for a while I had been working mainly "off the cards." For some time I had wanted to be legitimate and after what had happened recently I was determined now to become a fully paying member of the community but as always first I would have to earn enough money. I quite fancied getting meal tickets and vouchers for leisure activities as a benefit with a new job but it was more likely that I would get the freedom of being freelance as a benefit with the price for this being to pay for my own social and health insurance.

I had made my bed so I had just better lie in it and just because Dasha had been murdered I couldn't use this as an excuse for my own shortcomings. It's all very well to think like that but sometimes in life you just need a something to go right, what they call a lucky break and that can be the catalyst for change. I remembered what was written under Dasha's name at the funeral "jen chtěla žít a mít trochu štěstí." (I only wanted to live and have a little bit of luck.) Well, as much as I needed some luck these words prove that it doesn't always happen and just because I had been on the wrong end of lady luck recently didn't mean that things were certain to change. In life there are no rules concerning how things go, they just happen. Some things we can control, some we can influence and others we can do sod all about. I wasn't sure exactly which of these 3 categories the Bering Strait project fitted into but I thought that it could be the catalyst for a positive change.

First of all I would have to be fit to swim. The conjunctivitis was long gone, the tick I managed to remove but the ear infection? Well to be honest it was worrying me.

I'd had mild pain in my ear from time to time for the last year or so but thought nothing of it. It wasn't my habit to go to the doctors unless there was really something wrong with me. I had reluctantly been 2 weeks ago and the thought of going again seemed ludicrous. I managed to obtain some herbal ear drops from the chemist and the pain subsided but I still had a feeling that I would end up at the doctors and worse that I would maybe have to give swimming a miss for a few days or maybe even all week. I was soon planning cycling and running as the alternative but the biggest worry in the back of my mind was that I would get on the ship in Chukotka only to fall ill and be unable to play a part in the relay. I have always trusted my own body but just lately it has been behaving erratically which several people have put down to the stress of the last few weeks having a negative impact on my immune system. It was hard to disagree given the evidence. I didn't realize I was stressed. I knew I was deeply sad and I told everyone that given the circumstances I was ok. My head was fine in my opinion although I had to admit I had started to become interested in murderers, particularly serial killers and I was spending time watching documentaries about the moors murders, Nielsen and the Yorkshire Ripper on YouTube. In some way I think this helped me to understand the evil that had taken place in New Zealand and I felt better or at least comforted when I saw that there were other people whose lives had been ruined by acts of evil and some of them in perhaps worse ways than mine. It reinforced my belief that I had to eventually live on and I was firmly concentrating on the near future and the Bering Strait.

Will we or won't we – Deja F*****g vu

My eye deteriorated rapidly to the point where I visited the chemist on Monday and then on Tuesday I reluctantly sought medical advice as I started to become worried. I managed to keep swimming without problems, which was something but this seemed to become irrelevant to a certain extent and finally the water in the Vltava had warmed up. This meant that all swimming was now simply swimming for fitness and endurance but was no longer related to cold hardening. I was confident of my abilities in cold water and had experience of big temperature drops at least twice in the last year, the first being my trip to Lake Bajkal and the second being the Alaska trip before Christmas. It was enough to have the experience of the icy water both mentally and physically. The shock would be big but I knew it would be ok.

On the plus side money was supposed to be coming to Leonid Kokaurov in Alaska from the Russian side, either from some kind of credit or from a media deal, or perhaps even both. Knowing how anything is possible in Russia I hoped for the best whilst at the same time preparing for the worst. Sure enough there was some problem and nobody could really pinpoint as to why Leonid didn't receive the money; but as far as Alexandr Brylin and the Russian organisers were concerned it was full speed ahead and we would be swimming the Bering Strait. Meanwhile Leonid's mood had visibly changed and he was now in a tight position trying to get all the necessary bureaucratic work done without the necessary money. His reputation was at stake and I knew how he felt as I had battled for almost 10 months to find and keep international swimmers interested in this project and to have several still hanging in there was some feat, but it would mean nothing if we didn't swim. The situation was causing me a little stress especially when it seemed that there was a problem with my tourist visa in that I need a humanitarian visa which corresponded with the Chukotka permit! I pondered how to solve this and it actually started to look like a trip to London was on the cards. I knew how the Russian consulate operated in Prague, that is to say that if you have everything in order you can get your visa without problems but the moment you need something unusual it can be a problem even for Russian citizens. I had visions of trying to cancel my visa and simply being told "Niet!" The truth was that I would have the correct supporting documents from a high level and it would be fine but the way things were going I had to cover all angles.

Even with several of these minor issues they all paled into insignificance at thought of my beloved Dasha and her untimely and horrific end in New Zealand. I went back to her wonderful family for a short visit and to bring fresh flowers as I didn't know when I would be leaving the country for the Bering Strait swim. We all felt the same deep sadness in our own ways as we all had our relationships with Dasha and it was good to be around people who felt the same. I had been back in Prague for 3 weeks and now it was over 5 weeks since Dasha's death. I think most of my friends and acquaintances thought that I was over the worst of it but the truth was that it was just the same as a few weeks before. I was ok but I had a deep sadness hanging over me. That's my way of describing it whereas the psychologists refer to it as grief. Well, it doesn't really matter what word we use, as a word is a just a series of letters, more important in my opinion was to describe the feelings accurately.

During this time my eye infection (conjunctivitis) started to clear up. I had a bit of cold but I was fine, only a few days later to wake up in the middle of the night with a throbbing ear ache. I was certain that this had been caused by the Vltava River. The day before I had tried out some new goggles and they had been terrible. They hadn't tightened the straps enough and they were leaking profusely. I battled on and I lost an earplug in all reorganising and adjusting. The water was already up to 18c so it wasn't cold but it was that very night that I woke up in pain. It seemed to me that everything was conspiring against me and even the Vltava River was taking a hand in it!

The following night I was awoken again but this time it wasn't physical but more mental as I had deja-vu like visions of going to Petropavlovsk Kamchatsky only to be unable to get on the boat like last year. PK isn't a nice city but it is surrounded by incredible nature. But that natural beauty isn't easy to get to so it needs cooperation with locals in the form of a driver and often a guide. I knew if I went to PK again that I would be unable to stop myself from making a trip into the back country which would be a nice diversion but there was something about Kamchatka that was worrying me. I can only describe it as deja-vu! I pondered how I would deal with a late cancellation this year. Last year I was annoyed but this year with my personal situation I would be prone to more erratic actions. I tried not to think about it but the size and difficulty of the project not to mention Alexandr's modus operandi made it a possibility. I was now about 80% certain that we would go and then if I got on the boat I would be say 90% and then once in the water I would be 100%. I don't like to quantify such actions into percentages as we are really talking about qualitative things but I would say that these numbers accurately represented my opinions in the first week of July.

Bering Blog 17 July

2012 has been a difficult year so far. Actually difficult doesn't begin to explain it and the words of any language are inadequate to describe it.

I always expected it to be difficult until the end of May when everything would become easier. Sometimes life is inexplicably cruel and having got through to the end of May a personal tragedy overtook my life in the form of the random murder of the person closest to me.

Almost two months on and I am carrying on as best as I can. This means I am now on the way to Petropavlovsk Kamchatsky (PK), one of the oldest cities in the Russian Far East, the main city of the Kamchatka peninsula, the land of fire and ice.

PK is situated in the Avacha bay, a natural port and although nobody could claim that the city itself is attractive, the surroundings are stunning as there are magnificent volcanoes everywhere you look. The Avachinsky volcano is popular with tourists yet the most visually stunning in this part of the peninsula must be Koryakske, a stratovolcano with an almost perfect conical shape; it is best viewed from the lower slopes on the western side of Avacha and from the lunar like landscape of the Avachinsky pass.

However, I am not just there for the volcanoes as wonderful as they may be. In around 10 days the Russian ice breaker Akademik Shokalskiy should arrive and myself and 29 other ice swimmers, as well as a support team of around 20 should board this ship and sail north through the Bering sea, up the Bering Strait to the restricted border region of the Chukotka Autonomous Okrug. The reason is that we plan to swim a non-stop relay across the Bering Strait aiming to land at the native village of Wales in Alaska, USA. This project has been a few years in the making and last year our attempt never left the port at PK due to technical issues. This year we hope to get to the start point, Cape Dezhnev, the most easterly point of the Eurasian continent situated at approximately 66°4′45″N 169°39′7″W

A great deal of work has been done by the Russian organisers to obtain permission for a mobile border control at the remote starting point in the form of a ship, without which it is impossible to swim from this place. Cape Dezhnev is a rocky and exposed headland, punctuated by the remains of an old village and a monument to Semyon Dezhnev who in 1648 sailed down the Kolyma River to the Arctic Ocean and rounded the cape, continuing on into the Bering Strait to land somewhere near what is now known as Anadyr. Thus the cape now takes his name. Also known in some atlases by its Russian name of Mys Dezhnev. (mys = cape)

As for the swim itself, the sea ice has retreated from the Bering Strait and the water temperature will be probably around 5c. However, it will be much colder on the Russian side, as low as 2c and maybe a bit warmer on the US side, up to 7c. Having said this, we cannot make too many assumptions about conditions until we are there at the starting point of the swim. It will be tough, it has never been tried before but there are 30 experienced cold water and long distance swimmers who are ready to attempt this crossing in a non-stop relay.

Exciting as it is, the magnitude of this project in terms of the remoteness of the location and also the bureaucracy to be negotiated on both sides and of course the huge amount of money needed to realize it (a ship for 54 people plus crew doesn't come cheap for a start) means that until I am on the ship at Cape Deznhev and cleared immigration, having obtained an exit stamp on my visa I don't want to say too much about it. The main organisers of the swim are Akvais sport federation from Blagoveshchensk and their driving force Alexandr Brylin. He is backed by former submarine captain, Oleg Adamov and more importantly the Russian Geographic Society and General Arthur Chillingarov. The latter is a famous and much revered and respected Russian polar explorer, with many achievements to his name. I have been working as a member of the organising committee to coordinate the international swimmers and also in conjunction with ACTI and Leonid Kokaurov in Alaska USA.

More news to follow soon…

Preparing to Travel

On Wednesday the 11th of July I decided to start fully preparing for travel to Kamchatka. I needed to gee myself up and I needed a break desperately to clear my head after the events of 26th May in New Zealand.

Deep down I knew that such positive action would have no bearing on the relay. It didn't matter where I was it would either happen or not but PK was the meeting point so better there than somewhere else.

I hunted for all my Kamchatka contacts and my SIM cards. The contacts were no problem but I couldn't locate the SIM cards. This made me anxious as I knew I had a ready to go SIM card with some credit and I knew the phone number. It would help me. I started to panic as I always do when I can't find something although I wasn't too bad. I just told myself it's no problem you just go to the MTC shop and buy another SIM card.

By 10pm I had reserved a flight but I hadn't paid for it. It was the last one and I got a call the next morning telling me I had until 6pm to make the payment. I hadn't been able to reach my friend in PK who would help me with arranging trips to the volcanoes yet and I wasn't sure if I was going a day too early. It was a tough call and made tougher by the fact that on Thursday morning it became apparent that some of the swimmers were up against it not just with regards the participation fee and other expenses but also the timeframe in which to obtain the visas. Speaking to Nuala Moore on the phone and she was really stressed. I told her to take one problem at a time and tackle the visa first. I counted 12 days until they had to fly, meaning 8 working days. It was surely enough, but likewise I understood the anxiety. For the Russians everything seemed ok and let's face it they are used to dealing with all kinds of shenanigans especially when they need the coveted US visa. For my friends in Blagoveshchensk it means 2 separate trips to the consulate in Vladivostok, which I guess is in total 8 days by train over 4 journeys. Those with deep pockets can fly but that would probably be about £1000 for the 2 return flights. Driving may be possible but also not easy with the vast distances and difficult road systems. In our countries we are not used to this and I wonder what other things go on in Russia that we don't know about or wouldn't understand. It's such a vast country with so many ethnic groups and languages even after the break-up of the Soviet Union with the loss of vast territories such as Kazakhstan.

Ram Barkai also had doubts though he remained pretty cool which was his style and I liked it.

In the end I went and paid for the ticket so I was on the way to PK! Better there than Prague to swim the Bering Strait! I believed that the volcanoes of Kamchatka would help me and it's true that I was keen to get back to Kamchatka and explore some more of its wonders.

Leonid Kokaurov sounded positive when I spoke to him and as usual that filled me with confidence. The owners of the Akademik Shokalskiy, our ship for the crossing had sent him some more documents. He was pretty pleased with this and I started to really believe the hype. Leonid didn't even seem too concerned that he had only been sent $5,000. At least he had been sent something was the way he looked at it. This meant he had so far received $12,000 of the agreed $110,000. I estimated that he needed about another $50,000 in order to pay Tom Router of Alaska maritime agency. He had already opened up a line of credit for about $25,000 which had made him feel uncomfortable. Tom Router is also a friend as well as a business associate and the old proverb don't mix friendship with business was sounding like a good one.

Meanwhile my ear infection was getting better but all week I had been limited to land work, meaning running, rowing machine and weights. I felt good but I wanted to get back in the water. On Wednesday after my workout I walked 50 metres down to the riverbank and got in just to cool down and wash off the sweat. I stood there, barely moving and the water felt pretty cold. Well I could be facing water of just 2c in a little over 2 weeks! I laughed to myself and although I know the power of the cold I wasn't bothered, in fact I was looking forward to the drop in temperature.

En route to PK from Moscow

Flying over the vastness of Russia and after an hour we came to the Caspian Sea and a beautiful view of the wetlands surrounding its northern shores that seemed to go on forever. Distances are big in Russia the biggest country in the world by far.

Talking to Leonid Kokaurov while I was waiting in Vienna airport and he had started to inspire me to think deeply and positively. He was definitely having a small but tangible influence on me as a kind of mentor. He has experience of living in many places and is bilingual as is his wife Natalia. Crucially he doesn't bullshit or come across as patronising and I would guess that he has had a very successful life. He had already hinted as much when he told me in a completely understated way that "I have never failed with a project before."

So I had almost 9 hours in the plane from Moscow to PK. I thought a little about Dasha of course and what a great person she had been, she had contributed to our world and it was so cruel what had happened, but happened it had and nothing could be changed. Although I have a great affinity to and affection for the Czech Republic and its people I have begun to wonder if a new chapter in my life will open elsewhere? Maybe it's even possible that I keep Prague as my base but expand my horizons. Leonid had an idea for us to start an extreme cold water swimming school in Anchorage, Alaska. I knew it was an idea with potential and if someone like Leonid could back it then I felt that we could really do something. It also reminded me of how pleasant I found Anchorage when I was there and how down to earth the people were. I remember what John Byrne from the Institute of the North said, "You know here in Alaska we all wear many different hats." I understood him and I knew that whilst Alaska was the 49th state it was also maybe the final state as well as still being something of a frontier. I had already had the feeling that I might fit in there and now I was beginning to see a way forward.

This idea was given more credence when I read the readers' letters in Time magazine. They were all concerning the recent demonstrations in support of illegal immigrants in the USA. One person pointed out that these migrants were coming from countries such as Mexico and Korea, whose economies were on the up, but the people still desperate to get to the promised land of the USA which to quote a cartoon I saw in a recent geographical journal is in the boorish stage of capitalism (neo liberalism), middle aged capitalism, fat and slobbing out on the couch mockingly saying "What are you going to do, Leave me?" The USA is still economically powerful but on the wane and the reader's letter predicted that in the future the roles would be reversed with perhaps US citizens migrating to the new economic powers in search of a better life. It was already happening in Europe if you looked at my situation. I had consistently said that while I didn't have a bad life in the UK, it wasn't that good either. After some travels I have been in Prague, Czech Republic for most of the last 4 years and there I have found my happiness and what I believe to be a better quality of life. Prague is a great capital city and the Czech Republic a beautiful land with people to match but it is still seen incorrectly as "Eastern Europe" and a former soviet satellite state. I wonder how many expats there are like me? I suspect there are a few but not too many. But truthfully maybe it was time to delve back into the "Western world or perhaps better described as the "traditional Western European world". I still didn't feel ready for the UK, NZ was of course totally ruled out for the foreseeable future, leaving a few options though the only one that appealed or even made me think in this way was the frontier of Alaska.

During this plane ride I also skim read the best bits of Sir Ranulph Fiennes' autobiography; "*Mad, Bad and Dangerous to Know*". I was spurred on by the fact that the Bering Strait had even beaten him. He made it to Wales and spent some time there and even had the legendary Russian explorer Dmitry Shparo organising things on the Russian side but in the end his planned crossing by adapted amphibious land rovers never happened. The plug was pulled for financial reasons. But the outcome was the same and the project was never realized. I wouldn't say that there is a jinx on Bering Strait crossings but they are few and far between and the area is a difficult one to operate in.

Although I wanted to swim across the Bering Strait, I was just as excited by visiting Chukotka and having the chance to spend some time in Alaska without any constraint. I did plan to travel back to Prague by the end of August, maybe around the 25th but I only had a verbal agreement to start work again as an English teacher and I could easily change my plans. I felt that the journey of my life had suffered a big crash with the death of Dasha but now I was getting back on the road and I wasn't sure what was coming next, a series of adrenaline fuelled hairpin turns or a major crossroads, or possibly even a combination of both. I was sure something was looming but maybe it was just the Bering Strait?

Waiting in PK – again

Well it's another case of a deja-vu as the relay appears to be in trouble once again here in PK. However, there is a very good ship (Akademik Schoklaskiy) waiting to go and the documents, needed for our entry into US waters, are also ready. It is now just a "nimnozska" – a problem with money.

This really is only for the connoisseur of Russia, those uninitiated will probably fail to understand as the conflicting and confusing information comes thick and fast at regular intervals. Pinpointing the exact problem is quite difficult but my educated guess says we have a superb example of a big Russian mess on our hands. I am laughing a little as I write this but it isn't so funny especially not for the international swimmers who came a long way to be here and it wouldn't have been their first choice destination this summer that's for sure.

All is not lost but I have just heard mention of US visas for the Moscow media people being ready on the 31st of July which is 5 days away so I hope they can meet us in Anadyr. I am not sure how long the international swimmers will want to wait about and it will be interesting when the truth is revealed. Right now they think we are going in a few days and that all is well. Some of them are on quite tight time schedules so I think things could get interesting. Speaking from experience I think this mess will take a little while to sort out but while the ship is still here there is hope. Leonid and his work in Alaska, however, is another matter entirely. The need for a pilot vessel in US waters which has to be booked and paid for is a top priority right now and Alaska maritime agency are asking for money. If they don't get it in a few days we could be facing an impossible task in entering US waters and arriving at a US port due to the lack of a pilot vessel which is needed by foreign vessels according to US law.

Kamchatka 2012

Another July and another arrival in Kamchatka. This time Alexandr Tarakanov met me at the airport and we made our way into town by bus. My first brush with Russian bureaucracy was in the mobile phone shop as I tried to get a new SIM card. The Uzbek guy was pretty interested in who I was and where I was from but it was all quite funny. I didn't care if there was no address written anywhere, this was a phone shop and not an official office. After that funny little episode it was time to drink tea and eat biscuits with Alexandr in his flat before going into town for a walk round the bay which was very pleasant in the hot weather.

I couldn't get hold of Viktor but that wasn't a major problem. Alexandr soon connected me with his friends and we arranged to meet the next day.

After a decent night's sleep Alexandr went off to guide on Avacha volcano whereas I made my way to the Pacific Ocean for a short trip, crossing a river and going through bear country to get there. I didn't see any salmon in the river and thus no bears either. It was good to feel the strength of the ocean and the strong sea breeze after the high temperatures in the city. I looked north into the Bering Sea and apart from another part of the peninsula there was nothing. We were in for quite a trip, an adventure, of that I was sure and off I went back to the city with the black volcanic sandy beach and open ocean still fresh in my mind.

I had made contact with Viktor but first I had to meet Anya and arrange our trip for the next day. This involved shopping for food and discussing transport, timings and itinerary, all fairly standard fare and this passed without incident which of course all changed when I ran into my old friend Viktor Godlevski!

After a quick embrace Viktor told me (in Russian) "There is a problem; Chillingarov has said we are not ready. Now you must write a letter to him and I will fax it directly to him in Moscow. These are the orders of Alexandr Brylin!"

After the initial shock or surprise and disappointment at this negative turn of events I relaxed and began to write the letter. I was experienced enough in the ways of Russia to simply get on with it and not worry about it. But what a bizarre situation as we sat in Alexandr Tarakanov's flat and tried to construct the letter with Viktor giving me ideas in Russian. I made a blunder and referred to Chillinagarov as general, because I was sure he was, but I was quite wrong, a source of amusement to Alexandr Brylin when I saw him a few days later and told him.

Nevertheless, news came back from Alexandr Brylin that I had written a great letter and all would be ok. The phones started buzzing and sure enough good news came the next day in the form of Leonid Kokaurov receiving the Certificate of financial responsibility COFR letter. With Viktor we went to deliver an air ticket to an Uzbek guy. Viktor is a policeman not a travel agent but I don't ask too many questions, although I know he had helped this guy get work. We were invited in to eat ploff and soon there were 4 Uzbek guys, only no... there were 5, no 6, no 7, 8, 9, 10... loads and enough ploff for everyone crammed into the small room of the small flat. It might have freaked some people out but actually I have seen just the same kind of living arrangements in the UK. Poverty and different living styles exist everywhere it's just that in some places there are more rich people and in others more poor people.

This eventful evening wasn't over yet as we went back to Viktor's where we of course drank vodka, ate and he showed me videos of winter swimming in Kamchatka but perhaps more importantly of himself dressed as Ded Maros, the Russian version of Santa Claus. Highly entertaining stuff and eventually I got to bed and managed 2 hours sleep before starting off for the back country with the guys the next morning.

We left almost an hour later than planned which was ok as it gave me the chance to catch up on emails and messages. It was at this point that I started to feel the beginnings of a backlash. I got an email from Nuala Moore and she seemed pretty upset that she wasn't coming which I already knew. She had time to get the visa, just, but in my opinion she had been completely spooked by Russian organisation which is totally understandable!

Then Andrew Chin was skype messaging me and he was gutted and said if only he had been given more notice. Andrew is a nice guy but I have to say that I called him back in April and said send me your passport details if you have any intention of joining us as this could yet happen this year. Then he and the others from South Africa all declared themselves out a week later. The key to this is that the reason they did that was because of conflicting email announcement by Alexandr Brylin and Sergey Novikov. They chose to take Novikov's advice and it was down to him that they had declared themselves out. Andrew mentioned that Novikov was saying things but that so far "He was being very politically correct!" This made my blood boil, not with Andrew but with Novikov, he was so power hungry and venomous in his spiteful words and attempts to ruin other people's work. According to Leonid Kokaurov It seemed he even had the audacity to call the

Russian consul in Seattle and say that the project was stolen from him! Absolute nonsense, the truth always comes out. This was a man who was convinced he could recreate the conditions of the Bering Strait in an indoor swimming pool in Seattle! Alexandr Brylin may be at times difficult to deal with but he is neither criminal nor fraudster. He may have an ego but so what – he has a great heart. He was right about two things and the first was "Hahaha, Novikov mnogo govorit" (laughing, Novikov talks a lot) and the second was "Divide et impera, this is what Novikov is trying to do."

Anyway as our vessel the Akademik Shokalskiy left port in Vladivostok, on its way through the Okhotsk Sea to Petropavlovsk Kamchatsky, so I also began a journey, but overland into the backcountry of Kamchatka to the wilderness of Mutnovsky volcano.

I don't want to get off the topic of the Bering Strait too much but I think Kamchatka is the perfect starting point for our Bering Strait expedition. A visit to a place such as the extremely active crater of Mutnovsky volcano is enough to remind and reinforce man as to the power of nature.

Volcanoes produce weird and wonderful landforms and on this occasion it was a bonus on the trek from the little valley of geysers to meet a small glacial lake. I am not an expert on the cryosphere but it seemed to be the outlet of a small glacier. I made a mental note of the location so that I could come back the next day as first I had to make a trek to the active crater of Mutnovsky, an otherworldly experience in itself and typical of Kamchatka.

The next day I made my way back to the lake. It wasn't ideal for a really good swim as it was only about 12 metres long with a huge piece of ice in the middle. However, it was sufficient for a little training in extremely cold water and I was in for 10 minutes. Kamchatka is experiencing a very warm summer this year and with the sun blazing down, rewarming the body afterwards was obviously much easier than in winter conditions.

It felt good to be in the icy water again and I thought about the Bering Strait and the immense challenge of multiple immersions in such cold water. It is not to be underestimated.

Late that evening I returned to Petropavlovsk Kamchatsky.

As I have already explained I arrived back to PK and immediately the next morning I was met by Viktor.

Typically things were looking slightly tricky following the problems with money and with Chillingarov showing little confidence in the expedition.

The good news was that the Akademik Shokalskiy was in port at PK. Me and Viktor went there to make some arrangements. The captain invited us for coffee and we talked, he was friendly but underneath all was not well. Yet again, a money problem, a delayed bank payment. I must stress at this point that some money had been received and the ship had travelled as expected at our command to be ready in PK. The first mate showed me around and we talked about the use of the zodiacs. (*who knows what would have happened if we had gone. The Akademik was a good ship and well capable and proven in these waters, regularly sailing in the North pacific, Bering Sea and Bering Strait, but we needed perhaps a bigger vessel.)

However the ship was in port and we had to put any issues aside which were not ours to deal with; for neither I nor Viktor were involved with finance. I had seen the contract for the ship but that was it, soon the international swimmers and in fact other swimmers from Russia would be arriving and it was my job to be at the airport with

Viktor and assist in meeting people. Of course I was the "international coordinator" and indeed I was responsible for those who were coming. It was a small but strong group comprising of the 2 Estonians Henri Kaarma and Toomas Haagi, Ram Barkai of South Africa, Paolo Chiarino of Italy, Jackie Cobell of the UK and the Argentinian Matias Ola. Luckily we had buses to transport us and Viktor had everything under control.

We worked together to pick everyone up and deliver them to their accommodation. Of course everyone asked me "When will we get on the ship?" My own opinion was that perhaps we would not get on the ship but that was only my opinion so I simply said definitely not today, probably tomorrow or the day after but don't worry you will be just around the corner from where it is docked. Indeed the small hotel or rather hostel was just a few hundred metres from where the Akademik Shoklaskiy lay at anchor. This satisfied everyone. The international swimmers were tired as they had been travelling for a while to reach PK and most were soon resting.

The next day we had to meet the press, go for a swim in the bay all organised by Viktor. However, first we had to have lunch, yes, a nice lunch followed 30mins later by a cold water swim. I would have preferred a little longer to relax after eating but there was no choice. |For once in Kamchatka I wasn't the centre of media attention which was natural now that others were here, although I actually felt ever so slightly jealous even though at the same time I felt like something of a local.

A question came from Matias Ola: he was not happy with his accommodation and I immediately realized that I was dealing with someone who was used to high standards. I assured him that this was just temporary.

It took a few days for everyone to gather and this gave the organisers some breathing space. A trip to some hot springs was arranged but the skies were overcast and I sensed that our fate was also looking the same way.

The swimmers were moved to various flats around the city except for the international swimmers who went to hotels.

Finally I got the bad news from Ira that we were sunk and that the swim would almost certainly not go ahead. I was disappointed but I said nothing as I had been expecting it now for a few days. It was Thursday and it was expected that Alexandr Brylin would arrive from Moscow on Friday to tell everyone what was going on. Now everything was a complete mess, including me, the hapless international coordinator and extreme swimmer unable to do anything but reassure people that all would be ok. The weather was terrible in PK and it really suited the situation. None of the volcanoes could be seen due to the cloud cover, it rained intermittently and the air temperature was just above 10c.

Finally, on Friday at around 16.00 we assembled at the sports centre for a meeting. International swimmers were still talking about getting on the ship and it made me feel bad in many ways. Here I was again in PK, again in a hopeless situation, but I was alive and well so I was philosophical about it. Finally Alexandr arrived at around 17.00h. He looked pretty tired and apprehensive and that was what I expected. It was clear that he was not a happy man. Finally everyone assembled and Alexandr gave his statement. Irina translated it and the upshot of it was that the swim would not go ahead due to the Russian ministry of foreign affairs making it very clear that taking the vessel into US waters was a big risk which they strongly advised against. The main reason for this was due to the Sneerson case which is explained in the following press release from the organisers:

Ice-swimmers couldn't cross the Bering Strait because of American court's verdict.

The Bering Strait dividing two continents and two largest countries in the world has always attracted enthusiasts of extreme sports due to its unpredictable and severe conditions. Highly unfavourable climate together with a strong and changeable current caused by the confluence of two oceans make the strait an insurmountable barrier for a swimmer. But for those who don't seek for easy ways the Bering Strait is a real plum, it is their dream.

For two years ice-swimmers of the Amur regional public organization "AQUICE-sport Federation" have been preparing to connect the Russian and American coasts by a swimming relay.

On 25, July, 2012 the participants from Great Britain, Czech Republic, Italy, South Africa, Argentina, Estonia and Russia gathered in Petropavlovsk-Kamchatskiy where they were awaited by the support ship "Academic Shokalskiy" which belongs to the Far Eastern Regional Hydro Meteorological Research Institute and is a property of the Russian Federation. Everything was ready for the expedition.

But at the last moment, nearly on the very start of the relay it turned out that the most serious obstacles are put by people, not by nature. On 26, July the organizers of the swimming relay received the documents which nullified all the large-scale preparation work. All the jobs devoted to freight of the ship, all the permits from the Russian Frontier guards and the US Coast Guards, attracting sponsors, recruiting the swimmers, letters to the officials and endless phone calls even at night – everything was crossed off in one single moment.

The documents included a letter from the Ministry for Foreign Affairs of Russia which informed the organization committee that 'due to unfavourable to

Russia verdict made by the Washington court during the so-called 'Sheerson case' there is a real threat that any property of the Russian Federation unprotected by the diplomatic immunity will fall under a security arrest. It refers as well to the ships which enter the US waters and ports. Taking into account the threat in October, 2011 the sailing vessel "Nadezda" had to cancel a visit to San-Francisco and Honolulu and the same decision has been made this year regarding the sailing ship "Sedov".' Moreover, in this letter the Ministry of Foreign Affairs strongly recommended that Russian ships should not enter the American ports.

The second document was the telegram from the Head Office of Roshydromet. It was not advisory in nature, but contained a direct order: "Therefore we ban the Far Eastern Regional Hydro Meteorological Research Institute as an operator of federal property the use of the ship 'Academic Shokalskiy' for working within the program of the Amur Regional Public Organization 'AQUICE-sport federation' in the Bering Strait outside the Russian waters."

The owner of the ship proposed to make a swimming relay a bit shorter and swim from Cape Dezhnev to Ratmanova Island but this program would not satisfy the sponsor of the event.

This could be regarded as the end of the expedition. But the swimmers whose dream to cross the Bering Strait remains a dream are not going to give up. "If something is easy, it's not worth doing", says Ram Barkai, a well-known South African ice swimmer. And the Russian swimmer Andrey Sychov adds: "The Bering Strait for an ice swimmer is like the Everest for a mountaineer. It's prize number one."

The organizers and the participants of the project are grateful to all the organizations that supported the idea. They are determined to realize the project next year or *even later. They believe that their hot hearts will help to overcome the cold waters which separate Russia and America. They are sure that the swimming relay is a wonderful means of establishing good neighbourly relations between all countries of the world.*

After this we were all fairly deflated. There was a small chance of taking the vessel to Cape Dezhnev and making a swim to Ratmanov (Big Diomede) Island and I for one was in favour of this plan. I therefore went with Alexander Brylin, Yevgeny Noseeyev the kitesurfer and Alexandr Yurkov to the vessel to talk with the captain. Now time was a problem, regarding where the vessel had to be. I could see that the captain was not looking too favourably upon this idea. Already we were several days behind schedule and he needed to get the ship back to Vladivostok. After this I went to a disco where the other international swimmers were and explained the possibility, albeit slim, of swimming to the Diomede Islands from Cape Dezhnev. Henri immediately dismissed the idea and did not look too happy. Ram was thoughtful whist Jackie in her own typical way simply got on with it and treated everyone to some amazing dancefloor moves!

I was woken up the next day by a phone call from Dave Cobell, Jackie's husband. It was 7.30 in Kamchatka so in the UK it was still early Friday evening and Dave being as supportive as ever towards Jackie, he had heard of our plight and come up with the idea of taking a friend's fishing vessel from San Francisco or Seattle. He was extremely helpful but I had to explain that unfortunately due to the issues of crossing borders and not to mention the need for a larger vessel that was already in Russia it would not work. Dave soon realized this but credit to him for not giving up and trying to help us even if nothing could be done. After this I was soon on my way to meet the others and the whole day was spent organising tickets to get everyone home. This was not easy and took several hours. The other international swimmers went home via Lake Baikal whereas I opted to stay in Kamchatka. At one point I was trying to arrange the trip to Cape Deznhev to make an ice swim there after Ram showed some interest but I had to stop after it became a logistical nightmare involving criss-crossing the Russian Far East several times to reach a point some 200km north east. The idea of going via Moscow stopped me in my tracks and I admitted that it was not feasible to take air transport to Chukotka. The chosen route back for the international swimmers was via Lake Baikal and was expensive at the last minute, unlike when I had booked it in advance with a 2 week interval the year before. I felt rotten, the weather was bad and here I was spending my time in a travel agency.

Then it was decided that in the evening there would be a party at a local restaurant. It went as expected and speeches were made. I tried not to say too much and just made it clear that we were still in good health. Next, something predictable happened as while Alexandr Brylin was giving his speech, Tatiana Alexandrova, at the end stood up and said something along the lines of "Don't worry, God did not want us to do it this time." At once, many of the Russians began to murmur in agreement and soon all were standing rejoicing in how we were not meant to do it this time and that God had stopped us and maybe even saved us from a watery fate. This reaction did not surprise me and I could not argue with it but at the same time to say that I agreed would be a lie. I have to say that this was quite a powerful experience and probably an excellent example of belief in fatalism. I couldn't argue with them because I couldn't prove them wrong and in all honesty that kind of belief is maybe not a bad thing whether you agree or not, for it binds people together and allows you to get on with things. It takes a very strong character to apply this in the aftermath of say a bereavement but nevertheless in a case such as a failed swim this fatalism is well suited. The situation, although a little bizarre whereby everybody started to stand up and rejoice in how God had maybe saved us from a watery fate reminded me in some way of the previous year when it was accepted that things had gone wrong and that the main thing was that we were still alive and well. We are lucky that we can try to do such things as swim across the Bering Strait. I thanked my Russian friends, for without me realizing it completely at the time they had taught me a valuable lesson, and I don't mean about seeing the important things in life (I had already learnt that in May) but rather togetherness and how a common belief can unify and support.

The party continued but I left just before midnight. It was agreed that the next day we would meet at 11.00h and go for a swim in the ocean to finish things in the right way.

The next day we travelled together in a marshrutka (minibus). As we took the bumpy road that led to the Pacific Ocean I talked with Paolo Chiarino while Alexandr Brylin held a conference with Ram with Ira acting as interpreter. It was obvious to me that even after the failure to realize the Bering Strait swim again Alexandr was looking on the bright side as he engaged with Ram. I chuckled to myself during some of the misunderstandings as Alexandr asked "How can I join your association?" and Ram replied "Swim 1 mile in under 5c water." The reply from Alexandr came "Why?" Ram replied that those were the conditions. Alexandr then shrugged and said "Well, I have swum almost 2km in zero water." The scene was already set for further meetings in the coming winter swimming season.

When we arrived at the ocean it was windswept as usual. Everybody started to get ready and flags were unfurled. There was quite a good atmosphere although I felt rotten as quite frankly it seemed that nothing would work, even my clothes felt more tired than usual. I had been in Kamchatka for almost 2 weeks and perhaps the stress was beginning to show. Nevertheless I joined in the mass swim and it turned out to be great fun. We were even joined by a seal which added to the excitement. Matias Ola appeared to be in his element and enjoyed showing his freestyle stroke.

Afterward there was a fair bit of shivering as the water was around 10c and the wind was still blowing hard but there was also much elation, you'd have thought that we had actually swum across the Bering Strait rather than simply had a short swim on the coast of Kamchatka!

After photos with the flags we got back into the buses and headed into town. There was time for one more meal before we took the others to the airport and of course it had to be in an expensive restaurant! I wasn't interested at all and just ordered a bowl of rice.

There were more goodbyes at the airport and exchanges of gifts. Finally myself and the Russians retired to one of the flats and soon the discussion was the chance of taking the ship and swimming to the Diomede islands. I made my feelings quite clear, and that was that failure to leave Kamchatka again would be terrible but if we could at least make some headway towards Alaska it would be something of a success. After much discussion, and a great many phone calls we agreed to sleep on it. The next morning we met again at 9 and the expedition was officially cancelled and ended for 2012. I tried in vain to gain passage on the ship to Vladivostok so I could at least see the Kurile Islands but the paperwork was already done and what's more it was agreed that nobody should travel on the ship due to the fact that there was a need to recoup some of the money that had already been paid for the charter. All this took up the whole day and the only thing left was for me to accompany the others to the airport with Viktor the next day. And so on Tuesday it was just myself and Viktor left in Kamchatka. Typically I got some kind of sickness and I was pretty out of it for 2 days before arranging travel to the peace of the volcanoes. As for the swim across the Bering Strait it now appeared to be further away than ever and I also feared for my reputation. 2011 was ok but this time I was very much part of the organizational team and it was my name that had been attached to the project.

I sought solace again on the volcanoes and finally 2 weeks later I returned to Prague to rebuild…

Winston Churchill said

Winston Churchill said "I cannot forecast to you the action of Russia. It is a mystery wrapped in a riddle inside an enigma." I already concurred to some extent with his synopsis and after the events of around 10 days ago I think that this phrase is an accurate and fair way to sum things up. Sometimes Russian people say that everything is possible in Russia and sometimes they say no, everything isn't possible, but this is just a paradox and in the so called land of wonders nothing surprises me.

Russia has a great tradition in naval exploration, particularly in the Arctic and the Far East.

Why does my heart feel so bad?

"Why does my soul feel so bad?" The lyrics to the song by Moby. It sums up my feelings right now.

Hard to explain the feelings now I am sitting back here in
Prague after my month in Kamchatka. I had a good time again on the volcanos but we again failed to get a ship out of PK harbour. It wasn't my fault but I can't help feeling that everybody is secretly pleased and laughing at me. I don't really care but after what happened to Dasa I would just like something to go right.

I experienced more magic on the volcanoes of Kamchatka, again the magnificence of Koryaksky from the slopes of Avacha, and the beauty of Vilyuchinsk combined with the fire of Gorely. But this time I was on Avacha in good weather and the beauty, colour, smell and texture of the crater was joyous. I was also treated to an otherworldly ascent into the fumarole field and crater of Mutnovsky. That's high on the list for a second visit as I was limited on time after a late start and a long hike from Mutnovka thermal power station.

Then a trip to Tolbachik and another dimension of volcanoes and volcanology opened up to me; first the heat of the cinder cones and the quiet desolation of the dead forest. I understood the potential power of a volcano and I grew ever more respectful of their power and not a little bit more scared – definitely no bad thing. The crater of Plosky Tolbachik was high, windy and vast, with the northern side highlighted by a glacier and a view across to the giant Kamen, the second largest on the peninsula.

Just when I thought all was over the next day I was resting, leaning on some tundra when the sky cleared and Tolbachik came into view from the northern side. The word great is overused as an adjective and therefore has little emphasis so I will describe this sight as magnificent, imperious greatness. I felt great contentment and a degree of security to be looking up at the enormous volcano from around 1000m above sea level.

I will be back for more and top of my list is of course another trip to the summit crater of Avacha not to mention reaching Klyuchevskaya and Shiveluch as well as many other natural wonders to be found in Kamchatka.

Sunday 19 August 2012

On Sunday 19th of august I sat at my computer not knowing what to do, or should I say still not knowing what to do. However, there were a few things on my mind that were certain, one was to swim the Bering Strait and the other was to go back to Kamchatka and get on some more volcanoes. Both of these would have to wait so the question was what to do in the meantime?

Not easy but somehow I had to get the motivation to pick myself up and start again with something that paid me money. It was either that or live in the woods which although I don't mind, (I often go to live in nature for a few days or even a week) I didn't see as a realistic lifestyle option at the moment.

The end of August

It was the end of August, I was back into some kind of swimming rhythm, I had been to the Zillertal Alps for some adventure and I had even agreed on some new work to start soon. However, I was still consumed by lethargy and a feeling of dissatisfaction and frustration which was rather unpleasant. Worse obstacles seemed to be coming up which I couldn't get over, life seemed to be turning into a huge puzzle or a maze and I felt trapped and a little lost. Even worse than this I felt alienated from people in some way. A person must help him or herself and harness the power in some way. However, some of the nonsense advice makes me angry as it is so easy for people to offer all kinds of wild, profound and seemingly inspirational advice but I get the feeling that most of the time these people didn't experience a tragedy which knocks you in so many ways. I am actually ok but I can feel the lack of confidence and uncertainty oozing out of me here in the city. When I'm out in nature I feel better, more harmonious and nothing seems to matter. However, now is not the time to leave for a life in the mountains. I need to overcome these minor difficulties and rebuild, and I need to somehow complete the task of swimming across the Bering Strait in an international relay.

Beringia, From Pleistocene to present day
(US national parks service)

10c July isotherm (CIA World Factbook)

Gipanis 2011

Training swim, Kamchatka, 2011

Press conference, Kamchatka 2011

Celebration after training swim, Kamchatka, 2011

Confusion in Kamchatka, 2011

Petropavlovsk Kamchatsky

Mysterious Bering Strait, Alaska, 2011

Alexandr Brylin & Jack, Bering Strait in background, Alaska, 2011

Lunch at school, Wales Alaska 2011

National park offices, Anchorage alaska, 2011

Speaking to the Russian community in Seattle

Jack swims in Lake Bled 2012

Lowpoint, Jack, 2012

Akademik Shokalskiy,2012

Jack training in a glacial lake, Kamchatka 2012

Avacha bay, Kamchatka

Vitus Bering

Georg Steller

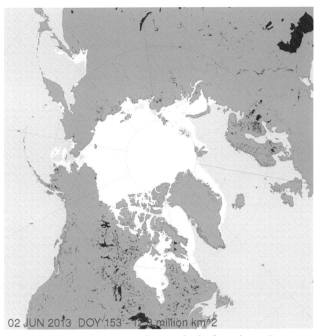

Arctic sea ice extent, 2 months before the swim
(Above and below images courtesy of the National Snow and Ice Data Center,
University of Colorado, Boulder)

Sea ice detail, 6 weeks before the swim

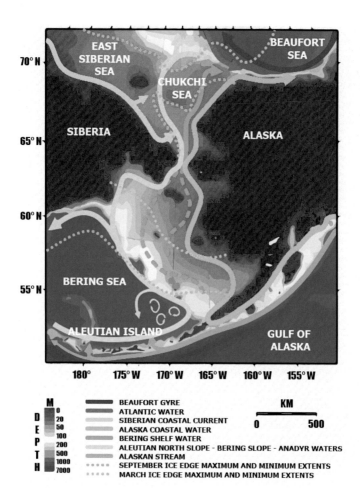

Ocean currents in the north Bering Sea & Bering Strait

(Image courtesy Washington University)

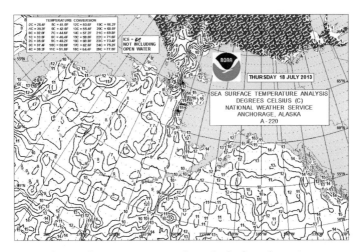

Sea surface temperatures 2 weeks before the swim

(Image courtesy of National Oceanic and Atmospheric Administration (NOAA))

Lend lease exhibit, Yakutsk museum

Shamanic ritual, Yakutsk

Traditional Itelmen dance, Kamchatka 2013

Irtysh 2013

Kamchatka coastline

Alexandr Brylin & Jack, Provideniya bay

Providenya bay

Border control approach us, Provideniya

Captain of Irtysh

Oleg Dokuchaev

Morning exercise onboard Irtysh

Seagulls in the Bering Sea
(Photo: Olga Sokolovna)

Cape Dezhnev, easternmost point of Eurasian continent & swim start

Ram & Ryan after reccy swim

Paolo, Craig & Jack, ready to swim

Paolo swims

Hard work in the waves

Relay handover, Paolo & Anne-Marie

Doctors examining swimmers after another icy immersion

Big Diomede Island

Walrus Rookerie, Big Diomede

Swimming into yesterday across the dateline

Climbing aboard the zodiac after another immersion

Fog in the Bering Strait

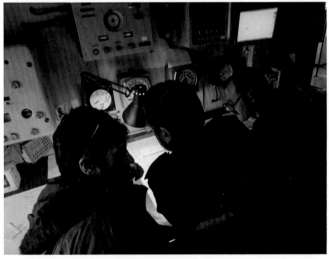

Navigation meeting

Skiing or swimming!

Swimming to the USA

Zdenek uses Czech honey for energy

Waiting for the handover in the waves
(Photo: Olga Sokolovna)

The end is in sight, Cape Prince of Wales, Alaska, Westernmost point of the American continent

Mass finish, approaching the beach in Wales, Alaska
(Photo: Stacey Mueller)

Jack & Craig at the finish
(Photo: Stacey Mueller)

Team at the finish

Zdenek at the finish

(Photo: Stacey Mueller)

Jack & Jackie at the finish
(Photo: Stacey Mueller)

Memorial plaque, Wales, Alaska

Locals & Zhoung in Nome

Our swim, connecting continents, from Eurasia to America

(Map data: Google, DigitalGlobe)

Bering Strait Sept 2012

Just when you think things can't get any messier they do, but that has become a trademark of this project.

Alexandr Brylin is now (understandably) hell bent after two successive failures in 2011 and 2012 on realizing the swim. But it does seem that he won't change his ways. In my opinion this doesn't bode well, although with him still trying combined with "everything is possible in Russia" this can't be ruled out.

In the meantime Oleg Dokuchaev is preparing his own attempt in 2013 bringing Sergey Novikov back on the scene in some way.

Apparently Alexandr and Oleg worked together on the great Amur swim of 2010 but in typical fashion nobody can agree who was in charge of that swim and who organised it. I haven't met Oleg Dokuchaev but the impression I am getting is that although he maybe has a big ego like Alexander Brylin, he is possibly a better organiser, though I have no proof.

If two failures weren't bad enough the international swimmers can now pick from 2 teams – a quite ludicrous situation in my opinion, although one could say it's just a 50/50. Some would say it is no problem either way but I cannot see how both swims will be able to go ahead unless one is starting from the USA and they meet in the middle.

Meanwhile in Prague, I am still picking up the pieces after the tragedy in May. The Vltava has just started to cool a little but not much. It was still 15c last week when I swam 2km and could feel a little coldness coming to my toes – reminding me of what it will be like when the water has cooled by more than 10c!

Rebuilding in Prague, no Tyumen trip for me

In the autumn of 2012 I was concerned with rebuilding my life. I knew that I had to go slowly and get on with things. I declined the chance to socialize extensively as I really didn't feel like it. I had enough teaching work to keep me going but not too much as I needed time for my own studies and projects and also I needed a minimum amount of stress following the events of May. I was recovering quite nicely but the fact was that my life was in tatters and I was still emotionally confused. I knew this was natural so it wasn't a problem, my only concern being that I enjoyed myself and felt happy with my life. In October I contacted Karel Wolf and offered him my volcanoes of Kamchatka presentation for his travel festival Kolem Světa. He accepted it and this gave me something to work on which was great especially as it was connected to the Bering Strait project. I have already said that I declined the chance to be in the organising committee in 2012 but it was still a crossing that I wanted to make. I was contemplating a future solo crossing by skis from Russia to America. I estimated that I would be ready in around 7 years if ice conditions would still leave it feasible at this time. It was only a passing thought and I remained committed to participating in the swimming relay if it would happen.

In November I slowly started to try meeting people and I even used a web dating site although my experience with this wasn't too good. I slowly started dating girls and I was helped by the presentation at Kolem Světa which I gave in Czech language. Although I made some enormous mistakes it went down very well, as I was able to laugh about my mistakes. I felt that maybe the worm was turning, the winter swimming season was starting to "warm up" and I was also helped by several relaxing trips to the forest with my friend and fellow winter swimmer Matej and a few others. It was one of our favourite pastimes, sitting in the forest, roasting sausages on an open fire and talking about many diverse subjects as if we were professors in the science of life.

Meanwhile an invitation came via Alexandr Brylin to swim in a competition in Tyumen, Siberia. Not only did it clash with the Schengen swim but quite frankly I wasn't ready to travel at that time. I was more concerned with rebuilding my life in Prague. I referred Alexandr to Andrew Chin and before long Ram and some of the others were arranging their trip to Tyumen. I was right that things were changing. One Thursday we had a meeting with my friend Mirek Fajfrlík about a photo exhibition that we were planning. Martina was there to help us and although I had met her some years before it was only for a short time. Mirek said to me "Das jsi nejaky aperitif? Treba Jamesons?" (Offers an aperitif of whisky) "Ok" I replied and the tone was set. It was lunchtime and after we had finished our lunch and started on coffees along with more Jamesons I got an SMS through that my afternoon lesson was cancelled. Fine, I accepted that I would stay in the pub for a little longer. This lasted until about 11pm. Jana (Dasha's younger sister) came at 9pm and stayed for a while. Then we went home and I checked her new place out. I was happy with it and made my way back to my own flat. It was around midnight and I had drunk several beers and many, many Jamesons after an 11 hour session. I munched on some bread and wrote Martina a message, telling her it was nice to meet her etc. the next day I was up at 6am to go to the Pool. Later that day I met Martina again with Mirek. Then I went alone with Martina for a walk and I started to like her. She didn't want to speak English but it didn't seem to be a problem. We started meeting more and more which was good for me. The next week I visited Prostějov before the Schengen swim for a meeting with a few people and all afternoon I was texting Martina. It felt good. She invited me to her flat for Christmas which was also good. This relationship lasted around 3 months and during this time I felt pretty happy. She had her volleyball and I had my swimming. Both us were busy so it was ok. This relationship was probably never destined to be long term as Martina wasn't keen on speaking English. It ended abruptly after my Spitsbergen trip. It was my mistake but also there was an issue with the language barrier.

As for the Spitsbergen trip it was a big success and was another good thing that came about from the Kolem Světa event in November...

28th November 2012

Sometime after the summer and as the autumn began to start so increased my desire for the paradox, extremes of fire and ice manifested itself – volcanoes and winter swimming.

I became more and more annoyed with people except when I was in the forest with my friend Matěj and a few of my language lessons which were a great help to me. Aside from that I was greatly soothed by looking at my volcano pictures from Kamchatka as I prepared for my lecture and photo show at the Kolem Světa festival in Prague. It went very well so I was very happy with that but I soon realized how strong the feelings were inside me. The suggestion by Tomáš Prokop of a photo exhibition was a good one and soon I found myself sitting in the front room of the polar explorer Miroslav Jakeš, contemplating a winter trip to Svalbard. This galvanised me and the next day I was rapturously viewing my pictures from last year's trip to the Bering Strait, almost salivating as I thought of the mysterious and wonderful arctic, bolstered by my childhood memories of watching *"The Snowman"*!

Then, bang I was back on fire and again almost frothing at the mouth as I heard within a week that Etna had erupted with strombolian activity and then Plosky Tolbachik erupted again after a near 30 year break.

I simply couldn't wait for the Etna trip, it was giving me some focus but then! Ching! I had wangled my way into doing a Ram Barkai authorised ice swim at Lake Windermere in February!

Regarding the winter swimming I was going well but just to add to the fire and ice paradox at the same time I was experiencing problems. I once failed to make the 22minute limit for 1km and I started to become angry with those who were wearing neoprene caps. Again, a paradox as I considered the old adage "If you can't beat 'em, join 'em." Maybe I should give in and buy a neoprene cap, but of course that would be no good regarding the training for the ice swim. I contemplated this ice swim whilst I was in the water at Hradec Králové and to be honest I wasn't 100% satisfied with my ability to get the mile in 3c water although on other occasions I had been happy.

The truth of the matter is that I am a slow swimmer with a very low speed over anything more than 50m, and although I can swim 10km and upwards in open water I am undoubtedly more talented at travelling over ground. This is extremely important for slow swimmers like me when thinking about doing an ice swim as we must spend longer in the water. I know that I wouldn't bat an eyelid at doing the mile in 3c water if I could get it in around 25mins but when I am looking at 35 or maybe even 37 minutes I know it will be a major challenge. Definitely achievable without danger but very difficult and not to be taken lightly. During some conversations I even scared myself with my own comment and logical reasoning about what is and isn't possible. I had been studying biogeography and I had looked at various animals and of course it was quite clear that the Homo sapiens was not at all suited to swimming let alone swimming in cold water. Compared to the great sea mammals such as whales, walruses and then that beast that is the polar bear the human being looks like a bunch of matchsticks at worse and at best a few branches with a birds nest in them!

I had just swum my 4th 1km winter swim in 4 weeks and I felt ok but at around 5c I was labouring towards the finish, switching to breathing every 2 strokes on the right side from my usual bilateral style. I was fine on exiting although I was thinking about the extra 600m at Windermere in a lower temperature and I had some worries but also I was sure that a good winter season would see me in peak condition by early February. I had learned over the last 5 years that around the start of Feb would be the peak with the need for a break somewhere around the end of February before something of a second coming with the slightly warmer water in mid-March. My feet were still bothering me and even though I had checked everything and they seemed fine, they were still staying too cold for my liking after an immersion.

Preparing for an ice swim

It was always my plan last season to do a low key but nevertheless official ice mile. Experience told me that end of winter/beginning of spring would be the best time for it with water around 4.5c. I know cold water pretty well and there is a world of difference between 4.5c and say 2.5c. Unfortunately last year the conditions went against me and I never got my chance to make the swim.

Now this year I have roped myself into an ice mile in the middle of winter at the first year of the 'Big Chill Swim'. Right now it's cold at Windermere and the average temperature for the lake at this time of year is around 3.5c, although this week should see considerably milder weather raise the temperature at least a little.

In a nutshell, 4c or over is a challenge but I have the experience for it. However, at under 4c it will become exponentially a bigger and bigger challenge and knowing cold water as I do I have no problem in saying I hope that the water will be around 4c. Anyway, we will get what we get from Mother Nature and we can't influence such things as climatic conditions, (at least not in such a short space of time).

More important is how to prepare for such a challenge and the perhaps surprising thing is that I have tweaked my training habits somewhat recently. It is clear to me now that it isn't necessary to constantly push myself to the limit week in week out. I naturally arrived at this decision and it concurs with the idea of the optimal time for hardening in icy water being between 10 and 12 minutes put forward by people such as Professor Zeman author of the book "*Human adaptation to cold*" (a book that ought to be translated into English). Not that I have been taking it easy. I have been swimming regularly in near 0c water and my other more unorthodox preparation activities have included winter rafting without neoprene clothing and the classic winter camping in adverse conditions.

Regarding the ice swim, I decided some 2 weeks beforehand that I am ready and that I don't need more training as such and that the best thing I can do is ensure that my body is in the best possible shape for the upcoming test. Yesterday (1 week before) I made a 9 minute swim in water around 0c with ice forming as I swam. That might be my last open water swim before the ice swim as I am thinking of cancelling my usual Wednesday training to leave myself in perfect condition. This is unusual for me as I always swim on a Wednesday, having failed to do so on just 2 or 3 occasions in the last five years.

Whatever the right way of doing it there isn't much that can be gained or lost at this stage and next Saturday I will see what happens, needless to say I am looking forward to it and I wish everyone else well in their preparations for the exciting Big Chill swim event.

Chill Swim **Blog**

I planned to do an Ice swim last season but unfortunately conditions went against me and I had to wait until February 2013 and the fabulous first year of the Chill swim event to go for the current holy grail of endurance winter swimmers only for conditions to again go against us as the water temperature rose from 4.6c in the morning to 5.1c in the afternoon. However with 2 turn buoys to be negotiated 20 times and a low sun this was never going to be easy but of course that is part of the thrill that is open water swimming.

I thought I had prepared ok and was in good condition... I know my limits and expected it to be difficult but I expected to finish due to my previous experience of 1km still water swims in lower temps. I got in and felt fine, the water didn't feel too cold, it felt as 5c water should when you have recently been swimming in lower temps. (However, we all know that 5c isn't "warmer" it's just "less cold") I felt fine although the low sun was messing up my rhythm as I sighted more often and perhaps it altered my breathing. After around 800m I got cramp in the legs, which is odd for me during winter swimming. Obviously I know how to swim with cramp and I dropped my legs a bit and kicked less. However, I am not blaming my performance on the cramp! I think on the 8th lap I switched to breaststroke permanently. I was still planning to finish and wasn't worried although I was perhaps getting groggy. I rounded the turn buoy to start the final lap and felt pleased that I was on the last lap, I still was planning to finish. Then somewhere in the middle of the course I took a stroke and nothing happened and I seemed to sink a little in the water. I stopped and looked around and I could hear a lot of shouting. At that split second I immediately decided I must get out (very strange as just a minute before I was happy to be on the final circuit with the finish in sight). The diver came in and touched me at which point my swim was obviously over, though somehow I made it to the steps unaided. I believe I was at my limit and needed to end the swim with regards the immersion time. On exiting I was of course very groggy and I think I made a great decision to end the swim and get out. I like journeys and this was an incredible one. The medical team took over and although it was against my wishes I wasn't really in a position to argue plus it of course felt good to have blankets thrown on me! The next 30mins are blurred as I was groggy although aware of what was going on and able to talk. I believe I was with the medical team for circa 55mins. When I left them I felt fine went to the hotel, had some tea and biscuits and decided to go to the sauna. As usual after an endurance winter swim I was extremely hungry and had no problem in eating an enormous plate of food from the carvery later that evening. I can tell you that the medical team managed my recovery very well. My thoughts after the swim are not much different to before it except that I have more respect for ice swimmers and also I believe that Ram Barkai has set the bar at a great level with the ice-mile concept. It isn't easy – mediocre endurance winter swimmers like me can probably attain it but it isn't easy at all. The faster more "elite" endurance winter swimmers will still find it a huge challenge but ultimately the extra speed means less time in the water and therefore less of the exponential difficulty that the increased immersion time brings. I thoroughly enjoyed it and I will get an ice-mile under my belt in the future! Well done to Ram, Haydn and Jackie on finishing the "nice-mile". I hope the sight of me coming out didn't put too many people off endurance winter swimming, although let's face it, it isn't very easy and maybe it's better that people know that!

Early Feb 2013 and it all starts going off

After the drama of the ice swim at Windermere, the 750m still water swim , even with water at 1.5c didn't seem too bad, in fact for me it passed without a thought, although I had to help some colleagues who were less fortunate.

Then, the following week 2 correspondences were forwarded to me. One from Jim Rowlinson regarding his dealings with a guy called Slava in PK and the second from Leonid Kokaurov about his recent exchange via email with Alexandr Brylin. At the same time an invitation to Murmansk arrived and a mysterious message from Andrew Chin, demanding our addresses for an invitation which I guessed was connected with Novikovs Bering plan. I knew Alexandr had been in Yakutia and he was obviously pleased as he had pitched to someone and had some agreement. Maybe it meant nothing although I knew that Yakutia was a very rich region and that he had maybe found a way forward.

The situation with Jim was a funny one; I had met him just 10 days before at a service station near Tamworth – a 76 year old ex-army guy. In his own words "Not blowing my own trumpet but I think I am quite good with people." When he said that I made a mental note to at a suitable time try to coach him on email etiquette as he had infuriated me in the past with his repetition of questions and his inability to answer my own after he had initiated the discussion, although in person he was charming and personable. However, this made me think again about imperialism and empire as here was a man who was clearly a part of that old world whereas I at 33 years old was if not one of the new generation, certainly in the transition phase. Jim seemed like a nice guy but I was ready to bet my last pound that he was a colonialist and that he would treat people in that typical old fashioned superior British way – and I mean no harm in saying that, I thought he was a nice guy, but let's face it British people were brought up to believe they owned the world and even in my own schooling, though we didn't get that kind of education, the history of the world was given to us in a diluted and incomplete form.

How relevant is this to the Bering Strait you may ask – and the answer is very relevant. I don't want to use Jim as a scapegoat because he is a nice guy but he is there and he didn't understand the Bering Strait region, geographically or historically/socially. When he was quoted some figure like £25,000 to arrange this project he baulked at it but the truth is that you must pay the going rate for things wherever you are in the world. The native people of Alaska and Chukotka were introduced to our way of life when the missionaries came over 100 years ago, they no longer live a complete subsistence life and in Alaska the kids wear baseball caps and want to play computer games, everyone drinks coke and alcohol has been enough of a problem that the villages are 'dry' by law. These things cannot be made by the produce of the tundra or the sea and money is needed even if some government support exists. So when westerners from the temperate regions come expecting the world to stop for their expedition it does to an extent – because there is a chance for business, to provide services and earn money – and why should it be given away on the cheap – it certainly wouldn't be in New York City or London or Amsterdam. (Just imagine a native Alaskan who has no fruit or veg but has seen pictures of Europe and all the crops, apple trees in gardens, grass, etc. now why do these guys insist on coming out here? They must be crazy but also have a lot of money? Or not crazy but just bored because they have such an easy life, they should try living here!) You get the picture, what I am trying to say – look at it from other people's perspective.

All said and done £25,000 is a lot of money to spend on a kayak crossing of an 86km probably fog covered strait between the arctic and pacific oceans, Eurasian and Russian continents, what some say is the end of the world. And that's the allure, the romance, but all said and done it really is just a body of water, an element of our earth like any other part of nature. Good luck to those who attempt it.

Anticipation of Svalbard

Back in 2010 I had first talked of the idea of a winter swimming expedition to the Svalbard Archipelago but that was as far as the conversation went. In all honesty, at the time I didn't really know how to realize such an idea only that it was possible and that therefore somehow it could actually be done. As usual time tells and a few years later this idea looked like it had become reality...

Travelling to Brno in a full car was always going to be conversation filled, mainly concerning that never to be exhausted topic among Czech winter swimmers of water temperature, however with Matěj Červený present it was to be made all the more interesting.

Matěj is a good friend of mine and he is a genuine guy, down to earth, funny and extremely tough – not to mention he also shares my loathing of wasting money. Another one of his character traits is his ability to brag and show off although he does this in a humorous way. Four other people in the car was enough for him. When I mentioned the Svalbard trip he made light of the amount of calories needed and claimed that he might not eat through the day. I know what he is like and he is capable of doing this but he hasn't been in the arctic yet so I was sceptical of his claims especially since I had had a taste of the arctic in Alaska in 2011. At least he was now resigned to taking a down jacket after at first claiming that soft shell would be enough! A wild claim but he is extremely strong and I didn't want to bet against him overcoming extremely adverse conditions. I remembered 3 years ago at about 1300m in the Giant Mountains on cross country skis, with wind-chill the temp was negative 25c and a near whiteout. He was wearing just a t shirt and it took him some while to succumb and go for long sleeves. I always joke that he is an incredible dryland winter swimmer!

The Matěj-dominated conversation turned again to winter swimming and we discussed the word in Czech "pokrmy" which means humble. He declared that he was humble in front of the winter water. We pretty much all agreed on this although I wondered why he wasn't so humble in front of the arctic and then I realized it was because he was yet to experience it. Another factor that our guide for this trip the well-known Czech polar traveller Mirek Jakeš was also rather laidback about everything even uttering a Matěj Červený like sentence when he said "People think Svalbard is terribly cold but it's not much worse than here really." However he did mean "here" as in mountains at elevations of over 1000m in winter and not the middle of the town centre.

The Svalbard trip was now nearing and the anticipation was building – what would conditions be like? Would there be open water/would we make a swim? Would we meet any wildlife? It was sure to be a tough trip in itself but at the same time it would also give me more experience before the potential extreme that might be the Bering Strait swim.

Svalbard

Yes, "It's polar life" we exclaimed as we sat warm and contentedly around a stove drinking tea in a small wooden hut on the west coast of Spitsbergen somewhere in between the settlements of Longyearbyen and Barentsburg! Myself, my swim club colleague Matěj Červený, the eccentric pilot Jindra Krasa and then the older Mirek Záveský , conqueror of some big mountains over 7000m and who could forget our polar guide himself Mirek Jakeš, 14 times to the north pole, 40 times on Spitsbergen etc. We were a fairly motley crew, and although we were something like a group of homeless with our tents on the edge of the city, and our visits to the wonderful church it didn't matter for a short stay.

The trip was turning out well. After arriving at 00.30 we made our way to town and slept for a few hours. In the morning we walked 10 minutes to the church for a meeting. It was horrendous as the wind was blowing and I donned my down jacket, complete with hood and ski mask. It was a relief to finally arrive at the top of the small hill where the church was situated. I dared not contemplate what lay ahead (although little was I to know that this just acclimatisation). As we listened to Mirek's tales the Pastor dropped in and offered us some coffee which we as the new (if temporary) poor of Longyearbyen gratefully accepted. 10 days later I was talking to the Pastor's wife and I had to explain that we simply didn't have any money so we stayed in tents. We may have been the poorest tourists but we were surely the strongest and most well adapted. In Barentsburg Vitaly who invited us to stay a night in his research base said that in his 4 years here he had never known an Englishman to arrive on skis so I was the first. In fact he remarked that Mirek was the only person who ever came on skis! Actually the only other people we met on our travels were on snow scooters.

The journey to Rusanov's hut was an interesting one and this was initiated by Matěj. In the morning, I heard him mention the hut on several occasions and then I saw him feverishly cutting firewood when really we needed to leave, this set the seed in my mind that he was aiming to reach the hut that day. We set off at 2pm and within an hour we had overhauled Mirek Záveský who had a 30 min head start on us. Several hours later we had ascended from sea level to a mountain pass over 700m high. It was a never ending climb and the view just before sunset was beautiful. The first downhill section was fun and everyone fell a few times before the angle of descent lessened and progress became steadier. The idea was to find a spot to camp once in the valley. Having changed skis I was using a new type of binding and I had some problems which led to a lack of speed. I was soon behind and alone as Mirek Záveský caught and passed me. An hour later I reached him. I asked where the others were and he said just ahead. I already had a feeling that we would keep going. I soon reached Jindra and Matěj who wouldn't admit to a desire to reach the hut. It was gone 9pm and very dark as we swept down a moraine and into the base of a huge valley, veering right that we knew led to the sea. Our estimates said 6km to the sea and at least 3km up to the hut. Tired, we kept going. At this point I was having problems with hydration and to a lesser extent nutrition. I had 6 snacks per day which was enough for 6 – 8 hours. For 12 hours it wasn't really enough so I ate some of my reserve food. Jindra also gave

us all some bacon which was nice. I had finished my tea –
again enough for 8 hours but not more. I began devouring
snow which is a temporary fix if anything. Then there was
real excitement on the way to the seashore as we saw a
light coloured animal in the darkness. A polar bear! I had
the flares ready and Mirek the rifle…however it was a false
alarm and was only a reindeer. This happened again but by
the third time we were already used to it although we
always remained vigilant just in case there was an ursus
maritimus on our tail. Now it was the hut or bust as we
reached the Coles Bay and the beginning of the abandoned
village. It wasn't the hut but we were on the right trail. We
continued spurred by the knowledge that it was apparently
only 1km to the hut from the edge of the village.

Finally at 2am we reached the hut of Vladimir
Rusanov, the Russian geologist who overwintered here
whilst researching the coal mining possibilities. He later
perished on a voyage somewhere near Novaya Zemlya.

The next day we realized that we had a possible
location for a swim. There was a safe entrance and exit to
the water with the ice and snow providing a series of steps
whilst the water was not too deep by the shore of this bay
and there was enough ice free open water for a short and
most importantly safe swim. We busily prepared for this by
collecting some driftwood in order to light the stove inside
the hut. Then we cut steps in the snow from the cottage to
the shore the air temperature was -18c with gusts that could
take it down to -37c. The water itself, being sea water was
well below zero, I think around -1.7c but later in the
evening we got a reading of -2.7c. This is possibly due to
the salinity of sea water.

The 3 of us, me, Matěj and Jindra got ready. We looked
a strange sight in swimming trunks, down jackets and
enormous Baffin polar boots.

At around 13.00h local time we carefully entered the
water and by 13.05h we were back out again. Less than 5

minutes but that was more than enough considering the conditions and that we were here at 78 degrees north in the high arctic. It was quite a buzz to swim in such a location and seeing as we were at his former hut we decided out of respect to dedicate the swim to Vladimir Rusanov who had perished 100 years before.

The swim itself was short but intense for the water bit and burned and soon I had lost the feeling in my arms. The water was clear and the soft ice on the surface was no danger, although it wasn't visible from the shore that some 30 metres or so out from land the ice was already more solid and for that reason we stayed close to the shore where conditions were best. This was not a time for heroics we just wanted to have a beautiful swim and we did.

On exiting the water, we now had to be extremely careful regarding frostbite. The wind was sometimes gusting and we got our boots and jackets on in seconds and soon made our way back to the hut and the warmth of the stove, more than satisfied with this experience.

The next day we skied on. A few days later we arrived at the town of Barentsburg, a town administered by a Russian mining company and as such a Russian town. Here lay the most northern statue of Lenin (aside from Pyramiden also on Spitsbergen which is no longer inhabited). I decided to get a photo of myself by the statue with the Bering Strait swim flag. I thought it a good omen for the swim and I was satisfied with our Spitsbergen 2013 polar swimming expedition, it boded well for the summer and the Bering.

Cehovice & Nova Paka

On arrival back from Svalbard I went straight out and bought some food. I chose odd shoes which should have alerted me to the fact that I probably needed some rest. I consumed almost 500g of meat with half a loaf of bread and 2 beers. Then Mirek Jakeš called me from Svalbard to tell me that Oslo airport had my camera – nonsense but still it caused confusion for a time.

Next day I was teaching all day and by then end of it I was glad to be going home for more food and rest. The tiredness and hunger continued into Thursday and again I was glad to get home in the evening. On Friday I had the chance to go to the pool, but when the alarm went off at 6am I was still half dead and I knew that more sleep was needed. Still hungry through Friday I had to be up before 7am on Saturday in order to go for a winter swimming race in Čehovice. I opted for 750m due to my tiredness. Many people asked me why aren't you going 1km and I had to say that I was probably doing well to be here today. I still felt a little sluggish. The water was 2.5c and although I started ok by the second of the 2 laps I was struggling and I was passed by swimmers who are normally far slower. I even defecated in the water and was thinking that it was the end of my winter swimming career. With no changing rooms it was a funny situation. Bob Pacl asked me why I was still wearing wet trunks, I couldn't tell him that they had shit in them but I thought about it as he was getting on my nerves. Finally we got back to the pub where I feasted on gulas washed down with a beer. Later I ate 100g of chocolate.

I moved on to Mohelnice where I left a piece of Svalbard coal and a small piece of reindeer skin by Dasha's grave. The next day I had planned another winter swim but wisely I decided on one more day of rest before beginning with training again on Monday. I was fed full of duck with cabbage and dumplings at Nadia's house, not to mention more beer, cake, pastries and slivovice. I got back to Prague feeling better. Sure enough I kick started my training again on Monday by running 6km to the river, swimming 1km and then some strengthening exercises. By the end of the week I was flying again and I noticed that I ran the 10km with hills at 44mins without being at maximum, a very good sign. Then on Saturday at Nová Paka, we had an ice pool to contend with for the season's final winter swimming race. The water was just above zero. Many people were concerned and there was talk of shortening the track or even making it an exhibition swim.

I had been back from Spitsbergen for 10 days and I was now beginning to feel stronger again and I was looking forward to the 750m with relish. A ridiculous amount of laps in the ice pool was in store.

The air hovered around zero and I wisely retired inside from time to time during the build-up so as not to get a real cold start.

Credit to the organisers they kept the format and we had heat after heat after heat as we swam the 750m 10 swimmers at a time. I won my heat with ease and the 37m course was helping me as it was like swimming in the pools. I was able to take short breaks at each turn which I think suited me. I felt good afterwards and was soon fully dressed and drinking tea. Others found it trickier but the truth was that it was only psychologically difficult as the water was 3c – still tricky but definitely it was the sight of the ice pool that was unnerving for people.

It was an excellent end to the domestic season and with the winter dawdling it seemed that the water would stay cold for some time to come. This would suit me, a long season followed by a short break before some acclimatization later in the summer before the Bering Strait. I knew the drill as this was the third year in a row that I had prepared for a July or early August expedition to swim across the Bering Strait.

8th April 2013

As I sat in my kitchen studying and thinking about the Bering Strait it was a repeat of 2012.

I started to chuckle as I listened to the Russian song Katyushka. It was Monday 8th of April and it seemed that there were now almost certainly 2 Russian groups trying to make the swim happen. The song really summed the moment up, the frantic up and down melody which was simply saying to me "Who knows what will happen next." At least this time I was somewhat in the background although I was still privy to information especially from the Brylin side through my friend Leonid Kokaurov. My only concern was that I had to watch what I said and to whom. The best thing was to remain as quiet as possible for the moment and not stir things either way – not easy as anything I added seemed to have some kind of double meaning!

I simply couldn't predict how this would turn out but I suspected there would be more twists and turns. I was amused now by the involvement of international swimmers and their associates such as Angelique, Paul Duffield's (Canadian ice swimmer) wife and social media expert. These people quite possibly had little understanding of what was in store. Even the others had now probably been brainwashed following red carpet treatment first in Tyumen and then in Murmansk. With these cities' desire to stage the world championships in 2016 they had to put on a good show and it was another case of a different Russian agenda. I still can't quite put my finger on it but the Russians have a different way to the British for example although there are similarities and parallels which I think may stem from empire.

I had seen an extremely angry letter (in Russian) from Oleg Adamov which was sent by Alexandr Brylin. Amongst other things the guys from Khabarovsk were described as amateurs and Sergey Novikov was referred to as an immigrant from Seattle! The fact that he was made no difference to his abilities although of course amongst the Russians it was insulting.

I sat back and listened to Katyusha (popular Russian song) again waiting for the next twist! I was fairly certain that it wouldn't be long in coming!

End of April 2013

As spring finally came and temperatures dramatically increased in Europe so too temperatures rose within the Bering Strait project. Luckily this time, although I was still caught in the middle I wasn't the only one and I had been careful to remain as neutral as possible while still supporting both sides. Interestingly the other international swimmers saw it as Alexandr Brylin vs. Sergey Novikov but I knew it was far more complex and that the real battle was going on in Russia between Alexandr Brylin and Oleg Dokuchaev. The South Africans had used their numbers well with Andrew Chin the front man for Sergey Novikov as someone who hadn't travelled to either Tyumen or Murmansk. The inevitable happened during the week beginning Monday 15th of April. I knew it would happen seeing as Alexandr had been in Chukotka and seemed to think he had an agreement for a ship and a plan to make his swim happen. I was not ready to support this since, like last year he was relying on money from too many sources, a flaw which I had flagged up (and rightly so) last year. Not only that, but of course there was the old problem of crossing the border. He came up with a plan to do this with the idea of chartering another vessel with a view to changing vessels at the 12mile zone. On paper it is possible but in reality I was convinced it would be a fiasco resulting in a failed crossing, meaning a failed swim. I still tried to support Alexandr, after all I had been involved with this project for a long while. I suggested an expedition to Bering Island instead or even to Ratmanov (big Diomede). Leonid was in agreement but it seemed that Alexandr as usual would press on in desperation. Meanwhile Novikov was starting not only to talk big, but to deliver, as a new website went online and official invitations were produced in Russia with tracking numbers. He was also certain about the logistics being taken care of by the military and even named the support vessel as a large medical vessel, an icebreaker named *Irtysh*.

Then I was accused by Alexandr Brylin of treachery and an argument ensued. I tried to be diplomatic but I would not back down. I was particularly angered when it was actually one of his own team members (my good friend Sergey Popov) who sowed the seed of joining the other swim. I went out to teach English and could barely keep my mind on the job, even arriving 2 minutes late for 1 lesson as I was outside drafting an email! When I got home I continued on with my diplomatic mission. Luckily it seemed some of the others especially Ram were in similar positions. The thing was they were probably feeling more torn as they had been guests twice in Russia for both the Murmansk and Tyumen events. However, what they didn't know (probably) was that this was simply a publicity exercise as these 2 cities were in direct competition for the 2016 world championships – and having international swimmers made them look better. Alexandr had been lucky; he had a chance to repair his damaged reputation with both the international swimmers and within Russia as he was the initiator of their participation.

Alexandr actually apologised to me during our argument which was unusual and from that moment I sensed a chance for unity. Then Ram posted a statement on the Facebook group stating the problem and that the South African team would support Novikov. I immediately agreed with his statement and called for Alexandr and his Amur swimmers to join us. I continued with my light diplomacy and I sensed that soon Alexandr would have no option. I like to think that my main piece of advice "sometimes we have to do things we don't want to do in the short term, in order to benefit in the long term" had some effect but the truth is that even such a pig headed man as Alexandr could surely see this time that he had no options. Some days later news came through that Alexandr Brylin and Oleg Dokuchaev would unite. I felt a weight lifted and I started for the first time to feel safe and also that maybe we were nearing the peak regarding organisation, like it was now in view, then it would be downhill before another big peak in the form of the swim itself. As usual time would tell. On the forum Novikov referred to me several times as a "veteran" and I sure felt like that. Many of the others were involved for the first time yet this project had been with me for two and a half years and I felt engulfed by it at times. This meant that I felt a strong sense that it must be completed and I hoped it wasn't just my desire but that it was actually becoming a reality.

Meanwhile I was visited by a friend of Elena Guseva, a certain Nadya Dudinka from the Urals. Over 60 years old but a marvellous and extremely sprightly not to mention still an excellent freestyle swimmer. Only about 5 feet tall but she had energy and that typical Russian toughness – that "it doesn't matter what happens, I can drink a lot, sleep very little, work a lot, but I will be fine." The more I thought about it the more I believed that we were mollycoddled and spoilt in the west. I was happy in Prague, a nice city; I didn't have or need many material things. The visit of Nadya was all the more significant as she had already swum the Bering Strait when she was a member of the swim team on the 1991 expedition. On the evening of May 2nd I started to feel unwell and I slept less than 4 hours. When I woke at 6am I decided that I should give the pool a miss. I made it to my 10.30 lesson but by the end of that I was heading towards autopilot. I arrived at the studio for the recording and I said very little as I was by now completely on autopilot.

However, now I had a challenge on my hands as I had to meet the visiting Alexandr Jakovkev for lunch. I found some energy for this and Alex and his wife Natalya are nice people but as Alex talked of many projects and businesses etc. I started to feel as though my own life was empty or incomplete not just emotionally but financially too. Not that Alex said anything bad but I soon got the feeling that he had large amounts of money compared to me who was about to spend 25% of my weekly wage on a meal for three of us. Never mind I knew I was only thinking like this due to my physical deterioration. I forced myself to walk them to Vyšehrad and then I got back on the metro to go home. I actually slept standing up which must have been a first. To make matters worse back home I felt worse and I couldn't concentrate on anything which was a worry seeing as I had now just 6 days to my biogeography exam.

As I sat in the kitchen sipping tea I hoped that a good night's sleep would see me in good shape for tomorrow and a return to the water. Before bed I wrote a short note to Jura and contemplated my still broken life. This Bering project had had some bearing on it although I couldn't put all the blame on the Bering, I had been trying to help Dasha's Mum (also called Dasha) for some time with her stress and I had failed. Although I didn't feel to blame for what happened I felt more like a pawn in game who could see what was happening but was powerless to do anything about it – some people would say that the strong would do something about it, but I don't know; I did what I thought was best. My dealings with the Russians had sapped my energy but taught me many things. The Bering project and the people involved were not so much my friends but people I was associated with through the project itself. At the third time of asking I badly needed to complete the task and move on to something new even if the ultimate goal would again involve the Bering Strait. One thing was certain and that was what Steven Munatones said back in late 2011 "Be careful with so many people involved there will be huge politics." It had been like that but surely now the worst was over...

I felt a little better the next morning, at least well enough to go for a short swim so I met the Latvian delegation again, put on a brave face and made a short swim with them in the 8c Vltava.

June 2013

I needed a break and I took one at the end of May, travelling for a long weekend to Campania region of Italy specifically for the volcanism and the trip was fine, allowing me to clear my head nicely for the coming summer.

Returning from volcanic Campania to a flooded Czech Republic was an interesting change. The Vltava had burst its banks reaching a peak flow of 3200 cumecs – around 15 times that of an average flow for the river. The river channel itself had swelled to at least 3 times its normal width and trees and bushes on the floodplain were submerged. Swimming wasn't possible -unless you had a death wish.

Meanwhile other than this naturally enforced break in open water swimming the Bering Strait project seemed to be coming to something of a break or at least a stalemate. This time it was an argument over collecting information for visas between Novikov and Irina. I just simply sat and waited knowing that most of the others were more than a little perplexed by the constant contradictions which were something I had become accustomed to.

I decided on a short trip to England for my friend Stu's wedding party. I didn't have the money but I needed to catch up with some old faces even if it would only be for just over 24 hours.

I made it to the party having booked a cheap flight from Brno and I used a combination of walking, hitching and bus to travel from Stansted airport to Peterborough. We drank a lot and had a laugh. Reverting to old ways when I would buy and sell various things

I sold some tobacco which helped subsidize the cost of the flight. Sitting in Luton airport I was fairly pleased as money wise I had done ok. However, this changed when I got back to Prague and realized that I had lost my camera. My Fuji xp10 which was waterproof, shockproof and freeze proof didn't have the best sensor or lens but I knew how to use it to the max and extract the absolute best from it. Now I would have to pay 3000czk to get a new one. A week later my not so smart phone decided to break down on me. It had been on the cards for a while and quite frankly I think it was the second Kamchatka expedition that really did for it. Anyway, I dug out my 6 year old trusty Nokia and struggled with the buttons and its slow nature. I was frustrated and at this point I said to myself "You need to find sponsors, now is the time."

James Cook languages in Prague had been my employers in 2008/09 and again since 2012. Naturally the school was named after the famous British explorer. I was no expert in obtaining sponsors but I knew that you should always look to what and who is around you as that was how I had been successful in the past when I found Czech beekeeping association through Dasha's mother, and they ended up sponsoring one of our club's swimming events.

Somewhat reluctantly I decided that seeing as James Cook had sailed in the Bering Strait and named the strait after Bering, named Cape Prince of Wales and generally explored the Alaskan coast a great deal, practically founding Anchorage that it was a 'no brainer' to ask the language school to get involved. Even so, as I said I was reluctant as I had been through so much with this project and in 2012 especially I felt that my reputation had suffered. I didn't want that again and not on my own doorstep. Therefore when I met with the boss of the school, Ondřej Kuchař, I enthusiastically sold the project, I couldn't help but do anything else, before backtracking and saying that I would only look for cooperation if we succeeded and even then only if it was really in the interests of the business. Ondřej was keen but didn't like my idea of trying to promote James Cook languages externally, seeing it as more of an internal thing so I wasn't sure how it would turn out. Later I was pleasantly surprised to get an email saying that they agreed to sponsor me for 10,000czk. This sponsorship game was easy after all!

Facebook

While I was gaining sponsorship, internet politics were hotting up through the medium of Facebook.

I've already mentioned the role that Facebook played, and if Facebook regarding the Bering Strait was synonymous with one person then that was Sergey Novikov.

He chose this as his tool to take control and then manipulate the international swim team with the help of Andrew and Ram from South Africa who invited swimmers into first a private debate in the form of a shared message followed by the creation of a group "Bering Strait swim". This private group which Novikov referred to as a blog became the place where all information was disseminated instead of using email. I watched with fascination as the transparency of Facebook was a great place to witness the wonderful workings of Sergey Novikov's mind! I remember that he had told me that his background was in construction and aviation. Judging by many of his posts and comments one could deduce that he was quite poorly informed about many things. In fact it became apparent to me at one point that he was incapable of making appropriate comments on almost any subject save for blatant criticism or straight praise. His continual errors in using the English language started to become amusing for me too, although the most amusing things were the fantastical ideas that he from time to time posted regarding logistics for the swim. It all started early on when he said that we would be taken by military helicopter from PK to Anadyr. I didn't doubt that it was possible but I was sure that it was impossible in one flight and that it would require a stop at Ust Kamchatsk or somewhere close. Flying direct 2000km by this kind of helicopter was not possible. Then later on he became involved with some people in Russia and he came up with his great notion of the Baikal training swim. Strangely it got talked about in this way ("Baikal training swim") without any vote or suggestion of the idea. I felt somehow guilty as I had already used Baikal as a training venue in 2011 and some of the other swimmers had been there in 2012. Novikov became adamant that we should all go there and when I made a few small but telling queries regarding the logistics by commenting in the group he went absolutely mad and vented his spleen in a long rambling, incoherent post which was to become a trademark of his for the next few months.

He soon backtracked and made some kind of apology although by this stage he had probably already started his slippery slide that would eventually lead him out of this project. Andrew contacted me and had also been having big doubts about Novikov.

During this time I took it upon myself to become slightly more involved in a very minor but perhaps ultimately crucial way using Facebook. I took it upon myself to start posting one new Russian word per day with an accompanying picture from my involvement in the last few years. It gave the group some much needed content and also allowed me naturally to post a little more. My aim was to become something like an invisible moderator and the real manager of the group but from a distant and unofficial position. I decided to do this because I could see how Novikov was using the power of Facebook and that he potentially could cause problems. In the end I was proved right because after he left the project several swimmers including Claudia Rose and Paul Duffield refused to take part in the swim.

I was gaining a lot of knowledge and experience and I saw what a phenomenal thing Facebook was. One of the funniest moments of course involved Novikov, in fact there were several incredibly comic moments in which he was at the centre. Novikov called me on Skype and asked me if I had copied and pasted comments from the private group and forwarded them by email. Now, if you imagine that there is a private group and then there are other people who are also discussing say through email with members of the private group it is pretty obvious that some things will be cut and pasted and forwarded on. Why would you even question that? After asking such a question it was clear that Novikov was in trouble.

Then a letter came through saying that he had been removed from the project and that Leonid Kokaurov was now in charge of ops in the USA. Paul Duffield posted this emailed letter in the group and now I sat back and watched. Novikov as usual hit the like button and I couldn't help but comment at the irony of him being the only one who had liked a post in which he himself had admitted that he had been fired. Paul Duffield referred to the project as a circus and was clearly bemused by the situation. I didn't bother but I did feel like referring him back to our first message correspondence about this project in which I tried to gently warn him about what might happen. Ram chipped in by saying "It has been a circus for a long while". I was laughing now, as I imagined Novikov as an incompetent ringmaster trying without success to control his animals, perhaps whipping himself in the process. A few days later and as I remarked to Alexandr Jakovlev the truth that I (and others no doubt) had always suspected about Novikov was coming out, he had lied, and lied and lied again...and then lied some more. I started to visualise him as Pinocchio and

I was guffawing with laughter and feeling devilish being extremely close to posting some picture of Pinocchio. In the end I didn't do anything of the sort and kept my laughter to myself. The main reason for this is that I am not a nasty person and quite frankly my conclusion was that another of my suspicions was true. Sergey Novikov was a man with psychological problems. If it was true then I wanted him to seek help and get better. I certainly didn't want to ridicule him even though he had been a huge pain in the ass for nearly 18 months not to mention a big waster of time.

He got desperate near the end and was talking about going to Sergey Shoygo the minister of foreign affairs. I thought about the saying "No smoke without fire," and how he had complained last year to the Russian consulate in Seattle. This worried me. However, this was classic Novikov. He wanted to go to Shoygo and if that didn't work he had only one option left – Putin. I concluded that he was finished. He tried saying that he had everything under control but in the end it was just hot air, he screamed down the phone to me that "Maria from Finland knows everything!" On the inside I smirked and translated this to mean "Maria is nice and listens to me so I just rant and rave at her until I run out of energy."

A few days prior to this he had already annoyed and amused me with his "I am consulting with x, y and z" What he really meant was "these people still listen to me so I use them to sound off!" I sincerely hope he has found peace now. He did his best, he was a character and as much as he blundered continuously he did help to bring people together so he has to take some of the credit for that even if he also did his best to break these people up consequently. Maybe he was also badly treated by people in Russia but he also lacked the real knowledge that was needed.

2nd July 2013

In the main dish of life, the swim across the Bering Strait is nothing but a side order or perhaps just a condiment or even simply a napkin, however those little things can be quite important and add somewhat to the enjoyment of that main dish.

Therefore I was completely caught in limbo with regards to the Bering Strait swim and its politics. It looked like there was going to be another "Crisp" (the racehorse) moment on the route to the start. I could feel it. Novikov had been thrown out at the whim of General Moiseeyev. The other side appeared reasonably well organised now. Meanwhile of course Novikov was plotting his offence and it came in the form of various letters to Shoygu the big guy in the Russian ministry of foreign affairs. What was about to happen, I couldn't predict only that these people simply wouldn't stop the name-calling and accusations. It was incredibly juvenile and undermined not only themselves but it started to undermine their nation. This habit of sidling up to politicians, getting their signatures and so on made me start to think that nobody had any real authority over anything. Alexandr Brylin had made errors it was true and it was also true that he had a huge ego but on the flipside I had always been unsure of Novikov and I had serious suspicions over his mental wellbeing. If I was right about this then there was no way that he should be in any way involved in this project. He needed professional help to get himself and his life back on track. I had no room for sentiment but at the same time I didn't want to get involved in this issue.

I needed to realize this project this year mainly due to the connection it had with the passing of Dasha. I was over this terrible event and after a failed 3 month relationship I was ready to meet someone new and bring some much needed joy back into my life. I saw things more clearly now and although the new main dish was starting to smell better after having been badly burnt previously I really wanted to have that side order to go with it.

I sensed that Novikov was having problems and that he was now clutching at straws but I could not be certain of this. Now he was working with Vergara, Rose, Jakovlev and Maria, well I couldn't care less who he was working with as the situation was absurd. He thought he had some power but quite frankly if he was hiding behind those 4 swimmers and claiming to have a consensus then he was wrong as nobody had asked me.

July 7ᵗʰ Another Chapter

As I thought about all that had gone on and my own role in everything I started to really question everything and wonder what was the reality of the Bering Strait swim.

A few days previously I said out loud "It is my destiny to go to Alaska." I am not sure why I said it but I started to believe it. My life had taken an amazing turn in the last 6 years and especially since 2011 things really started to go crazy, then in 2012 things were turned on their head to the point that now I didn't really know what reality was anymore. I knew what I liked and what I didn't like – sadly somewhat I was beginning to find the natural world as more trustworthy than human beings. I justified this by saying that although "Plants and animals were competitive they couldn't love you but also couldn't hate you unlike a human being who was capable of both." I saw my old friends gradually settling down and here I was with little time and little money and still a heart that if not broken was still in need of redemption after the trauma of 2012.

I perhaps need to be more competitive like my namesake the Jack Pine that was capable of colonising everything in sight in the pioneer phase of plant succession.

But maybe it really was my destiny to go to Alaska across the Bering Strait. Perhaps it would be the making of me. It was true that in November 2011 I got a good feeling in Anchorage. Now I had learnt more about our world and its people through my involvement with this project. I had just about enough money for the flight ticket to the Russian Far East and a flight home from the USA. In between who knew what would happen. In fact I wasn't ruling out another visit to Kamchatka. I could feel the power of the Russian Far East and this year I wanted to make the most of it. I had read more and more about the likes of Dezhnev, Bering and the naturalist Stellar as well as James Cook and various other explorers and native people. For me this area and the seas surrounding it were the most exciting in the world. A further twist was added by my continuing fascination with the previous ice age – the Pleistocene epoch – quaternary glaciation and its impact on our 21st century Holocene earth. When sea levels were lower and ice stretched half way across the northern hemisphere the Bering Strait became a land bridge and there was a huge exchange of flora, fauna and people between Eurasia and America. Our crossing mimicked this original migratory route. It also mimicked to a certain extent those early explorers and the difficulties they faced outside of Antarctica and parts of the high arctic

This was one of the most difficult places to travel in the world. As the clock ticked and we waited for the ok to obtain our visas I pondered what would unfold in the next month or so, what adventures I would have this year and where I would end up. The schedule seemed simple but experience told me that the reality was likely to be quite different. Mentally I made the decision to be prepared for the possibility of an extended trip and another adventure into both the familiar and the unknown.

7th July 2013

Regarding the organisational control and the role of Sergey Novikov, as I have already mentioned finally matters came to a head and a letter was sent, signed by General Melnikov, stating that Sergey Novikov had been removed from the project.

I expected a response from Novikov and prepared for it. Sure enough it came although it was short lived as it seemed that Admiral Sidenko had also decided that Novikov was surplus to requirements. He (Novikov) talked about going to Sergey Shoygo but this was simply the last throw of a desperate man, or maybe second last as he could always go running to Putin.

By July 7th it seemed that all had played itself out. Understandably the North American contingent were unhappy as the "Rug had been pulled out from beneath their feet" as Lelane Roussow-Bancroft put it. Now they had to find their way across the Pacific to the starting point in the Russian Far East. Far more time consuming and expensive than the Eurasian team travelling from the west to the east of the continent. The blame for this mess lay solely at the feet of Novikov. His ridiculous promises would now go unfulfilled. He had never revealed who would fund this venture and when asked a few simple and relevant questions he had failed to answer them. The writing had been on the wall for some time. Of course some people would argue that I or someone else should have stepped in earlier but the truth is that it had to be allowed to play out in this way. I was happy with how I had handled things and that my predictions were fairly accurate. Alexandr Brylin had been lucky with the Tyumen and Murmansk events making him look good. He needed it as Novikov, if he had done one thing well it was to take control of the international swim team back in the autumn, utilizing Andrew Chin after I declined the role. This set things up nicely as Novikov had the swimmers but at the same time Alexandr Brylin had a kind of emotional or at least a genuine "swimming" hold over them. When Alexandr made his audacious plans known in April after the initial arguments everything fell into place culminating in the formation of one project in Russia and ultimately the end of Novikov. The word circus was used a few times and I couldn't help but laugh as I imagined Sergey Novikov first as a clumsy ringmaster and then as an even clumsier clown!

Meanwhile I started to get a little disillusioned by the selfishness of some of the other swimmers. I made a post in which I analogised the Bering Strait and life as food but it seemed to fall on deaf ears as some completely misunderstood what I meant. Quite frankly I saw the swim for what it was – a nice event but really it wouldn't mean anything big in the scheme of the world. Maybe if we were successful we would have the chance to say something. I saw it clearly, the swim was nice, crossing the Bering would be great but it couldn't beat love with a woman or perhaps starting a family, the latter something that I suspected must be the best thing in our lives. It is worth noting at this point that following the horrible events of May 2012 I now had a fresh outlook on life. I believed in biology as our guiding light through life and the need for procreation. The only thing that worried me was that society in the west was perhaps changing, that people were changing on a small scale, maybe just to even things out and I couldn't say how long it would last but |I believed that even in this way that biology was the cause and at the same time I hoped that I wouldn't be the victim and that I would continue the Bright family line.

Giant Mountains (Krkonoše) Training

With prospects for the swim looking bright it was now time to turn attention towards some preparation beyond the normal regime for the time of year. My fitness levels were fine, I was ready for a long and difficult trip but I knew that I would benefit from summer cold water training, as much for the mind as the body to put me in the best shape for the challenge ahead.

The late winter and early spring had been kind to the winter swimmer in Prague, ensuring that we were still swimming in 8c water at the end of May. But then Mother Nature intervened in the form of a flood. The Vltava was now to be un-swimmable for a month. At the end of June the water quality had improved and so had the temperature – 16c, pretty useless except for long distance training. Now I had to adjust my training accordingly and the one thing I needed was cold water.

I know the Giant Mountains (Krkonoše) in northern Bohemia very well, being a regular visitor to the area. Therefore I knew that around 1100m above sea level there was something of a small natural swimming pool on the course of the white Labe River. I travelled by bus to the mountain resort village of Špindlerův Mlýn and immediately it started pouring down with rain. I didn't fancy getting wet just yet so I stayed in the porch of a hotel watching the sky. The forecast said that at around 6pm it would stop raining and it did almost to the minute. I made my way out of the village and followed the course of the white Labe upstream. 1.5 hours later I had found my spot. I also found an excellent place for camping and got my small one man tent up in the middle of the trees but only a few metres from the river. Unfortunately due to the rains the river was flowing very quickly and there would be no swimming but it would be possible to at least immerse myself in the cold water. This was enough. I was here for a cold water immersion and not actually swimming training. I was extremely careful as I was well aware that one slip could lead to me hitting my head on a rock, losing consciousness and dying. When you are naked you are more aware of things like this and I certainly didn't have a death wish. Nevertheless I got my immersion in staying almost pinned to the edge of the river as the water rushed past me in a frenzy. The water was around 7.5c and I stayed in for 15 minutes. I was happy with this and now I could have some dinner and relax. The next day I repeated the feat and again felt good. Mission accomplished I was still able to handle cold water. I knew this anyway but it is a great boost to the psyche to have these kinds of sessions especially in a wild environment away from the city.

That's the adventurous life:
July 21ˢᵗ 2013

The next week I upped the ante and travelled to the Tatra Mountains in Slovakia, my goal being a high mountain tarn where I would be sure to find extremely cold water.

After almost 8 hours of walking from the foot of Ziarske Dolina and up to the peak of Baranec, a short descent into the next valley before ascending up towards Rohac I finally arrived at my goal Jamnicke Pleso. I had been forced to take a difficult but scenic route involving around 1800 of ascent over the day. I wished I had studied that map a bit more closely instead of making the mistake of relying on tourists markings for the trip into the valley and out again. However, there wasn't much that could be done and even with hindsight it would have been a waste of time – I simply had to get on and make the ascent!

Needless to say a rest was in order when I arrived so the first thing I did was to inflate my sleeping mat and lie down. All day the weather had been fine if a little cloudy but after 20mins of lying there I felt the wind change and I said to myself "better get that tent up." It was an instinctive feeling – and not a moment too soon I had the tent pitched as the wind started to blow a gale. I got inside as outside it was unpleasant. After an hour I went for a walk. Still blowing a gale. I reinforced the tent with stones and got back inside. There would be no swimming or any kind of immersion in the lake tonight.

I got the stove on and made some dinner and then a flask of tea.

Lying in the tent with wind howling around me I thought that this summed up the reality of the adventurous life. Sometimes it was just a few minutes of excitement – followed by hours of waiting and boredom. This was a perfect example. A big ascent to reach the lake and then I was tent-bound due to the weather for around 12 hours. In the morning the wind dropped a bit. It was still horrible outside but just about bearable whereas unbearable had been the best way to describe conditions the night before. I made breakfast and a flask of tea and decided that the best way to do this would be to pack everything up and then go for the swim before leaving.

I prepared everything and got my stuff buried in the tundra a few meters from the lake. The dwarf pines would help shield me from the wind after exiting the water. It took some guts to strip down and even more to get in the water but it was worth it. The water was under 6c and I stayed in for 15 minutes. I didn't really swim but once again as with my previous trip to the giant mountains this wasn't swim training as such but rather cold water immersion to make sure the body remembered what it was like.

I felt good and strong as the cold water coursed around my body penetrating my skin and slowly my layers of fat reaching my bones, taking the blood to the core and causing an ache in my extremities. I knew the feeling well and at that moment I had the feeling that I've had many time before in this situation "Oh god, that's cold" I said to myself, followed by "Ok that's no problem you know how to handle it." I stayed in for 15 minutes before exiting and it was a big success. I felt good and protected by the thick dwarf pines I got dressed without problems and after a quick few sips of tea I was ready to go. The wind was blowing but I wrapped up well in my Columbia Omni heat long johns and merino base layer. Soon I was climbing towards the pass at around 2000m high and the blood was circulating nicely.

Later that day I arrived back to the town of Poprad and travelled through the night onward to Prague. It was now less than 1 week before the departure to Russia and I felt ready.

Bering Report: days waiting, days at sea

Monday 2nd September 2013 and I am sitting at my desk a week after coming back. Now I am ready to report what happened.

The last week has been a blur and it was finished by a weekend trip to the Alps and the summit (3776m) of Wildspitze, then a few swims. The previous few days I managed to arrange my stuff, pick a few photos and teach a few English lessons.

Actually the previous 2 weeks in Alaska were also a bit of a blur as I made a hiking trip around the Seward peninsula and explored Anchorage and visited the State Fair too, riding on the railroad, but of course all that is another story...

Fri 26th July

After swimming at the outdoor pool, I wondered when I would next meet such swimming luxury. Libor, one of my pool colleagues kindly gave me a lift to the embassy where Zdeněk was already waiting in the queue. We received our visas without problems and then I felt that a weight had been lifted from my shoulders. Now I was calm and I finally felt I could really see an end to this arduous project. After teaching one last English lesson I did a few final chores, (the typical last minute purchases) and returned home. I calmly prepared and packed everything. It takes longer and longer, mainly because I have so much equipment and clothing. Half of it is good but half of it I use only rarely, but who could get rid of a nice waxed jacket?! The charging of various batteries and the collation of the electrical equipment also takes time, prepping and cleaning and checking everything. Finally at around 3am I was able to go to bed after I applied for the USA online visa for myself and Zdeněk.

I was tired and ready to sleep and my mind went back to a similar Friday evening 2 years ago when Dasha helped me and cut her finger, me feeling guilty as I rushed to catch the metro, she was such a great girl.

On the bus to Brno I saw a Czech documentary film about the North Pole which featured both Mirek Jakeš and Lewis Gordon Pugh. Mirek I know personally whilst Lewis I had also met in an attempt to involve him with the Bering Strait project. It made me feel good when I saw them in the polar environment. We finally got on our UTAIR flight from Brno to Moscow after a 3 hour delay but we didn't really care as we had a day to wait before our onward flight to Yakutsk. I took advantage of the hot weather as I knew that we wouldn't get 30c midday sun in the far north even if we might get near polar days.

It was good to fly with UTAIR on their CRJ200 even if they only gave us baguettes and they were 3 hours late. I practised my Russian with one of the air hostesses. UTAIR is a Russian firm operating all over the place and therefore I felt it a fitting start to our expedition and I took a chocolate wrapper as a souvenir. I was happy and I thought about all that I had enjoyed and endured over the last few years. I felt almost like the Bering Strait swim personified! It also occurred to me how important our virtual friend Facebook had become as a means of communication. I got it on my borrowed smartphone and whereas email was trickier Facebook was simple allowing you to reach one person or many people at once, certainly a powerful tool. I used to look down on it but now I accepted and embraced it.

I was surprised that my Russian held up quite well as we enquired about first mobile phones and then our flight which was confirmed for the next day at 7.30pm. We found a quiet place and slept. The next day we met Henri and Tomas and then many others too. The following morning we were met in Jakutsk by Alexandr Brylin, Ira and Semyon Petrovich a diminutive and charismatic man from Yakutia, looking every part the classic soviet sportsman. The only unpleasant thing in Jakutsk occurred outside the airport as Zdeněk wanted a photo. I spoke to a local guy as the others made for the buses. Next thing I knew another guy took the camera and started talking quickly in English. I immediately didn't like him and more importantly didn't trust him. I lost a camera only 2 months ago and this new one was a week old, no way was I losing it. I went straight to him and said firmly in my best Russian "мы большой группой, дайте мне камеру" – "We are a big group, give me my camera" – he shit himself when he heard that, especially in Russian, "Ok" he said, his smug smile dropping as he ran off. Nearly a bad start but things would only get better, Yakutian people proving to be extremely friendly and excellent hosts.

The first day started with many museums which was fine. I began to really like our No. 1 host Semyon Petrovich. He was extremely pleasant as were the two young translators Masha and Nadya. Later in the afternoon as we toured an art gallery, Oleg Ivanov suggested a small breakaway trip to an ice cave. I was more than happy to do this and I thank Oleg for driving this trip. After spending around an hour and a half on various buses we found our way to the outskirts of the city and the ice cave. Well, it was fascinating and a great way to continue the slow build up to our expedition. Jakutsk is the biggest city built on continuous permafrost and lies some 450km south of the

Arctic Circle. It is well known that the coldest place on earth (outside Antarctica) is Omyakon in the Yakutia district. We found ourselves by a small hill and basically they have just cut into the hill and created a real living museum of permafrost. It was interesting and cold, also beautiful as we wandered amongst the human made sculptures including a life size bed, reindeer, Father Christmas and many other things. We frolicked and had fun with Zdeněk and Masha particularly enjoying it. They even shed some clothes whereas I preferred on this occasion to stay well wrapped up. Paolo and Jackie left early and after around an hour we made our way back. The weather had changed and now the wind was blowing and the air temperature was around 12c. We waited for the bus and I decided to leave my jacket in my bag, more training was necessary. Vladimir Nefatov said to me "This isn't training it is simply freezing"

Back at the hotel there was of course vodka and food before the next day which would be full of official engagements starting with a Shaman's blessing. This was a nice and genuinely authentic event. We all drank Kumis (fermented mare's milk) and ate bread. Next up was a press conference and anyone who was in any doubt about the seriousness of this expedition soon had their doubts blown away by the grandness of this event. It was in the senators' office building, with named places for us to sit at complete with gifts of books and various chocolates and fruit for us to eat, not to mention simultaneous translations through headphones. I sat next to a general and had a short chat with him. He told me he wasn't coming but pointed to someone else who was, an older man sitting at the back who turned out to be a sailor turned journalist. He came along to document the trip for Yakutia, whose government was kindly sponsoring the expedition by providing transport from Moscow and the supporting programme in Yakutia. After much frolicking and photo taking amongst the grand surroundings the press conference opened with music and video. Various people spoke including the vice governor of Yakutia (the governor was away) and the military supervisor of the project. They spoke a lot about the arctic and it became clear that Yakutians were proud of their arctic connections, after all they have an arctic port, Tiksi, lying at 71 degrees north. This port is the gateway to the Laptev Sea, an area which likely holds 20% of the world's untapped hydrocarbon resources. It didn't take a genius to work out that Yakutia had to get their fingers in the Bering Strait pie and why not? Not only the arctic link and the permafrost but there was a monument to none other than Semyon Dezhnev who settled in Yakutsk after he returned from his 1638 expedition. It was also a key stopping place on the lend lease route which saw the USA provide warplanes and other equipment for Russia during World War II. It was a nice gesture by the swim organisers to connect our swim to lend lease which was a successful example of cooperation between Russia and the USA. In Yakutsk there was an impressive museum about lend lease.

Our swim was dedicated both to the 365th anniversary of the Dezhnev expedition and also the lend lease programme. The press conference was more of a break in between photo shoots as the cameras went wild. I got a bit fed up with it and was slightly annoyed with Zdeněk who continually demanded photos in true Russian style and by this I mean photos with anyone and everyone, as many and as often as possible. One particular time as I tried to get a picture of myself alone I had to say after 3 attempts "No just me on my own!"

After a swim with flags and more gifts it was time for the first big team meeting. It was decided that we leave at 8.30 the next morning for the airport. After a beer in a local pub – typical for the Russian Far East in that it wasn't a pub but a restaurant, (it is not usual for normal people to drink in pubs) it was bedtime and soon my alarm was telling me it was PK time. By the time I got through check-in and onto the airplane I was a little tired. I sat next to Semyon Petrovich and we talked about swimming. I enjoyed our Russian conversation and he drew some diagrams to help me understand. He was trying to illustrate the dangers of sharks and the need for a shark cage as well as the dangers presented by killer whales. Personally I wasn't worried about sharks as the Bering Strait is too far north and too cold for almost all sharks except for the pacific sleeper shark which lurks around the bottom of the ocean. The Bering Strait is only 30-50m deep and with all the fast flowing currents I suspected that there wouldn't be much sea life unless we bumped into a migration. That said it is common knowledge that the Orca can be found everywhere and a pod of 4 or 5 had been spotted in the Norton Sound not far from Nome back in mid-July.

I took just a few more minutes before I could barely keep my eyes open and I apologised to Semyon and fell into a deep sleep. What a pity that I missed the rest of the flight although I got up and went to the middle of the plane for landing in the hope of catching a glimpse of my beloved volcanoes. No luck this time as there was too much cloud cover and when we landed I could just about make out Korayaksky volcano but it was just a faint outline, nothing more. Our reception in Kamchatka however, was strong. First we were greeted in a corner of the airport by a military cordon. Craig Lenning who is an ex US marine got quite excited about what he saw. For him it was probably a little unreal to be in the backyard of the old enemy, in Kamchatka one of their most secret places. We pulled our luggage off the military Boeing 737 and proceeded to the buses which were waiting almost on the runway with a convenient exit to the road. The next section of the journey was interesting in that it took forever. I know the area well enough and I am sure that the driver took a wrong turn just outside PK. Not to worry we eventually arrived at the bay, parking in the square an area not usually reserved for parking but we were under the protection of the Eastern military district so there would be no problem with traffic wardens or clampers. I followed General Melnikov who took us to the beach, then I saw the Itelmen dancers and a few minutes later a magical welcome to PK was coming our way in the form of song and dance. They timed it perfectly and I have to say that I felt it was for me personally my emotions were that strong, back in PK for the third time looking at the bay where I had swum so many times in the past. I even joined in the dancing and thoroughly enjoyed myself. After the governor of Kamchatka said a few words there was more dancing and we all received gifts. Soon we were swimming with flags and I couldn't resist joining in and I swam with a Chinese flag which was obviously amusing for everyone. Frankly I probably couldn't have cared less, in fact I could have been handed a swastika and I would have swum with it. The water felt good and I felt that this small but intense event had really kick started our expedition. I did an interview in Russian for the third year in a row with my seemingly old friend Dima from the radio and then we made our way to the Avacha hotel for dinner. My friend Alexandr Tarakanov the tourist guide made an appearance and I gave him a tube of Czech honey whilst he invited me to visit Tolbachik volcano with him if I could get back to PK by the 14th of August. I liked the idea and told him that I would call him. At the time I thought that it was possible that I could be back in time for this.

After dinner again we were back in the buses and a 30 minute supermarket stop turned into an hour. Still no sign of the volcanoes but it was at least fun to do some shopping as we literally invaded the supermarket. I took a photo of Ram and Andrew with a trolley that was completely loaded with booze. My comment was simply "Now I know what your secret is with the ice swimming." He just smiled and seemed pretty pleased with his catch. I drink occasionally but to this day I haven't drunk seriously with Ram and the other South Africans so I don't know if they actually drink huge amounts or if it is more talk than action. Eventually after a meandering drive around the Avacha bay we arrived at a secluded and private (military) part of the port. Irtyush was waiting for us and finally our aim of swimming a relay across the Bering Strait appeared more likely than ever to actually happen. Manpower is essential and this year we had it in the form of a 100 strong crew plus our own doctors and support staff, including Russian Special Forces members to pilot the zodiacs. The swim team was strong too, officially at 66 and this was a good idea. We also had the hardware, the Irtysh as our main vessel, along with a tugboat MB61 in case of problems. We were ready for the impossible, the attempt to reach the American continent from the Eurasian.

This had never been done before by swimmers. Lynne Cox had swum some 4.2km between the Diomede Islands but the full crossing of the Strait was yet to be conquered.

The light was fast fading and I snapped the moment before I found myself on board with everyone else waiting on the helipad like a bunch of refugees being evacuated from a warzone. The truth was that we were a bunch of crazy winter swimmers seeking to reach the new world. We had spent a good bit of time on the coaches and I coach-hopped enjoying everyone's company. I realised that I was well known to many Russian winter swimmers. I was something like "Jack from Kamchatka" or "Jack the Traveller". I didn't mind – it was about right I was the pioneer for this project when it came to getting the international involvement. I was the first one to join the Russians. I was quite proud of how we had in the end been able to connect so many people. This was just a romantic side to the real main dish which was the Bering Strait swim. Jack from Kamchatka, Jack the Traveller wouldn't be enough here – I would have to be Jack the winter swimmer, Jack the tough and Jack the fearless. I wasn't worried as I had been waiting for this moment for so long there was no way I would let anything get in the way of my full participation and that included sea sickness!

We had talked a little bit about the issue of seasickness and this was something that would be quite likely to play a part in the relay with our team being so large. Sure enough within a few days of sailing the reports from the medical team made it sound like we were a ship full of sick notes and that we were lucky to be on board a hospital vessel. When the chief medic reported that at the moment only half the swim team were actually fit to swim it was shambolic to hear. At least I knew I was ok…or at least I was on the surface. The truth was that I was suffering from seasickness but only a mild case. After about 4 days I stopped passing solids. I got on with life and enjoyed the 4 meals a day prepared for me. It was a luxury and every time I heard the announcement first in Russian then in broken English "the first shift is invited for breakfast/lunch/dinner/evening tea" I literally skipped along to the dining room to receive my food. Perhaps I am a pauper or perhaps I know what is important in life. I found the food to be nutritious. Porridge made from rice or buckwheat for breakfast. Lunch consisted of a soup and a main course of meat or fish with rice or potatoes or something similar. Dinner was similar, always a soup and often fish and rice. With both lunch and dinner we received a drink in the way of fruit compote. Bread and butter came with all meals. The menu was varied enough, light on fresh fruit but there were enough vegetables and I am sure many people like me supplemented the food with vitamin tablets. Some of the international swimmers seemed to find the food rather below par including the South African group who were clearly used to something different. Ram Barkai has a gluten allergy so it was often problematic for him although I always saw him eating so it can't have been that bad. Paolo Chiarino doesn't like fish and that proved to be a problem. Myself and the all-eating, all-swimming Estonian machine Henri Kaarma were often at hand to assist Paolo who learnt to say a couple of Russian words during our mealtimes including "Tolka kartoshka" (only potatoes) and "Tolka rys" (only rice). Matias Ola appeared not to eat too much but then again he did have his own 5 man support team. Actually it was difficult to take him seriously. We were a relay team and nobody apart from him had their own staff it was almost laughable. Then I found out from Christian Vergara that he wasn't able to finish his 10 minute legs in the relay. It turned out that he was very seasick. I imagine that for somebody used to comfort living on the Irtysh was not easy. The South Africans were also used to comfort but they were a different breed, able to overcome difficulties and get on with the job even if they weren't happy with things. On the very first night I got the impression that Maria might be problematic but once she found a cabin that she liked she was fine. Going back to the seasickness issue, and Rafal Ziobro of Poland was soon struck down and after the first swim he was confined to his bed for several days, coming out only at mealtimes and speaking very little. Several of The Russians also suffered a similar problem including my friend Andrey Mihailov who succumbed to the dreaded sickness of motion brought on by a long stay at sea. Melissa O Reilly of the USA works in the drug industry. She told me that she had no problems using various drugs to ward off the seasickness and that also she had no problem with sleep deprivation. A great looking girl, even the dark bags under her eyes didn't make her look any less beautiful and she remained strong and energetic the whole way through. I suspect she was rather clever about sleeping as sometimes I didn't see her for several hours so I am sure that she did get at least some rest. I take after my father and grandfather and only go to the doctor if I am on death's door and by the same token I turn my nose up at medicine. At the same time I am quite a hypocrite as in the past I have been known to dabble in many substances and not always for medicinal use. In the end I realised they weren't very good for my health and nowadays I prefer the odd beer or shot of strong alcohol. However, more often than not I am happy with a cup of camomile tea to relax me or a strong pot of black tea to wake me up. In fact 1 litre of strong black tea drunk over a morning is surely better than any narcotic when it comes to putting you on a high and raising concentration levels. That said, during our Bering Strait swim I never had any need for camomile tea as I never had time for it. I needed to rest as more often than not my alarm would be going off in under 2 hours. As for the pick-me-ups, I didn't need them. I was 100% focused. (More on my focus later)

Ship life

We left PK at night which was a pity as we didn't get to see the beautiful Avacha bay although of course I had had that privilege in the past so I could imagine and picture the three brother rocks as we passed them. We all went to sleep fairly late; I guess around 2am. I visited a few Russian rooms first and of course was invited for vodka. The situation in one room looked rather interesting and plenty of alcohol had been consumed. I drunk a few toasts and retired to bed. The next day we had some safety briefings and found our designated lifeboats and emergency assembly points. This was fine and well organised but I was dismayed that neither I nor my roommate Paolo heard the alarm! I enjoyed posing for photos and playing Bering Strait between Melissa (USA) and Masha (Russia) and it was especially good when Oleg asked the girls to show how much they love the Bering Strait! All good fun with two tremendous girls and excellent ice swimmers.

Then we had a general meeting followed by a meeting for the international team only. General Melnikov was the speaker at this meeting and in what seemed like a bizarre outpouring of emotion he proceeded to tell us about the project and his involvement. Oleg Dokuchaev soon left the room and Alexandr Brylin popped his head round the door only to disappear again. Melnikov was critical of Alexandr Brylin, critical to a lesser extent of Novikov and then praised Andrew Chin and the South Africans. The only thing was that he didn't give concrete reasons for any of his likes or dislikes except when he said that Novikov had done good work on the US side with translating documents and other such tasks. I bit my tongue and decided that it wasn't worth either making a query or contesting anything he said. Not that I wanted to contest anything it was just that he finished his speech with everything even less clear than it was before. He created more new questions than he answered and some of what he said could be described as more riddle than statement. One thing he did make very clear to everybody's amusement, mine included was that the T-shirts we were wearing and the ID cards we had been given were completely unofficial. It was written on them "Встреча солнца" (Meeting of the sun) and our current project had nothing to do with the old meeting of the sun project. The strange thing was that he had been seen with one of the ID cards around his neck! The previous day! So here we were on a ship going to make a swim across the Bering Strait from Russia to America and we had been given by a legitimate member of the team (Alexandr Brylin) some illegitimate merchandise – another example of how everything is possible in Russia. I wasn't overly concerned about this meeting with regards to our swim but it surely wasn't good for morale and Melnikov must have been aware of that. We could only guess that he was unhappy that he wasn't invited to speak very often at the events in Yakutia and therefore he wanted to assert his authority and let us know that he was in charge. We lunched and forgot about it. Later I asked Ira about the matter. Incredibly there was another Russian-only meeting later which Brylin and his swimmers were barred from. Then they were allowed in. Melnikov tried to ban Alexandr Brylin from the relay. How nonsensical when we were already on the boat, but as I said before anything is possible in Russia. I laughed a little to myself and realized that probably Alexandr Brylin needed taking down a peg or two. Perhaps this was the best way to do it; Melnikov, using the classic humiliation tactics of the military to do it but in the end his plan backfiring a little as Alexandr Brylin was supported by most of the Russian swim team. I would have also supported him, after all just because someone is a bad manager doesn't mean they can't be utilized as a swimmer, and after all swimming was our main goal here, the organising had been done, and it was now a case of navigating, supporting and swimming. When you simplify it into those three tasks it made the Bering Strait relay swim sound as easy as taking candy from a baby but as we were to find out, it would be nothing of the sort...

The next day I had breakfast and then went for a workout, nothing too heavy but a few weights and my usual abs routine. The South Africans were in the gym doing their own routine which was actually mainly for the benefit of their media man Alasdair. There wasn't much to do on the ship as we travelled north east in the direction of Chukotka apart from enjoying the sea air. Some people read books or listened to music, or simply congregated in the gym but I preferred to be outside. There were many dolphins swimming in the same direction as us and occasionally we spotted a whale breaching although this spectacle was always at a distance of at least 300m. During the afternoon I met Viktor Godlevski my old friend from Kamchatka. I got him telling me the story of how he got lost in a Canadian port, only speaking 2 sentences of English. I wondered if something like this was likely to happen when we reached Alaska after all it was no longer Russian America and it was necessary to have the correct documents, including visa for the Russians in order to enter the USA. That was for the civilians amongst us. As for the crew, they could (as Viktor had done in Canada) enter the USA for 24 hours if they had a courtesy of the port letter. Leonid had told me that Oleg assured him all was under control regarding this matter. Zdeněk and I also found time to present Oleg with a bottle of Czech-made Mead. He invited us for vodka and caviar. We had just eaten lunch; I would have opted for a coffee and something sweet but I can never turn down caviar from pacific salmon. In the USA they disregard it as a foodstuff, preferring to use it as bait whereas in Russia the rich salty eggs of the pacific salmon command a high price. They actually have more salmon in Alaska, Kamchatka has more brown bears but again Alaska wins hands down on natural resources with its oil and gas reserves. Kamchatka was the basecamp but Alaska the prize. Dwelling a little on the history of the Russian Far East and Alaska I concluded one thing:

The oceans and seas of our earth are the most inhospitable areas of our planet or at least they were during the age of exploration. The main paradoxical issue of having a huge amount of water which is useless for human consumption is somewhat negated in our modern era by the fact that many ships are fitted with equipment for the desalinisation of seawater. We humans are land mammals. We live on land. Looking at a map of the world and we all define areas no matter how big by the vast expanses of ocean that border them. Russia stretches for over 6000km and whilst the likes of Great Britain and Spain were using their superior sea power to travel far afield on the open ocean to claim colonies as distant as Jamaica and …. European Russians were still travelling overland to explore and colonise parts of their own enormous land. Eventually they got to Kamchatka but this was by boat, starting with a descent of the Kolyma river into the Arctic Ocean and then into the Bering Sea and Kamchatka. Years later the sea to the east of Kamchatka was crossed by Vitus Bering's second Kamchatka expedition and it was confirmed that America existed. Thus began over 100 years of Russian ownership of Alaska (the great land in Aleut language) before the 2 cents per acre offer from Seward was enough to tempt Russia into relinquishing its hold and thus confining its borders to the far east and the Kamchatka peninsula and Chukotka, both extremely remote areas but nevertheless joined to Russia by land unlike Russian America which was separated from the motherland by the sea. In the 20th century sea power is still used especially in logistics, primarily the transport of goods but as a look at the map will tell you, a country's border is defined by a sea if it isn't landlocked . Slowly but surely the old colonisers are losing those far away colonies. The sea is without doubt a great barrier, sometimes quiet and calm, in seconds it can become raging and dark, perhaps mountains provide a more visually stunning example of the power of nature but it is our seas and oceans that contain the most power.

That night we met at 8.30 and everyone was introduced. I got the first big cheer but that was because everybody knows me after my Kamchatka exploits, the legendary volcano trips, Russian language learning and of course who could forget the 7 men in a 1 bedroom flat in PK. I was popular with the Russians but now there were many more foreigners with the team and I could no longer be the star which suited me fine. I didn't want or need the attention; it was for me simply a case of getting the job done. Later, back on my bunk I thought about the last few years and all those crazy moments. I made a brief note of them – losing my card in the machine in PK, getting invited for fish soup on the beach in PK, a crazy night in Avacha village, my first swim in Avacha bay, Viktor and the lies at the press conference, the force-feeding again from Viktor, the deflation in 2012, the disco after the 2011 failure, the training swims in 2011, the farce of the Paratunka visits, the letter writing, various people's antics,, there were so many things. I could actually feel the end of the journey coming and maybe the most danger, drama and excitement. That night I had a marvellous dream about a river full of salmon. It seemed to be a very pleasant dream and I took it as a positive sign for our upcoming swim.

The next day we went outside for exercise before breakfast. It was much colder now that we were in firmly inside the 10c July isotherm and therefore we had now entered the arctic or at least the northern limits of the sub-arctic. The cold weather didn't bother me as I simply saw it as training for the swim.

Meanwhile all the whispered conversation and discussion centred not on the relay itself but the possible solo swim. I didn't think it would be a good idea but at the same time I would back a solo swim if it could be arranged safely without interfering in the relay and also if it was a majority who wanted it. In other words I was in opposition to the relay swim but I wasn't going to upset people or lose friends over it. Interestingly when I asked Ram about it he didn't seem to be such a big supporter of a solo swim, although he and his South African team mates were all being touted along with 11 others as solo swimmers. Amongst the others were the 2 Andrews from Tyumen. Both experienced ice swimmers from the icebox of central Siberia, their credentials in cold water were impeccable but would they be able to cope with the ocean in the same way as an ice hole.

Matias Ola was also supposed to be a solo swimmer. When I asked him how long he envisaged this taking he told me 1 hour. I replied that Lynne Cox needed over 2 hours and at that time she was still the female record holder for the fastest English Channel crossing. He thought for a moment and then said "Hmmm, no its just over 4km so I think 1 hour" I didn't bother continuing this conversation as it began to dawn on me that Matias was perhaps something of a fantasist. Undoubtedly an accomplished pool swimmer competing at a high level, but as far as he had told me his record in the open water for cold swims was about 25mins in 7c water. I couldn't work him out. He had a big project "Umir el mundo" (unite the world) but from what I could gather he was yet to make a swim of any note. (Now in

2015 he has just successfully crossed the Gibraltar Strait, so well done Matias!) Well, neither had I but then I wasn't the one with a big project and I was alone. Matias, on the other hand had an entourage of 5. This comprised of his trainer, a doctor, a nutritionist and 2 media guys. Matias was often absent for long periods and his team were more visible than he. He only ate with us sometimes and almost always looked unhappy. Guillame one of his media guys explained to me that after Matias swam next to an iceberg it was such a sensation that he became a celebrity overnight in Argentina. This explained the situation a little to me. I hoped that Matias would get what he wanted although I couldn't help but secretly snigger at him having his own support team unlike all the other swimmers.

As for the solo swim, I was sure that this was driven by Ram and Alexandr Brylin. I still maintained that once we actually got to the starting place people would change their minds on seeing the conditions. It is easy to talk about making such a swim from the safety of a boat as it leaves from Kamchatka but as the conditions worsen and the reality sets in things change. I also thought that the solo swim was not really being taken seriously in that people were rather blasé about what I was sure was an incredibly difficult swim. If 15 started how many would actually finish. Craig Lenning was one of the most accomplished members of the team with a very rough North Channel crossing to his name made while he was suffering from flu. He agreed with me, as did Alexandr Jakovlev.

Next day we had a meeting which settled the issue once and for all. I took a deep breath and said my piece. I gave my honest, unbiased and balanced opinion with big doubts over safety and effect on the relay. Luckily there were no arguments and within 30 minutes the idea of solo swim was just that – an idea, confined to the past. Oleg Dokuchaev had the final word and there would be no solo swims on this expedition. Oleg went up in my estimations after he made this decision. There was obviously pressure coming from somewhere but he didn't bow to it.

That day was a good day. I spent the whole day bar the meeting outside on deck. I needed my warm clothes, including mittens and a raincoat. The wind was getting stronger and the waves bigger. Now the temperature got down to around 7c before stabilizing at around 8c. A few people joined me and I was fine with that, enjoying the solitude of the ocean. There were many birds and I could tell that we were closer to the coast as the crested puffins started to reappear.

Later that evening Professor Ugarov or Mr Miyagi as someone had named him due to his pony tail revealed that he was also known as the Yakutian Santa Claus. He produced some cards with him pictured as the Russian version of Santa, (Ded Maros). Then he told us to write 3 wishes on the back. He guaranteed us that two would come true and then told us that we all had to write the first wish as our relay being successful. All good fun and once again resting on our bunks, myself and Paolo completed the cards. Alexandr Jakovlev insisted that we wouldn't reach Providenyia until evening but he obviously had the wrong bay loaded into his GPS. Just as Oleg said we would, we arrived to Provideniya in the morning. The journey from the Bering sea to Provideniya bay was interesting as we passed beautiful coastline just as I imagined Chukotka to be which meant only tundra and mountains, interspersed by waterfalls, patches of snow and various bird colonies. On the open ocean heading into the bay we also sighted a killer whale for the first time. Now that would be some animal to meet whilst swimming in the Bering Strait.

After a few hours we neared the port of Provideniya before coming to a halt and dropping anchor around a mile offshore. We waited for some time. There was a small problem. It turned out that the permits for Chukotka had not been downloaded and printed out. They were stuck in a virtual mailbox. Only the day before Oleg Dokuchaev had announced that we would go ashore at Provideniya for a short trip, to feel ourselves on land and buy any essentials that were needed. It was quite dramatic as "pogranicni" (border guards) came by boat and boarded the Irtysh. I just happened to be there when they arrived and I followed Oleg up to the bridge where some gifts and souvenirs were exchanged. How amazing that we could have very high level support from the chief of the eastern military district, Admiral Sidorenko who had provided the vessel as well as zodiacs, personnel and other things, yet due to some small error we couldn't make port in Chukotka. That just shows how Chukotka is a closed zone and has a large amount of autonomy.

Things became quite dramatic as we were ordered to our cabins. Various rumours started flying about the ship. I wondered whether things were about to start going downhill but I trusted Oleg he seemed to be pretty sure of everything. 30 minutes later we had lunch and during this time our passports were given back to us. I had an exit stamp so I believed that all was good. Then the international swimmers were summoned to the second dining room which had served as the customs and border control office. Most people were very nervous but I didn't care as I had been given my passport which had an exit stamp in it. I started filming but after a few seconds some of the others got extremely worried and told me to stop filming. This got on my nerves but I did manage to film later on from outside in the corridor.

Needless to say we all passed through customs and border control without any hitches. Now we were all equal, Russian and foreigners, in no man's land and heading for the wilderness of Cape Dezhnev the furthest eastern point of the Eurasian continent. As the expedition ventured into a more serious stage so the environment and weather changed too. Around the coast of Chukotka I saw a great many birds, auks, puffins, guillemots and something bigger a type of goose probably. The cloud cover was thick and I observed many changes in cloud colour and therefore thickness. I deduced that here nearing the top of the world it was difficult to predict the weather accurately but at least you could say that it would probably be damp, cold and overcast to some degree. The air temperature was now down below 5c and the water temperature in Provideniya bay was around 3c. It was obvious now that we were in the arctic as the increasing snow patches on the cliffs of the coastline confirmed.

A strong northerly wind was starting to blow as we powered on, just 10 hours to our destination. We arrived and hid the boat behind Cape Peek which is the rocky area on the south side of the Chukchi Peninsula. From here it is only a few nautical miles round to Cape Dezhnev the most eastern point of the Eurasian continent. The wind was strong and this was the reason for hiding the boat. In fact the weather prognosis wasn't looking too good when we went to sleep that night. I favoured waiting for potentially better weather in 2 or 3 days' time but I sensed from Oleg and others that there was an urgency to get the swim started. I had no real problem with this but equally I had cleared my schedule and was prepared to wait as long as needed to take advantage of the best possible conditions for our crossing.

Others as I had said were not so patient. My roommate Paolo was already talking about what day we would finish and what day he could get back to Italy and his family. He wasn't the only one but I just ignored it. Apart from this there were also people who thought this would be a holiday and probably hadn't brought enough waterproof clothing with them. Regarding the international swimmers I had left enough hints on Facebook with my maps and stories and photos. The Russians I am sure knew what they were in for but nevertheless some seemed rather light on suitable clothing.

As I have mentioned I'd spent the last few days mostly outside on deck. I probably spent a little bit too much time outside in the harsh wind when I may have been better off inside resting like many of the others. When I awoke with a slight sore throat I wasn't surprised and after breakfast I planned on resting for a few hours as judging by the wind speed (around 20knots) I doubted we would be starting just yet. I went downstairs to the doctors for the daily check-up and told Natalia of my sore throat. She pointed to a large glass jar filled with liquid for gargling and told me to come back with a bottle. I went back upstairs with a view to getting a bottle and procuring some of the mixture to help my sore throat.

First I decided to amble outside for a quick stroll, planning just a 5 minute stay outside. The next thing I knew there was a commotion on the lower deck and the zodiacs were out. There was a reccy mission to Dezhnev. Sore throat or not I simply had to go to Dezhnev. The first boat loaded up with Melissa and the kite surfers Yevgeny and his friend Sergey. Another boat was going and I simply asked Oleg and within seconds Alexandr Brylin was putting a lifejacket over my head. So much for the medicine and the few hours of rest! The mission was simple, go to Dezhnev, measure the current and the water temperature and then go west and measure again with the South Africans Ram and Ryan making a test swim.

There were 7 of us on our zodiac. Ryan and Ram in the back with the driver Leonid. Myself, another kite surfer Dennis, Viktor the fearless film maker and another crew member whose name I didn't know. This man was sitting on the bow or the nose of the zodiac and the water was pretty rough as we sped off in a north easterly direction as usual. This crew member was pretty seasick within minutes. I pretended that I hadn't seen it and tried not to think about my own health problems. As well as the sore throat I hadn't passed solids for 2 days, not that it was causing me any problems and I had mentally prepared to go through all but the worst seasickness without so much as a whimper. So far, so good.

After 20 minutes Dezhnev came into view or rather I should say the abandoned village of Naukan and the Semyon Dezhnev monument came into view. You see the Cape itself; the most eastern point is just a rocky headland with no landing place and thus nowhere to start the swim. We needed to get the swimmer onto land and start from there. Just below the old village Naukan there was a small pebble beach and it was here that we would begin the swim from. It didn't matter that it wasn't exactly the most eastern point as it was making the crossing longer rather than shorter. I of course was desperate to go ashore and explore but there was no need on this occasion. We had a job to do.

No major problems here, the beach was clear for a landing, no rocks or other obstructions. We made our way offshore by around 1.5 nautical miles out of the shelter provided by the cape where we could test the current and water temperature. After several minutes we got a stable reading on 2 thermometers that confirmed the water temperature to be 8.3c. Much warmer than we expected but this expedition was full of surprises and of course the water didn't stay like that for long. The wind was blowing hard, around 20knots and there was plenty of rain coming down, Yevgeny asked Ram and Ryan to swim for 5 minutes. They didn't look too convinced and I didn't blame them.

It looked like there would be no swimming when suddenly the pair of them started getting changed. I offered my assistance for when they came out and oversaw their procedures. It was agreed just 5 minutes and when they dived in I started my stopwatch. It was a great feeling to see the first swimmers dive in to the Bering Strait even though it wasn't me. Ram and Ryan showed tremendous guts to get in the water and great professionalism as they came out afterwards not needing any help and were soon dried and clothed. The result was a small northerly flow. When we got back we had a meeting. Ryan was invited to give his opinion. He said "We swum, conditions were difficult, the sea was pretty rough, but actually we were able to swim without problems. In my opinion if you are experienced in the ocean you will be fine but if you are not then maybe you will have problems." This proved to be a simple and wise synopsis of what was to come.

It didn't take long for Oleg to declare that the relay would begin with the first boat going out at 3.30pm. In fact his actual words were "Be here (in the sports hall) at 3.30pm ready to go out." The more time was going on the more I liked the way that Oleg was certain and purposeful about what he said. He was obviously a good speaker and I felt that it was a good influence on the balance of the team. I gratefully ate my lunch of soup and meat stew having had an early taste of the Bering Strait at close quarters. I was looking forward to the relay but I had the feeling that it wouldn't all be plain sailing.

So an American would begin the relay on Russian soil. That honour was given to Melissa O'Reilly, a nice gesture and surely the right way to start things. Our team was due in for the fourth hour of the swim so we had some time to wait yet.

There was a little more drama with one of the Yakutians carrying out a Shamanic ritual before the swim. He lit a candle, said a few word and then brought an offering of some special bread to the side of the boat where all the flags were flying before tipping the bread, paper plate and all into the sea as an offering.

It seemed to take an age for the swim to start but then we were anchored a few miles offshore. One great thing was the breaching of a whale some 300m from the zodiac and swimmer as the swim started. A symbolic gesture from

Mother Nature we hoped that the sea life would be welcoming us as guests and not welcoming us into the food chain!

Even through my binoculars there wasn't much to see but news filtered through that the relay was underway and soon the initial excitement died down and we relaxed a little and started preparing for our first immersions. I thought I prepared well. I opted for my GBR cap, favourite arena goggles and speedo swimsuit. Nothing unusual there, the main issue being the choice of goggles. The 'arena' goggles are my most comfortable for open water swimming and I only hoped they would handle the rigours of the Bering Strait. If not I had alternatives.

The more complex issue at hand was that of clothing. The air temperature was around 5c, there was often light rain in the air and the wind was constantly blowing. When we started it was around 20 knots, therefore when taking the wind-chill factor into account the temperature was well below zero. I expected nothing less and I decided on wearing my soft-shell trousers for warmth and insulation with my waterproof trousers over the top. For my torso I chose my merino wool base layer with my trusty club fleece over the top, covered by waterproof anorak that had already held up well against the rain.

The extremities are very important in the fight against cold so for my feet I chose to wear neoprene socks and neoprene boat shoes. The most body heat is lost through the head so after putting my swim cap on I covered it with a balaclava and woolly hat, both to be removed before entering the water. This left my hands and I took my ski mittens, already tested in the arctic and fine to a temperature of -15c. The next issue was how to store this clothing on the zodiac while swimming. The plastic bag is a wonderful invention and I took two decent sized ones along with my small backpack. Other things in the backpack included a torch, biscuits, chocolate and water, my emergency rations, plus survival equipment of compass and waterproof map, GPS, knife and flare.

I decided that it wasn't harsh enough to wear my ski mask but Craig Lenning upstaged me and looked similar to me but with the addition of this alpine accessory. Paolo had slightly less stuff but he improvised, using socks as gloves. He also had a very good woolly hat from the brand Head, made especially for open water swimming. It was very warm and could be pulled down over the ears with ease. The importance of keeping warm cannot be underplayed, both before and after a cold swim and that hat feels luxurious as you begin the warming up process, so generally the thicker, bigger and warmer the better.

We met in the sports hall in the middle of the ship an hour before our swim time. This room served as the assembly point before we moved downstairs to the platform which the zodiacs were using as a port. The waiting time was a little long but it was better like that as we sought to have the best possible organisation in order to get the best possible start on this mammoth task that we were facing. Finally our zodiac arrived and we boarded and made our way to the swimming place. It looked good, we had made quite a bit of distance in the 4 hours since the start. Toks Viviers from South Africa and the two Irish girls Anne Marie Ward and Nuala Moore were the team before us. They swam well and then it was down to us.

The Italian "Ferrari" Paolo was first up and he went well as did Craig of the USA although Craig had a small problem with the fastening of his safety buoy. These safety buoys were extremely useful and absolutely essential for this swim. Some other open water swims such as crossing the English Channel would not sanction the use of such a device as it can be held onto by the swimmer and therefore used as a flotation device. The English Channel is the Holy Grail, the Everest of open water swimming and rightly so due to its difficulty, a solo swim in pretty cold (16c-18c) water. However the Bering Strait swim was something completely different and as much as we wanted to follow English Channel rules it simply wasn't possible. All open water is different and so too the weather conditions, geography and geopolitics, thus having a definite set of rules for all open water swims is practically impossible.

To explain a little more about this safety buoy it is simply a 50cm by 30cm rigid inflatable bright orange coloured buoy which is then secured to a webbing strap, which in turn is attached to the swimmer, generally around the waist. It serves mainly as a device to make the swimmer more visible in a rough sea. The second purpose is that in an emergency situation the swimmer can actually grab hold of it and use it as a flotation device. It does not aid the swimmer but in fact hinders swimming by creating drag as it is towed by the swimmer, lying behind in the water.

Anybody who had any reservations about the use of such a device was soon left in no doubt as to its necessity after the first few immersions in the Bering Strait. It was stipulated explicitly by the organisers and also the "record man" Alexei that the safety of the swimmers was the most important thing and that on no account would the swim be a priority over swimmer safety. Actually this was something of a paradox as every swim represented danger as we were swimming in conditions that were outrageous. One of the South Africans commented that 10 knots was the wind speed cut off for Robben Island crossings. In the Bering Strait we were dreaming about winds of 10 knots.

The South African Team

Ram, Andrew, Ryan and Toks and their cameraman Alasdair. Their 5th swimmer of what they called the infamous five – Keiron had declined to participate for personal reasons.

So far I had only met Ram from their group and I had got to know him a little as I have already mentioned in PK in 2012 and at Chillswim in 2013. Two differing occasions that gave me differing sights of the chairman of the international ice swimming association.

When they arrived in Yakutsk it was after god knows how many hours of travelling from Cape Town and the far south of the Southern hemisphere. I introduced myself to Ryan, Andrew and Toks and Ram and I embraced. He seemed genuinely happy to see me and the vibes were good.

As our journey progressed so did the involvement of the South African team. They were held in high esteem by the Russian military and why not after they had twice travelled around the world for a weekend to swim in the ice at Tyumen and Murmansk, on the second occasion completing ice miles in some of the most severe competition conditions.

The guys proved to be good singers as well as swimmers and Ryan was also a guitar player and he held jam sessions almost every night on the ship. We already knew they were good drinkers and when I saw Ram with a trolley full of booze at PK it was clear that they meant business. After a few days on board Irtysh the Russians also knew about the SA drinking prowess although generally everybody socialized privately in their own rooms with few large parties. This was surely the best way as we had a job to do.

As individuals they were all fantastic and well liked by all on board. However, they seemed to take liberties as a group by wielding their collective power and obtaining some kind of control over the relay. There were many other fast swimmers including Sergey Popov, Christian Vegara, Melissa O Reilly, Toomas Haagi, Henri Kaarma, and Craig Lenning.

It is natural that a group of friends will be close knit so their behaviour was normal and the South African team backed up any of their opinions with great cold water swimming in the Bering Strait, setting an example from the outset after the reccy swim at Cape Dezhnev.

Bering report continued

Although extremely useful the buoys are a pain in the neck on the zodiac with its limited space. As already mentioned we needed rather a large amount of clothing, we were also supposed to wear bulky lifejackets though in reality only the zodiac driver wore his most of the time. The rest of us dispensing with them for practical purposes. The safety buoy was an added nuisance when going to swim as it had to be located, often untangled and then fitted and tightened or loosened. The design is not perfect as in anything but the calmest of seas the buoy often takes it upon itself to attack the swimmer, upsetting the stroke and occasionally wrapping itself around an arm. I devised a strategy for this and I secretly called it my "Bering Strait Buoy Drill". This consisted of me extending my pull to include a punch of the buoy at the end, ensuring that it didn't interfere any more with my stroke. Some had other ways of dealing with it; Ram Barkai of South Africa for example opted to tie the safety buoy around his ankle which negated any of the buoy's swimmer attacking tendencies although it almost certainly created more drag against the swimmer. In one of the early swims I watched Anne Marie Ward getting savaged by the safety buoy, I would have laughed but swimming in the Bering Strait was never a laughing matter even when something comical did happen.

2nd immersion

We returned pretty happy to Irtysh. There were a few people on deck to welcome us back with words of encouragement which made us feel good. This was often one of the translators, Raul and it was always very welcome. These people doing other jobs rather than swimming and simply offering a few kind words is really important and helps morale. We were quickly ushered through to the doctor's room through a few corridors that at first seemed like a labyrinth but in time would become very familiar.

Once inside our blood pressure, heart rate and a few other things were measured. Then it was off to the recovery room where girls waited with hot, wet towels. Sounds exciting and it was. All we had to do is sit back on a bench and start shivering (a normal process for the body to rewarm itself) meanwhile the girls would press the towels onto us in effort to warm up our cold blood before it went rushing back into the core. By this time the blood is already circulating but it definitely aids the recovery process and is probably better than the more full-on heat of the sauna. Some people believe in only a natural rewarming process and many of us winter swimmers in the Czech Republic follow that practice, with just a little time spent standing by the stove in our clubhouse after swimming. Zdeněk, for example shunned the Russian rewarming process declaring that he didn't need it. I told him that "When in Rome do as the Romans" and also "Don't knock it until you have tried it." He replied by telling me that now was not the time for him to be trying new techniques and that he was quite ok. I couldn't say much to that as he was right, he was in excellent condition both physically and mentally. I basked in the luxury of assistance and sipped from a cup of sweet tea as we had a short debrief with Paolo and Craig. Already a bond had formed and we were more than happy with our set up on the whole.

We arrived back upstairs at the cabins in time for dinner which was nice. As usual fish with rice and a soup. Naturally all accompanied by bread and butter. After drinking evening tea and checking the schedule to find that we were scheduled to swim again at 2am we retired to our bunks for a rest. Not much chance of sleeping but I did drop off for an hour or so. Then at 1am we were back in the sports hall where we were promptly whisked downstairs to the departure point. Craig was slightly annoyed as he received a knock at the door and the command "Ok 20 mins" only for someone to come back 5 minutes later and shout "Ok, come on let's go." Craig was a bit put out by this and I could see why. The preparation process was important and we all had our own ways of doing things.

Downstairs somebody handed me a bag of light sticks. Sure enough outside there was a kind of semi darkness, a twilight, or perhaps the best way to explain it was a blue kind of darkness, and although dark with low visibility it certainly wasn't a black darkness. One thing it was – cold. The wind as usual was blowing, I don't know how hard but that is almost irrelevant as it was always very windy. The air temperature was around 4c, and probably it had dropped a little due to the semi darkness which had started a few hours earlier. Sunrise was due soon. I was glad that I had my soft shell trousers and my balaclava and mittens to help me retain body heat before this second swim. The drama was now really starting as there were rumours about how a Russian swimmer had come back and was immediately on a stretcher and in the hospital. I didn't doubt this and I only hoped it would be the first and only such incident.

Now we were heading for the islands and they were both in view as we had come on a course south/southeast. A few hours ago we had hit the cold northerly current coming from the arctic. This had caused the water temperature to drop considerably and it was now below 3c with the last measurement being 2.8c. This was what we expected so in a perverse kind of way I was looking forward to this swim. It was a little dark and very cold and harsh, just what we expected the Bering to be like. The fear factor was now up a few notches as we waited pretty quietly in the lightly rocking zodiac.

In the front of our boat sat the starter and navigator, Vladimir Nefatov, a man I had only just met but I liked him from the word go. He was strong and reasonable and these qualities were about to be tested as our crossing progressed. He was pretty happy and pointed first to Russia (big Diomede) and then the USA (little Diomede). We were some way off the islands but their imposing shape was there to be seen. Paolo went in for his swim and when he came back in he looked cold. In fact he looked very cold and was soon shivering violently. Completely natural after such an immersion but nevertheless it let me know what was in store for me as if I needed reminding.

Actually I was well prepared mentally having waited for such a long time for these precious moments of swim time in the Bering Strait. Now it was time to rise to the challenge and enjoy the extreme conditions. I did just that, taking the baton from Craig and giving it my all in the icy water. I can confirm that it was extremely cold as my arms were numb rather quickly although all those years of winter swimming meant that my arms kept working and working well as I kept turning them over and over again. I thought a little about the cold and kept swimming. I decided in the murky darkness of the frigid Bering Strait that the short leg time of 10 minutes was the right decision from the organisers. Then it was all over and I clambered back on board. I didn't bother with putting any clothes on. This was normal for the last swimmers of each three person team.

The journey back was slightly chilly but with adrenaline flowing after the swim it was easily manageable. However, once back on board Irtysh I was shivering like my life depended on it and grateful for the assistance of the support team and doctors. I passed my tests with flying colours as did Craig but Paolo had a minor irregularity and was asked to return before his 3rd swim for a further check. This time it took us a while to recover and organise ourselves. We managed to lie on our bunks for an hour or two before we were awoken first at 7am by the captain's "Stavej" (getup) and then 30 minutes later by the more welcome "The first shift is invited for breakfast".

I enjoyed my porridge and put an extra spoon of sugar in my coffee as a reward for my night shift. Now we were starting to get to the serious business end of this expedition. It was no longer just a fun trip but we had work to do. I was revelling in it as I can only take so long in a passive role as a passenger.

After breakfast myself, Ram and a few others were invited up to the bridge by Oleg for a meeting with the captain. Now I felt like we were getting somewhere and that we were on course at last. Ram was in a similar mood to me, I could see he was concentrated on the job ahead and relishing the challenge. It was pointed out that we would soon reach the border, maybe this evening sometime and that we had a tugboat, MB61 that was looking out for us and that we could in turn use for navigation purposes. Right now it was several nautical miles away but well within hailing distance if there were any problems.

Ram was keen to get the message across that it was necessary for the zodiacs to stay closer to the swimmer and also to set a better course. This was a problem, especially during the semi darkness but it was the reality of swimming a relay supported by zodiacs in a rough sea like the Bering. I hoped that we would all improve our skills with regard to navigation as we progressed, but deep down I also knew that Mother Nature was playing the most powerful hand and would therefore have the biggest say in what was to happen. Another general meeting followed at 9.30am for everyone and after this it was something of a rush as we were due to swim again at 11am. At this stage it is worth pointing out that although we had around 8 hours between swims a sustained period of rest was almost impossible. In this last example we lay in bunks for 1 or 2 hours before breakfasting, attending meetings and then heading out for another swim.

Immersion 3

Paolo was given the all clear to continue swimming by the doctors. Daylight, and not a bad day in that at least it wasn't raining. The water was still extremely cold, somewhere around 4c but this time we could clearly see both islands albeit from a distance and we were all pumped up to give our biggest swims yet. It was about 11am and at this stage we were still keeping up with time and therefore it was the middle of the day and the time for high activity. The current was strong , we could feel it dragging us a little towards the island and for the first time the swim map showed an erratic zigzag shape, not just from our swim but for a few hours either side too. The waves were perhaps the biggest we had faced but we all managed to give big swims and it was a pleasant time to be in the zodiac, trying to make videos and take photos. All except Paolo that is who shivered too much to operate a camera successfully. The islands really did take on an air of mystery and beauty, being just large chunks of rock stuck in the middle of the ocean. The little one, particularly charismatic, with its miniature shape making it look like the smaller sibling of the other. Big and little Diomede were the right names and I prefer this to the Russian names of Ratmanova and Kruzenstern. Definitely this swim was so much easier psychologically and we even started to get a slight feeling of comfort as we were gradually slipping into a routine. Back on board Irtysh the recovery room was no longer working so instead it was a trip to the doctors for the usual check-up accompanied with a cup of sweet tea before we made our way to the sauna. I have to say that I enjoyed the latter more than the former. The doctors were very nice and I had known them for a few years but I started to tire of their questions such as "Are you tired", or "How do you feel" and their apparent surprise at my good physical condition. I know it was more that they were impressed but the thing was that I was in good condition because I train a lot and therefore anything less would not be acceptable to me. In this environment I felt I didn't really need any comments or help. Seasickness had come, my body had adapted and my sore throat of a few days ago was now long gone. Still the doctors were very nice and I always liked to see them, it was just the procedure that got on my nerves although deep down I knew that the doctors were 100% doing the right thing and it was just me being irritable. I only visit the doctors when I am on death's door, a habit I inherited from my father and he from his. It has taught me to be strong and to put up with things. I am glad of this but it does mean that I have less patience with obligatory medical examinations than those people who are perhaps more used to visiting the doctor. I have the same attitude with medicine, using it rarely, relying instead on natural methods or my body's own defences.

The sauna was a welcome relief and relaxation. I didn't look at the temperature but it was just right. Not really high but warm enough to reheat our frozen bodies a good amount in 10 minutes or so. It became our habit to have something of a de-brief in the sauna as we sat back and relaxed in the pleasant heat. Unfortunately the sauna often smelt of diesel but being in the Bering Strait we were able to put up with or adapt to most things and therefore this strange odour was soon forgotten about.

After this we arrived at the dining room just in time for lunch. A treat today as we had shashlik kebab and potatoes after the usual soup, today fortified with pearl barley and carrot as well as small pieces of fish. I like fish and that was lucky because it made its way into almost every meal, often more than once. We never received any dessert, just simple compote (fruit juice) and this alone was the only fish-free part of the menu. Not that I had any complaints, for the food was both plentiful and nourishing and what's more I didn't have to cook it. Quite frankly I could have stayed on that boat forever under these conditions.

Back to the cabins and we welcomed a guest in the form of Zdeněk and his camera as he insisted on making a video diary of events so far. He was extremely enthusiastic but me less so as it involved my skills as a translator in order that Paolo could participate fully. I found it quite demanding as Zdeněk babbled on in Czech like he was a TV presenter. That was fine but in my cabin I preferred simply to relax. It wasn't a big problem and I did my duties well enough.

A Blind Swimmer

Now I am not an expert in marathon swims and crossings but I still stand by my comment that if you wanted to choose the most difficult event to invite a blind swimmer to then this would be the one.

Firstly, he had to travel halfway around the world completely alone. Secondly he had to spend almost 2 weeks at sea on a boat that was a minefield of traps ready to catch out even the most eagle-eyed of us let alone someone who couldn't see. After a few days James was able to find his way down the corridor and get to the toilet but he needed leading everywhere. After a few more days he knew a bit more about where he was going but he still required a guide. This is where Craig Lenning came in. He was absolutely amazing. As somebody said "Craig really makes his words come alive so that he is able to describe everything that James had in front of him". Going back to our first meeting in Yakutsk and I was slightly worried that it might be me who would be responsible for James. He asked me to take him to the toilet so I did.

As I waited it dawned on me what it would mean to have a blind man with us. I mentioned to a few of the others that it would be necessary to work together to help him but in the end it was no problem at all and I found that I hardly assisted James at all for several days as he was simply inundated with offers of help. I noticed Alexei, the big Russian, ex-military a really great guy, a big bear of a man, always ready and willing to help James. I noticed how Alexei drank a lot of alcohol but also worked a lot and was always ready to do anything for anyone. This is a good example of a strong Russian person. Able to drink a lot, work a lot, sleep little, rest little, drink a lot, work a lot, endure a lot. I respect these people they have a good ethic and I believe that it comes from not being mollycoddled like so many of us in the West are. It is true that I also know many people from the UK who are like this but the Russians I have met do it just a little bit better, just a little bit more matter of fact. Even in Czech Republic the person I know who is most like this, the Mountaineer Petr, a veteran of many Kamchatka and Caucus expeditions and has spent a lot of time in Russia.

So Alexei was a great guy who was able to help James. I admire him just as I admired Craig and I also began to admire James although quite frankly he had an advantage a lot of the time in that he couldn't see the ridiculous conditions we were facing!

The main difficulty we had with this swim was the amount of logistical issues, in that we had to make hundreds of trips by zodiac which involved getting people on and off the zodiac from a small platform attached to the Irtysh ship. It was never easy but sometimes it was an adrenaline filled fairground ride and once it was Russian roulette style jump and hope for the best. Needless to say guiding a blind man from a rocking zodiac to a wobbling platform took some doing but I am pleased to say that it went off without major incident. Some others were more unlucky and an array of cuts and more often than not large blue bruises appeared all over the legs of our swim team.

Our original swim team was me, Paolo and Craig. We soon bonded and worked well together although Paolo I know resented going first and having to wait, shivering, for us to finish our swims before going back to Irtysh. I could have offered to swap but I decided that the "tough love" approach was best. You see Paolo is my friend and I happened to know that he was one of the best swimmers in the team. He has a great record in open water and was a former world record holder for distance in a lake. Although he sometimes complained about the cold he had taken to winter swimming perfectly well, managing to take a silver medal in the 450m at the world championships in Latvia in 2012. If I let him off here it would be a bad thing, I knew he could endure going first so I didn't offer to swap. Actually he was a typical swimmer who was perhaps nervous or even worried before any kind of swim but always able to go through it. He often shivered violently but this as we all know is just the body's way of re-warming itself and I am not one of those people who think that shiverers can't handle the cold. I would always back Paolo to complete his extreme cold swim. He was faster than me and I was of the opinion that it would be me that would crack before him simply due to his great speed in the water when compared with my more sluggish efforts. I didn't crack but sure enough he didn't change and just kept swimming the same every time like a true professional. I could see he was nervous before his swims but he never said so and he never said anything negative or tried to get out of a swim, he was 100% committed.

Craig Lenning was someone who I knew every little about before we met and I had only spoken to him on Facebook. He was clearly an accomplished marathon swimmer to say the least with solo crossings of the English Channel and the notoriously difficult North Channel to his name. He also posted a brief message about how he had been visiting mountain lakes at around 10,000m above sea level in preparation for the Bering Strait swim. The man was obviously a force to be reckoned with and I only hoped that his pleasantness as a man was at the same level as his swimming ability. I wasn't disappointed. One could say he was a typical American – loud and friendly but I don't like to stereotype people so I will just say that he is loud and friendly. His beaming smile and kind words were a welcome respite from the raging Bering Sea and I believe that he added security to our mini swim team of 3 on the zodiacs. He was the perfect person to room with James and his voice became James' surrogate eyes as Craig explained everything that was going on in a loud and visual way without complicating it.

Although the swim was going well, there was a small problem as we went into the fourth rotation and the second day. James Pittar still hadn't been cleared to swim. The reason being that his blood pressure had gone through the roof and the doctors were not at all happy with his health. This caused a further problem in the form of a vicious circle as he only became more and more nervous and irritated by this. Naturally it was a difficult situation for him and at this point in time I really felt for him. As we sat down for evening tea I watched him dispense with a knife and fork and eat an omelette with hands. But what else could he do the poor man couldn't see what he was doing. I didn't know what it was like to be blind but I knew what it was to feel lousy. James also had a habit of wringing his hands when nervous and he was doing this quite a lot, clearly very, very frustrated.

Andrew Chin came over and gave some kind but strong words in his soft South African accent. James agreed to relax and then later I saw Craig who told me the news that James would come and swim with us, meaning me, Craig and Paolo. At this point I felt quite proud as I expected the South Africans to manage this but Craig was to be James' buddy swimmer and he had decided that our team of 3 was a unit that would be best staying together. That was a real vote of confidence and another example of the leadership and human qualities shown by Craig during our trip. James still had to pass the medical examination which he of course did and then we were preparing to go. Our swim was at 9pm, actually during the twilight period. It didn't get dark due to the high latitude but there were around 4 hours of semi darkness from approximately 20.30 until 01.30. The reason for this was the fact that we had been ordered by the captain when we first boarded the Irtysh to synchronise our watches to Vladivostok time. Having spent 4 days heading north east we were now well ahead of our own Vladivostok time zone so that the semi darkness was coming earlier. This helped to add to the strange feeling that time meant nothing although discipline was kept by having our 4 meals per day. Outside of this though time seemed irrelevant and would become more so as we continued.

The head doctor Tatyana who I have known for a few years was none too keen on allowing James to swim and nearly came out with us. In the end she relented. I admired her professionalism but it would have been a travesty if James hadn't swum. Why his first swim had to be during the few hours of semi darkness I don't know although many people will counter this by saying that James had no idea as to the conditions of the light! I was thinking more about the difficult logistics of moving him into the zodiac, out of it for his swim and then reversing the process. As I have already mentioned it wasn't always an easy process for those of us who had full vision. One big positive was that our team of 3 was strong, we had bonded well and I saw how Craig operated and that he was capable of taking care of James almost alone while myself and Paolo quietly went about our business and tried not to get in the way, occasionally helping to carry something or clearing a path or securing a route. I may have made it sound like a mountaineering expedition, but it wasn't that tough though it was by no means easy getting on and off those zodiacs. So we changed things a little bit for the swim with James.

Paolo remained first up but I then went second with Craig and James swimming last and only for 5 minutes on this first swim. Vladimir Nefatov the starter allowed me to swim for 15 minutes to make up for the shortfall. I had no problem with this. The water temperature was now fluctuating around 6c and it felt fine after that icy second immersion when the water was well below 3c. The swell was quite big and it was another exciting swim as I could clearly see Little Diomede Island ahead and the twinkling lights of the village Inulik, population 100. I thought that it seemed much bigger; the lights promising shelter from the elements and a sign of life for the first time in several days.

The swell was big again and the current was starting to turn. Now we were nearing the border and at the same time, that change in the direction of the flow of water around the Diomede Islands as the water was funnelled in between them. Swimming second when James and Craig were coming next was the danger position. The reason was that as James prepared all eyes were on him. I looked behind a few times as I noticed that the boat was letting me get away by some 30m. I could tell that they weren't really keeping an eye on me. I didn't really mind but I knew that it considerably upped the risk and that my chances of something happening were being increased by this. Nevertheless I got on with my job and said little about it, certainly not when James was within earshot anyway. A job was what it was. We were working in a military way and all of us had to concentrate on our jobs to get the bigger job of the crossing itself finished. This meant that the job of the swimmers was merely one cog with the zodiac drivers, medics, starters, translators, cooks, cleaners, ship's crew all playing their part so that we could apply the finishing touches and do the swimming.

When we got back to Irtyush I quickly scampered up the platform leaving the others on the zodiac. There were 2 sailors on the platform and no room for me. I hung around at the top and waited for James to be pulled off the zodiac at which point I came down the steps to help him up with Craig not far behind. The recovery room had stopped functioning and it was now a sauna followed by a medical check or vice versa depending on how we wanted to do it. We opted for a celebratory sauna with even Paolo "I hate saunas" Chiarino joining in. We all passed the medical check again and felt good, buoyed by the success of James who was rather popular after breaking his Bering duck while the water was still pretty damn cold and the conditions – as usual – not far off horrendous. Little did I know what the Bering Strait would have in store for us on our next swim with James.

Later on in the week I was left with James at the dinner table. I helped him with his food, buttering his bread. It hadn't occurred to me that he wouldn't be able to do a simple chore like this. Then for the first time in a while I had to walk him somewhere. He wanted to use the satellite phone which involved us walking out onto the helipad. We went down the corridor and I went a bit fast. I told him perhaps somewhat cruelly from my position of sighted power that maybe it was time to up his pace.

Well it soon became apparent that this wasn't a good idea judging by the sounds coming from his mouth. At this point I changed my approach and closed my own eyes, telling James what I was doing. At this point we slowed right down. I managed to keep my eyes shut all the way around 2 corners before I opened them again. I had the luxury of choosing to do that and I hoped that by emphasising the change of speed caused by my change in sight that we would both learn something. I learnt to be more patient and I think James learnt that I am something of an idiosyncratic character. I might be stating the obvious but it is a totally different world being blind, not being able to butter a slice of bread or find your way around. I am sure over the years James has come up against all manner of situations and no doubt beaten them all. He never showed any fear during our Bering Strait crossing and was always ready to do his job, even when he was clearly angry at being prevented from swimming on medical grounds he kept his cool. It would have been so easy to think the world is against you and take on the role of invalid but instead in true endurance athlete style he came through it and always received the longest and loudest cheers, especially when we received our medals. Everybody got some applause but he actually received a concerted standing ovation.

Bering first stoppage, just before border

I felt good, James had swum with us on the 4th immersion and we had quietly welded together as a team. I now held Craig Lenning in high esteem and I would have no problems in working under him. That says quite a lot coming from me as I am more naturally shepherd rather than sheep and I will only accept who I consider to be outstanding leaders. (Whether I am right or wrong about people as leaders I don't know, but I will stick to my guns.)

Now it was about 11pm and with the semi darkness we stood a chance of getting some sleep. I ate a few biscuits with a little chocolate and lay on my bunk as did Paolo. We were expecting to swim again at around 4am. I wrote my journal content. However, I knew that conditions were worsening outside and just before midnight I got the feeling that something was going on. It was a strange feeling that I can't explain as I was thinking in one moment about several things, the maritime border, the zodiacs, the swimmers and the weather.

I readied my GPS and moved across the cabin to the window. Sure enough conditions outside were nothing short of atrocious. In the semi darkness the rain was coming down, the wind was blowing hard and more importantly I could see both zodiacs no more than 100 metres from the ship. They were bobbing around, clearly having trouble in the conditions and one had its spotlight on and was flashing it around madly. I couldn't see any swimmers and the spotlight was not pointing at the water but rather Irtysh. They were obviously struggling to get back in and needed as much help as possible. My GPS confirmed that we were right at the border. At this point I was overtaken by adrenaline and I started to get excited even though I knew that we had a problem with the swim. I wandered out into the corridor and into the sports hall, a strange sight I was wearing only my boxer shorts but I was adorned with a head torch, GPS, binoculars and camera! I saw Oleg who told me to go and get some rest. He exerted a calming influence over me and I went back to my bunk. We couldn't sleep but we nodded off, waking at 2am and again at 4am and 6am only to find out that the swim was suspended at the moment.

At breakfast Oleg told me to come for a meeting upstairs on the bridge. It was announced that the swim stopped officially at 23.53 due to gale force winds of 39knots, (22m/s) and rain, basically a storm which made navigation for both swimmers and zodiacs not only near impossible but extremely hazardous. The low light also made things difficult and it was the only feasible thing to do, stopping the swim at this point. A GPS mark had been taken just 500m from the Russia/US maritime border and as soon as we were able we would be back out. The format of the swim had now been changed from non-stop to staged relay. This decision was approved by Alexei the guy from the record books.

The weather prognosis was for a drop in the winds to around 20knots (10m/s) with just the occasional gusts up to 39knots (22m/s) so therefore we would start again at 10am. The current was still northerly although that was expected to reverse almost as soon as we passed Little Diomede Island. It was also agreed that the swim team would now be cut and that 30 of the best swimmers, only swimming freestyle would continue with the relay. We had no problems with this and we were ready to continue as soon as possible. I added that I had seen the conditions myself last night and that it was the correct and only decision. Ram hadn't seen for himself but he easily accepted what had been told and was eager to get out there with the other South Africans. They saw themselves as the top team and at times it seemed arrogant but the truth was that they were strong and also they never flinched from anything, just like me but I wasn't quite as strong a swimmer as those guys. I was strong enough and needless to say I was in the group of 27, 9 teams of 3 chosen to continue the relay.

After the briefing about conditions, the meeting took on a lighter yet still serious note or perhaps I should say, serious but mystical note as the kite surfer Yevgeny came in;. Our wind guru, our shaman from Moscow. Oleg commented that here at the border it was almost mystical that there was some kind of force at work here. Then Yevgeny was asked for his comments and he talked of a wall at the maritime border between the two islands, that here it was a make or break point and that it was difficult to break through. Certainly I had felt something strong last night at exactly the point the relay was stopped and I concurred with all that was said even if it did seem slightly far-fetched and nonsensical.

We left the meeting in good spirits, saying "Rabotyim" (we work) and then there was a short general meeting for everyone where the new plan was announced and some amount of rallying cries could be heard. We left for our cabins to prepare for more swimming. About 2pm was our scheduled swim time and it meant that we had to be downstairs and ready to go at 1pm. I ate lunch at 12pm but not too much. Usually I wouldn't eat a meal 2 hours before swimming but in the last year I had trained myself as I knew that in the Bering Strait I must be prepared for anything. This was a wise move as although there was supposed to be a 24hour buffet in fact it didn't really work like that and it was better to eat when you had the chance, to be sure of something hot. The kitchen staff, who were actually doctors, did their best and the service was excellent, there simply weren't enough staff for 24 hour non-stop service. I didn't care I was happy enough with the setup that we had.

The sports hall had been dispensed with as a meeting place although it still served as a noticeboard and information was posted there. Again we would be swimming with James who was now in a better mood as not only was he swimming but he was included in this slimmed down group of the best 27 swimmers. We would repeat what we did last time with Paolo leading off followed by me, and then James and Craig at the end. Waiting by the platform for our zodiac I noticed the fog start to roll in…

Now we get back to that scene that I described at the start, the panic of being caught out in the fog – lost in the Bering Strait. Thankfully that terror only lasted a short time and we all made it safely back to the Irtysh. With visibility at perhaps less than 50m there would be no more swimming for a while, certainly after having almost lost a swimmer in the fog. A GPS waypoint was taken and we waited for the gloom to lift.

Bering Report continued

Immersion 6

So, now myself and Paolo were deep into conversations in our cabin about how we would finish this swim and more importantly when. He really made me laugh when he said "I want to sit outside by the Med and drink an espresso. Then maybe go for a swim in the very warm sea and if I so much as see a zodiac I will go aaaarrgh." A classic comedic moment. Although I was loving every minute of this trip I still had to get back in the water after "Lost in the Bering Strait." The expedition was turning out to be everything that we had hoped for and much more besides as every swim brought some new drama. I can only describe it as a real 'Boy's Own' adventure. But what would it be this time…well the answer was jellyfish.

I got on the zodiac having double checked I had everything including water and food for 2 days, navigation equipment, clothing, flare, tools and torch. The only thing that I was missing was my own boat and a satellite phone. The former being impractical and the latter I was unable to bring into Russia. We did have 1 satellite phone on board but that was it.

Boarding the zodiac I looked at my team mates and I was more than happy, if something was to go wrong again I had no problem being with these guys. Likewise our driver

Leonid, I had travelled with him many times and he knew what he was doing. We got out to the place of the swim very quickly. One of the results of yesterday's mishaps was that Irtysh would now stay as close as possible to the swimming place. This was quite difficult due to Irtysh needing to either lie at anchor or travel around 4.5knts. Obviously we were swimming much slower than that and it needed expert seamanship in order to keep us all together, at around 500m distance between Irtysh and the swimmer.

Nuala and Anne Marie were swimming and having terrible problems with navigation, in fact Nula was standing up and directing proceeding. In the zodiac I could recognise the driver as being the guy who was seasick on our Dezhnev reccy trip. As for the starter-cum=navigator Viktor Godlevsky was doing that job at the time so the other could have a break, by Jesus they needed it too! Unfortunately Viktor was probably better off in some other role and quite frankly that boat looked like a circus act, fine except the Bering Strait was no place for a circus! I might be a little harsh there or perhaps I was by now completely used to the awful conditions. It wasn't easy to navigate and control zodiac boats. No more fog and slightly warmer water, of about 8c but the wind was blowing as usual and the waves were getting bigger as was the current.

As I said, today our surprise was jellyfish. The water below us was becoming a lovely clear blue colour, far lighter it seemed than on the Russian side. I thought back to the words of the US coastguard, Ryan Butler who we met in Anchorage in 2011. He stressed the importance of protecting the pristine Alaskan waters. I wasn't sure that there could be a massive amount of pollution on the Russian side of the strait seeing as this was one of the most sparsely populated areas of the northern hemisphere. It was true that with the reduction in the extent of sea ice in the arctic the area was opening up for transportation and particularly with regards to oil and gas exploration.

However, I wasn't sure exactly why there was a difference in the water colour but there was a slight, ever such a slight difference. (It could also have been connected to the sediment release from the rivers on the Alaskan side but then that would surely make the water cloudier, or it could have been attributed to the light as there was more sun starting to peek out at us although it never lasted long and we were faced with generally horrendous conditions.)

The presence of jellyfish indicated that perhaps there were more nutrients in the water and that it was more fertile, certainly the level of salinity and also the temperature had increased. There were many of these long, white, menacing looking beasts hovering just below us but luckily they were not coming to the surface – they obviously weren't hungry. It was unnerving as there really were many of them and it was especially concerning when the odd one came a little higher. These were not the only things we encountered, with Melissa O'Reilly perhaps having the most frightening of experiences. She met a giant sized squid and had quite a lot to say about it when she got back on board Irtysh:

"The pinkish-yellow squid was as large the zodiac boat from which I had just plunged into the dark icy waves but I did not attempt a second look. The creature was lurking 15 metres below me and its smaller friends and relations were a mere arm stroke below me. I knew exactly what it was the minute he came into view through my clear goggle lenses. What a rookie mistake to use clear goggles when swimming in the middle of the Bering Strait. Had I not read the manual? The clarity in the Bering was terrifying but would lend itself to me sprinting each of my relay legs from the start as if my life depended on it. And swimming over such a nefarious looking giant made me kick and pull through my usually smooth freestyle stroke like a woman possessed.

Speaking of possessions, I vowed at that moment to use my dark tinted goggles for the remainder of the swims. I had already swam enough times in the Bering Strait over the course of several days, for an interval of 10 minutes in the frigid and volatile waters where temps ranged from 2C (35F) to upwards of 10C (50F). Thankfully I only had hopefully two more swims of now 15 minutes each, and hopefully without any sightings of the local residents of the sea.

As my sprinting session came to an end, I high-fived Masha for the relay hand-over, shouted to her 'Davai!' (Let's go!) Trying not to show any fear that could be detected from my voice and I swam over to the zodiac which was being tossed around in the exponentially growing swell which was now pushing 6 metres. I threw my entire body up onto the stern, trying to get my toes out of the water for fear that someone hungry below would mistake them for a snack. Leonid, our Russian Spetsnaz driver, and Alex, our skilful skipper yelled at me to get seated safely in the back of the zodiac but I continued to hold my beached whale position and while gasping for a breath yelled 'Kak govorit po-russki giant f*cking squid?!' (How do you say in Russian giant f*cking squid?!) My reply from Leonid was 'MEEELEEEESSA, DERZHIMSYA!!' (Meeeleeeesa, hold on!) and we sped off after Masha who was already cutting through the folding waves ahead of us in the direction of Alaska.

Only after we got back to our ship, Irtysh, that I learned 'squid' in Russian was 'kal'mar'. Hardly the correct term for what I had just swam over with a heart-rate spiking close to 200bpm. When I tried to explain the kal'mar I had seen was gigantic, all I got in reply was 'Ahhh, tak bol'shoy kal'mar' (ahhh, so a big kal'mar). The only calamari I know are breaded, fried and dipped in marinara sauce; so very glad that I did not become this creature's appetizer," said Melissa.

We were luckier than the girls from Ireland as our driver plotted a better course in the ever growing swell. The sea was now starting to turn visibly nasty whereas in the past it had been using one of its secret weapons – the cold – against us. We had also faced strong winds and waves but now it was different, the swells were bigger and bigger and actually with the slightly warmer water the swim took on another aspect, it was now fun and adventurous in a different way and it also took a different kind of courage to get in the water. The sea felt more alive now and this was characterised by an ever stronger current coming straight at us from the South – the fearsome Alaskan current.

On speaking to Nuala later she told me of the driver's struggle to navigate a good course for the swimmer, I sympathised with her; I had seen it with my own eyes. Then Nuala said to me "You know it is getting difficult now, the sea is really rough, and yesterday I was throwing up in the water." She then used one of her favourite phrases when she said "We just keep going, it's only arm over arm". At this point I must explain a little bit about these two amazing ladies from the Emerald Isle. Both of them for want of a better expression look quite big but marathon swimming is a sport where appearances can be deceptive. Anne Marie having crossed not only the English Channel but the North Channel solo, a feat which few people have achieved. Nuala had also swum in many marathons including the 26km Lake Zurich swim renowned in Europe for being one of the most difficult freshwater swims around.

With regards to our Bering Strait crossing these two ladies actually may have had the best preparation when they were involved in an incredible round Ireland swim back in 2006. They were part of a team that swum round Ireland, spending something like 16 hours per day either in the water or sitting on a zodiac. That takes a special kind of toughness perhaps similar in some ways to what was required of us in the Bering Strait. Therefore when someone like Nuala Moore turns round and says "it was tough yesterday" you take notice. In fact there wasn't one single person on the boat who was uttering anything different and we all knew how tricky it was getting. Even Ram, renowned for his devil may care attitude after swimming in places such as Antarctica and an ice swim in Murmansk was in agreement that it was one hell of a task to cross this Bering Strait.

Getting our money's worth was an understatement. Jellyfish aside, there wasn't so much drama during immersion 6 and my confidence was now fully restored following the previous day's mishap. Once again I was champing at the bit for more action although not until I had been in the sauna and had my dinner and evening tea. That goes without saying that if a man cannot enjoy evening tea on a Russian navy ship then something is wrong. In fact the only thing that was wrong was that the evening tea lacked "pechenie" (biscuits) and "Konfety" (sweets), but at least there was sugar so for me sweet tea was enough with bread and butter and whatever else they rustled up. I have to say that the mutton pasty was so strong tasting that I struggled to eat it all. That was the only time I had any kind of problem with the food.

After this 2.30am swim I was fully expecting another immersion sometime in the morning and my main hope was that I would get not only a little sleep but perhaps some breakfast too. Our usual procedure of arrival to the ship followed by doctor's tests and sauna went fine. Luckily there was some sweet tea in the doctor's room in order to take the taste of sea salt from our mouths. Again another debrief in the sauna and this time again I had to leave some of my clothes in there so that they would be dry for the next trip. I was now firmly attached to my combination of merino base layer, club fleece, raincoat, soft shell trousers with waterproofs over the top, neoprene socks and shoes and balaclava, hat and mittens. In the early days I had been using my trusty old down jacket but now it was too bulky and I didn't need it.

All this stuff required some organisation and it took a few more minutes of the precious time so that once we had done all that needed to be done we finally climbed into our bunks at 5am, leaving the usual 2 hour sleeping period before the wakeup call. It seemed that whatever the schedule 2 hours of sleep was the norm. In fact I think our bodies had accepted and adapted to this somewhat strange regime.

The news as we emerged for breakfast wasn't good. The swim had been suspended at 6.19 due to big problems with navigation resulting from a strong current coming at us from the south somewhere, what was to become the infamous Alaskan current. There was no big disappointment as we had already faced two stoppages and the relay was now staged rather than non-stop. However, I could see concern on the faces of Oleg Dokuchaev, Vladimir Nefatov, Alexandr Yurkov and the crew up on the bridge as I was summoned up there. Now I was given a small mission. I was to go out with the 3-strong South African team and measure their swim distance. We could call them the South African 'A team' but that would be unfair on their 4th member Toks who was paired with Nuala and Anne Marie.

For once the weather was pretty nice and I would even say that it was pleasant although the wind was blowing as usual and I opted to take my down jacket as I was on research rather than the "action" of swimming which required my other clothes. After initially overrunning the coordinates due to some poor communication in Russian and English we got to the where the last GPS mark was made and came back somewhat to allow for any deviation. We had no problem swimming more but swimming less was not on. I was sitting in the front on the left hand side as

Ryan went in first. I watched him and I watched the water, together they were moving nicely together or so it seemed.

It was quite difficult just by sight to tell how far he was moving but he looked good. Glancing at my GPS and the results were mixed but conclusive. Ryan was swimming an excellent course in that he was not deviating but swimming straight, that was very positive, however, the negative was that he had made only 350m in 15 minutes. It was a similar situation for both Ram and Andrew who made no more than 300m each. We travelled back to Irtysh in the knowledge that one of our strongest teams had made around 1000m in 45minutes. So around 1km per hour was not such a bad result, meaning that perhaps if the weather was good we could finish in 24hours, except that non-stop swimming had not been possible since the first 2 days and now we were into day 4.

Even though it was approaching 12noon ship time and my adapted body was ready for lunch I headed of course straight to the bridge with my GPS results. It was decided that we continue and I was soon heading back out for my 7th immersion. But first there was a general meeting. It was decided that now we were at a critical stage and that with the swim running into a fourth day that we needed to change our strategy a little. Therefore it was decided that now only the 27 strongest swimmers who swim freestyle would continue on with the relay and therefore swimming around every 7 hours. The swim time was upped to 15 minutes as the water was warmer. Some people favoured sticking with the 10 minute leg in an effort to keep the tempo as high as possible. I understood this but I also thought about the 5 minute less which meant in the long run more rotations and therefore more complicated logistics. Ram was very vocal at keeping a 15 minute leg and now it was becoming clear that he had more influence over this swim than possibly anyone else bar the captain and Oleg.

Happily as expected I was included in the new list. Unhappy to a certain extent our team had been broken up, although I was now with my club colleague Zdeněk, who in the past had been in the zodiac behind me. The third member of our new team was a Russian, another Alexandr, this time Alexandr Komarov. I didn't know him very well, having only met him on this trip but he was a nice guy and we soon had an understanding. Alexandr (Komarov) was well prepared in what I will say was the typical Russian style for this expedition, which meant, everything is fine, nothing is a problem, let us get the job done. I admire this attitude and I had been using it myself. It had worked well and as I have already mentioned I had surprised myself a little as to how well I was handling everything. Alexandr (Komarov) also had a pretty good camera with him which meant that over the course of our next few swims we would get some pretty good video footage.

After the reccy with the South Africans it took a few hours to start swimming again after the meetings. When we got back in the weather conditions were different. Now the wind was blowing harder, 20 -25knts and the waves were starting to roll. The water may have been less cold at around 8c but being out in those rough seas with strong winds and rain in the air meant that there was no let up and we were still going out looking as though we were on a skiing holiday and not a swimming expedition. We came back in having made some 500 or so metres. This was now becoming par for the course and it was slow, hard work, but we plugged. The situation continued to deteriorate and the north wind blew stronger and stronger.

Breaking the Alaskan Current

After we got fairly quickly to the halfway point I started to laugh at Claudia Rose's prediction that we would not be able to make the crossing due to currents. However, we were soon to be at the mercy of the strong Alaskan current. A simple name, but not a simple current. At its worst it came from the south or south east and proceeded to move north/northwest in all kinds of directions. 7.5knts was the strongest recorded speed and at this point it seemed to be producing an eddy like feature which caused the swimmer to go backwards and the zodiac to become unnavigable. Alexandr Jakovlev was onboard this zodiac at the time and said "It was crazy, we were just going around in circles"

It was just after our 7th swim that this incident with Jakovlev bringing in the boats happened.

This was at somewhere around 65° 3687 C, 168° 31893 between Little Diomede Island and the Alaskan mainland.

There was no other option but to make a GPS mark, bring the zodiacs in and regroup. It was one thing to fight a current when the wind was also blowing at around 20knts but it was another to lose a swimmer or a crew member doing so. As usual there were no complaints from anyone. This was perhaps the lowest point of the relay. We could see the American coast clearly, less than 20km away when visibility allowed but the new world was proving difficult to reach. The land of opportunity was still just a dream for us. But then to coin a couple of old phrases "There is no such thing as a free lunch" and "The best things come to those who wait." Nevertheless, I was starting to doubt if we would succeed. A current of 7.5knts wasn't just strong it was frightening. It is worth mentioning that the ocean while being extremely simple on the surface is conversely extremely complex underneath with physical features such as bathymetry, geology and plate tectonics all playing a part in the movement of water as well as the wind at the surface and the moon influenced tides. A current is not necessarily constant and can change quickly therefore the report of a 7.5knt current, although true, was something akin to a tabloid newspaper headline proclaiming something like "Treason" when all that has happened is a member of the royal family has worn a swastika at a private fancy dress party. Poor taste perhaps but not a threat. In the case of the current it was at one moment in that one place 7.5knts but it wouldn't always be, indeed maybe it could get up to 8knts, which wasn't something any of us wanted to contemplate.

Morale was obviously low and some of the Russian swimmers were particularly unhappy as they had already been knocked off the roster due to either a lack of speed or an inability to swim freestyle. Actually there was another reason and that was seasickness. Some had little ocean experience and were amazing swimmers in the "prorub" (icehole) but the ocean was a different matter entirely. It was frustrating for all of us but those that hadn't swum for a while and badly wanted to, felt it perhaps the worst of all. I had no time though to sympathise with anyone, my only concern was that we had to do it, to get through this current and make it to the American continent. It had been 2 years of explaining failure with regards to bureaucracy and I didn't want to explain yet more failure even if this time it was down to Mother Nature. I could almost see the doubter's half smiles and hear their comments, smirks and questions – Why?… Why didn't you…?

There was quite a big meeting about how to do it, how to get through. This involved several people using a pencil to annotate a nautical chart that was on the wall on the bridge. The captain talked about the coming shallow water and at this point I got an insight into the dangers faced by large vessels in the shallow Bering Strait. We did have the tug boat MB61 with us but we didn't want to call it into action or even worse have our Irtysh end up capsized like the Costa Concordia. It was agreed that we would have to meet this current head on and go south with the idea that we could be brought north around the cape or from off the cape into the village of Wales which is bordered by the Cape to the South and the beginning of the Prince of Wales shoal and the shallows punctuated by sand bars and spits to the north.

An idea that was first touted by the captain seemed interesting and it was to allow the current to take us north into the shallows before turning back when the current stopped, allowing us to swim freely to shore. Craig Lenning agreed with this idea and also made his own marks on the map. Then Alexandr Jakovlev took the pencil and made a few notes of his own. He had been out earlier with Yevgeny to measure the current closer to Wales. He mentioned that he had met a current of perhaps 3.5 or 4knts around 8km from the shore. In this case it would be a very difficult current to break through and could lead to us being pushed north. I had visions again of Shishmaref and a drift to the North Pole. That Prince of Wales shoal was also a worry as I imagined the dangers of the shallow water and the sand banks both to swimmer and vessel.

In the end it was clear that we must get through this current and pay attention to how far north we were pushed, avoiding this if at all possible. Oleg then stated that he had been in touch with Admiral Sidorenko and that he believed in us. It was good motivation knowing that we still had the top man backing us. The captain, Viktor, added that he wanted to start cold water swimming himself so this was also a nice thing to hear from a tough Russian sailor. He went on to say that he believed that we would be the first swimmers to break through this current and that nobody in future would be brave enough to repeat this. At the time I agreed with him, we were fighting a big uphill battle and the cost of this project meant that failure was not an option. Whatever would happen to us in the coming hours anybody trying this in the future would have to bear all these things in mind. Ram agreed with everything and we left the meeting in good spirits even if we were still worried about being at the mercy of this mysterious and powerful Alaskan current. I thought of the old sayings my parents had told me when I was younger "All good things come to those who wait" and "There's no such thing as free lunch." The thing was that now it was nearly 12noon and here on Irtysh there was a free lunch.

Perhaps of all the immersions, number 8 was the most emotional. The wind was blowing from the north, the swells were big and we swum with them as we met the current head on. We could just about make out the American continent in front of us through the cloud and mist. I swum flat out but unfortunately I went in a north westerly direction. That course was 110. Zdeněk went on a 120 course which was bit better and he moved a little to the west. Alexandr (Komarov) had a similar result. Vladimir Nefatov told us how we had fared and there was much disappointment and frustration having just given everything for 15 minutes in an extremely rough sea with jellyfish all over the place. Now the cold water didn't bother us, although still very cold we would have swapped it for ice water if we could have had just a slightly weaker current.

I was almost in tears as I was thinking how the New World was taunting us, we wanted to reach it so much but it simply wouldn't let us in. Strange feelings but real, this swim was becoming an incredible adventure, a journey through not just an extremely hostile body of water a physical and mental journey for all of us personally. Just a few days ago we were thinking about making a non-stop relay between the continents in just over 2 days, perhaps with 3 or 4 immersions each. Actually many of us, me included hadn't put a figure on how many immersions we would need but the general feeling was for the numbers mentioned.

Now we were in a staged relay, almost 5 days in and looking at more than 8 immersions to get the job done. The fact that we had changed the format from 'non-stop' to 'staged' didn't bother anyone as it was simply a case of survival and getting the job done somehow. As long as the swim was unaided then it was fine in our opinion. Obviously, those from the channel swimming fraternity wouldn't think so but then we weren't in the English Channel. This was a totally different challenge in a totally different area of the world in terms of climate and geography. One thing that was similar was that they are both straits and as such there is a lot of water moving around and currents could be strong. Their bathymetry was different though and the Bering Strait was extremely shallow with a slope down into the deep arctic and pacific oceans at the north and south ends respectively. The English Channel remains the Everest, the ultimate prize in marathon swimming but to compare with the Bering Strait would be folly.

Here we were facing a different challenge as we prepared to go in yet again, not knowing when this endless merry go round of soup, no sleep, horrible weather, even more horrible zodiac rides, and of course the scary immersions themselves and then running the gauntlet of getting back on the boat from the zodiac as it lurched and reared. Then there were the doctor's visits and the sauna that smelled of diesel. But this wasn't really bothering the core group of us swimmers who were just getting on with things. We were now well used to the routine and we had adapted to it.

At this time I met Alexandr Brylin who had already stopped swimming, he was a classic example of a tremendous ice swimmer in the hole, one of the world's best, but in the ocean he struggled to operate as efficiently. We talked seriously about how to get across. One idea was that I would make a trip to Wales to speak to the native people and get some advice. Well, I favoured a phone call first but the idea of going on an excursion by zodiac wasn't a bad one, but I favoured trying little Diomede as that was the place where they had the most knowledge of all, being isolated from the world, 25 miles from Wales, 2.5 miles from Big Diomede and some 30 miles from the Russian coast. They made Wales seem far more cosmopolitan.

However, the reality of the situation was that we had got ourselves into this mess and now we would have to get ourselves out of it. I had a couple of ideas about the reactions we might get from native people if we asked for help and it was opinion that they would first say that we were mad to even be out in a boat in such bad weather and that swimming, well, we were even madder. Secondly, I expected that if they would take a boat out that they would want perhaps $500 per day which is both usual and reasonable for providing such a service. Yevgeny Noseeyev agreed with me about this and it raised an issue – this project had everything at its disposal but no ready cash. What could we possible offer them? A ride to Wales or Nome on the Irtysh? Some bread? Some chocolate? I didn't know and as much as I wanted to go on such an excursion it was unlikely to be useful.

I urged Sasha for someone to call Leonid which they did finally. There was talk about tides. According to my information it was a negligible tide with just 1 high and 1 low per day. Leonid Kokaurov put the Captain in touch with Tom Router of Alaska Maritime Agency and he gave what information he could regarding the tides and currents.

Now things were starting to get not only serious but a little bit blurred, working out what time and what day it was, now this wasn't easy anymore. At least we were still held together by our Vladivostok time and our call to the dining room 4 times a day. Oleg Dokuchaev as ever remained in good spirits even if he was under extreme pressure. This project was worth $2.5 in terms of the value of what had been given by the Russian far eastern Military district. Nobody could contemplate failure.

As we were looking at one of the maps up on the bridge Oleg chuckled and asked me where it was that I fell through the ice in Wales. I laughed and found the spot immediately. It seemed a long time ago now that I had received my arctic awakening, warning and emergency training in Alaska back in November 2011. Oleg didn't regard me as fool but instead rightly as a man who was driven to achieve the goal and get the job done. I could only see one way forward and that was to Alaska. I was in quite a serious mood as were the South Africans. Andrew Chin was a man of few words but he always spoke realistically. He was worried about our ability to break through the current. If we could only manage a few miles in an almost 24 hour shift then when would we actually reach the Alaskan shore?

After the talk about my falling through the ice, I dropped my guard a bit as we were downstairs waiting to swim and I loudly told everyone about my experiences with frostbite after my swim in Nome. Ryan Stramrood mentioned that he had also had some problems after one of his marathon ice swims in Murmansk and Tyumen. There was a sense of understanding, both us knew what it felt like and had a respect for what the cold, icy water could do. There is no way to hide from cold water it is too strong and too honest and if you are immersed for too long in extremely cold water it will do you some damage.

10.08.13 immersion number 9 big waves

The wind had become extremely strong and was not predicted to subside but this was beneficial for us as it was a north wind which would help us fight against the current coming from the south. It was sometime in the morning that we went out, without our breakfast, myself, Zdeněk and Alexandr (Komarov). The zodiac ride was interesting and the boat reared up and down. The sea was fierce and the waves were like weapons of anger released by the gods of the sea such was the fury we found ourselves in. This as always was going to be an interesting immersion. The water was up to around 9 or 10c and that kind of temperature posed no problems for us hardened ice swimmers. In fact it was almost an embarrassment that we were only swimming for 15 minutes, except this was the Bering Strait and quite frankly it was unnerving at best and terrifying at worst.

The waves were definitely getting bigger and bigger, the zodiac ride taking several minutes even though we were perhaps less than 1 nautical mile from Irtysh. The waves were so big that the zodiac was moving on a vertical plane but not much on the horizontal. It made for an exciting and varied ride that wouldn't have been out of place in a fairground. I was starting to feel a little weaker than normal, maybe it was the lack of breakfast but I had managed to eat some biscuits and chocolate so I'd had some kind of energy boost. For this reason and this reason alone I spoke to Vladimir Nefatov and told him that I had no problem swimming my allotted time but if I slowed down or couldn't make ground he should pull me out after 10 minutes. The experienced starter knew what I meant and agreed without hesitation. He was a reliable man was Vladimir Nefatov and I trusted him to do the right thing.

I had also been sluggish getting undressed but I was soon in the water and turning my arms over, trying my best to keep a smooth rhythm and streamlined shape as the waves crashed around me. We went on a course that took us parallel to the waves which made for an eventful swim. At least once I got absolutely gazumped by a large wave that left me with a gobful of saltwater and gasping for air. After such a gazumping (and that's the best word I can think of to describe it apart from the phrase "attempted drowning by the Bering Strait") it took a few seconds to get going again and this swim was difficult, the constant pounding was harsh and took its toll. I pushed as hard as I could but I wondered if my efforts were having any effect. This was the one time in particular when I had the feeling of being just a tiny insignificant human in a huge and powerful body of water with little power over my swimming destiny.

My time was up and Zdeněk jumped in and we tagged with me making my way to the back of the zodiac. Now came one of the most difficult tasks I had faced, namely getting into the zodiac when the waves were 3 or 4 metres high and seemingly growing. Two or three times I got close only for the zodiac to rear up like the uncontrollable beast it was. This was pretty damn scary and I feared for my safety. I managed to briefly get a hold on the boat but I was soon violently thrown off before I could get a second hand or foothold. This was like climbing but in the middle of the ocean.

Vladimir came over and finally I got a hold and hauled myself up, at this point Vladimir provided an extra arm and I kicked my way to the relative safety of the back of the zodiac. A few seconds later, gasping for breath and I was asking Vladimir, almost begging to know how much I had swum, he told me – 50m, in the right direction, so at least that was something. I had apparently spent 10 minutes swimming on the spot and then the current had let me through and I made 50m in the last 5 minutes. Well, I wasn't happy but I had at least made some ground in the right direction even if this was an average speed of 200m per hour. Zdenek and Alexandr (Komarov) managed a little bit more than me, 70 and 90m respectively so maybe the current was weakening gradually, after all we were of similar swimming speeds.

I was quiet and contemplative, angry with the new world for not letting us in. As we made our way back the fun started and the waves started to get extremely big and were rolling for a long time. It was quite something to watch although it was almost impossible to document well with either photo or video and I had given up trying, instead concentrating on getting back to Irtysh. Again the zodiac lurched up and down. We made it to 100 or so metres from Irtysh and this was where the driver of zodiac needed great skill and patience in order to bring the zodiac in to Irtysh and the platform. So far I had got back on without problems but this time it was a different story.

When it was my turn I watched the platform and zodiac changing heights as one minute I was much higher and the next minute it was vice versa. I did my best to pick the right moment but suddenly I was dangling off the end of the platform and the guys had to work quickly to pull me in. I got away with a few bruises and hobbled up the stairs. The South African team were waiting and they looked pretty apprehensive which is saying something, I couldn't speak much, it was obvious from a quick glance at my face and then the sea conditions to know what the state of play was, surely it wouldn't be long before another stoppage.

Irtysh was rocking violently and as I went to the doctor's room I peered into the sea and watched the enormous waves. It was quite incredible and I felt a range of emotions at once, fear, respect, disbelief and amazement. Here I was getting another lesson in the work of Mother Nature. I stumbled upstairs and wasn't able to say much apart from "I want a coffee and some porridge" and then just laughing. Breakfast was long gone and I tottered back to my cabin looking and feeling like a complete drunkard. For around 30 minutes I was completely out of it. Sure enough after the South Africans swim the relay was stopped. I could feel the waves getting bigger as Irtysh started to rock with more and more force.

The maximum height of waves recorded that day was some 7metres although when we made our GPS mark to stop the swim they were around 5m. This was quite big enough and on that day we swum through incredibly rough sea conditions and big waves. It had been dangerous for a long time and we were swimming by Bering Strait rules so this meant that the danger didn't start after a risk assessment but rather after you reached your fear threshold. As I said the canteen was closed so I had to make do with mineral water, ship's biscuits and chocolate. I lay on my bunk and tried to relax but Irtysh was lurching violently from side to side. We are talking about a 150m vessel here so you can imagine that the waves were now enormous. I'd had the chance to film these waves but apart from it being very difficult technically I really didn't feel like it. I should have gathered myself, persevered and made the film as it is these moments that are important. Hindsight is a wonderful thing but I can say now that I don't really regret not making that video as I know what it was like at the time.

There were similar moments during the swimming too when the camera went away as keeping warm needed full attention. Then there were times when we were simply shivering too much to make reasonable documentary footage, especially Paolo who on the 3rd swim was instructed by me to make a video of my swim. Unfortunately he had now been out of the water for 10minutes and being a contender for 'cold water shiverer of the year' – his footage was authentic but shakier than a long term drunkard a few days without a drink.

With the ridiculous sea conditions the swim had obviously been stopped again. We were now getting to the peak of what had become an old fashioned adventure in the style of Dezhnev, Bering or Cook. It is hard to explain it exactly but this expedition was completely unique and would surely never be repeated. It was only made possible by Russian desire and manpower, a throwback to Bering's second Kamchatka expedition which required 2 large vessels and many crew members. We had a swim and support team of around 90 and the crew of Irtysh which numbered 100. So we had nearly 200 people at sea in attempt to be the first people to cross the Bering Strait in its entirety by swimming. Now, more than ever I felt I was half swimmer, half old school mariner such was the courage needed to get into the zodiac for each mini swimming expedition. In some ways it would have been so much easier to swim longer legs with the water now around 8 or 9c but although the getting in and out of the boats was tricky, the 15minute swim was trickier. The waves were simply battering us.

During the semi darkness later that evening the tension was palpable, Nula Moore and Masha the Russian TV reporter had messages in bottles to throw overboard and what's more there was a notice that there would be a disco at 10.00. The first of these events I could accept, even if I had no interest in participating but the second event seemed preposterous and I made my thoughts clear, when I said "Ship's rules, quiet after 10pm." I knew people were frustrated and needed to relax but at the same time we needed to keep our military like discipline and complete the crossing with the Alaskan shore and the finish now so close. Thankfully the disco didn't happen and now all eyes and ears were focussed on the wind and waves.

Final day...final drama...

At 2am, Alexandr Jakovlev and Yevgeny Noseeyev went out for a reccy mission and before long the swim was back on with the first shift going out at around 4am. I had been in my cabin talking to Paolo and I was sure that today would be the day. We began making ground and the waves were big as usual. I had a good swim even if I felt tired, once again my only sustenance being ship's biscuits, chocolate and malkinskoye mineral water.

Finally our prayers were being answered and we were making ground towards the mainland. For me there was one more twist...I was due out again around 11am and as usual I was ready to go and waiting on the apron only to be told that I was off the rota and that I should rest. My immediate reaction was utter fury, especially when I saw Rafal Ziobro appear to take my place. He was no doubt a faster swimmer but during the difficult middle part of the relay with cold water and fog he had been largely absent due to sickness. Luckily I bit my tongue as he is a nice guy and played his part in the relay and by taking my place he was just following orders.

I shot off to find Oleg Dokuchaev, with my immediate mission to get back on the rota as soon as possible. I went first to his cabin but he wasn't there so I headed for the bridge. It takes some time to get around the maze of corridors on the Irtysh and after my initial 2 minute of fury I calmed down. When I got up onto the bridge I learned that

Oleg had left via the other side. At this point it needs to be stated that I am an endurance athlete, not the world's best but nevertheless that what I am. I've skied for 7 days in the high arctic, completed mountain ultra-marathons, swum winter swimming marathons and swum various 10km races with my record being 18km and also cycled marathon distances over multiple days, summited big mountains and trekked alone in the Siberian wilderness for several days. As such I can accept when I am a totally spent force although that has to be where I cannot physically continue like when I collapsed and passed out on a roundabout in France after yet another marathon day on the bike or when I got out just before the end of the mile winter swim at Lake Windermere, but try telling me that I must stop and naturally I simply cannot accept it.

Up on the bridge I met Alexandr Brylin and actually just by talking to him for a few minutes I relaxed. He hadn't swum for 2 days yet he was relaxed about it, pleased that we were nearing the finish and that we would finally reach our goal. Then I saw Yevgeny and he also had a calming influence on me. We took some photos and I peered through my binoculars towards the native village of Wales which was now coming into view. I made my way downstairs and finally found Oleg. As usual he was beaming a big smile and greeted me warmly. I made it clear to him that I was always ready to swim and he knew this and told me to relax and save my strength for the finish, he said that the bulk of our job was done it was now just a case of finishing it off.

My hot headedness had now worn off. I had been heavily involved with the swim, having been on 2 reccy missions, helped James Pittar, and also saved us in the fog with my GPS as well as at times giving some words of much needed encouragement. To miss one rotation was disappointing but not the end of the world. I could hold my head high safe in the knowledge that I had been one of the big contributors in this project over the years in myriad and sometimes invisible ways. As much as I wanted to swim I accepted that I was in the top 21 swimmers for speed but not the top 15 and it would be these people that would swim first. However, it didn't work quite like that because the current slackened with 8km to go and Alexandr Jakovlev came off navigation duty and instead took a stint in the water. He is the same speed as me. I didn't begrudge him another swim now it was easier after all he had done a lot of hours navigating and supervising in the zodiacs.

It has to be said at this point that such a swim is really all about a team effort, an absolutely massive one at that. It isn't about individual swimmers or even groups of swimmers but everyone together and the whole team, including the crew and the support team. So many people worked behind the scenes on the ship, in 6 hours on, 6 hours off shifts from tasks such as mechanics to zodiac driving, cooking, cleaning, navigating, medical duties and even fishing. (On reaching Nome I tried to show our appreciation for the crew by having a whip round and buying them all a small souvenir from Alaska, just as a small gesture of thanks.)

I relaxed in my bunk for a few minutes before ambling down to the canteen for lunch. I was now looking forward to the finish. I sat down next to James Pittar and got stuck into the soup. We chatted and generally had a nice lunch. Then James said he wanted to go outside so I began leading him to his room. All of a sudden all hell broke loose as Craig Lenning came running down the corridor telling James that he was going swimming, followed by a running Andrew Chin and Ryan Stramrood. I wasn't sure exactly what was going on but they were all very excited. Soon they were heading downstairs. I started to get an uneasy feeling and then I met Nuala who had a real look of concern on her face. She said to me "They are going to finish it." I couldn't understand that as were supposed to be having a mass finish, swimming with flags together to the shore. She told me "They are going to finish it, the 4 South Africans, Craig, James and Melissa." I told her that I thought that was strange because it should be a Russian that finishes it. At this moment I realized I had seen something like summit fever on the water as the finish was in sight. The zodiac left with those aforementioned swimmers on board.

I made my way up to the bridge trying to turn around in my head what was going on. Just a few minutes ago I had been enjoying lunch and now I was contemplating a confused and potentially wrong finish to the relay. Up on the bridge I met General Yuri Melnikov and the record was soon set straight. We spoke in Russian and I understood everything clearly now as I listened to him intently while he explained how the finish would be. He said "When we reach 1200m from the shore we will make a GPS mark and return to the ship. Then we will have a general meeting to arrange the final part of the mission, but I can tell you that it will be a Russian and an American that finish it and the rest of you will join with your flags." I was again calmer after hearing this and I started to wonder what on earth those guys were thinking of if what Nuala had said was true. If they did finish the relay then they would probably be better off staying in Alaska rather than coming back to the Irtysh as the general had been quite clear in the how the format of the finish would look.

Well, finally the boat came back and there was a little more drama. They hadn't reached the USA and finished the relay. I confirmed with Craig and James that their feet hadn't touched the bottom and therefore without a doubt the relay was still on. There was a strange atmosphere pervading the boat, something like euphoria and relief as we knew that we were about to finish this historic swim after at times it looked like the odds were favouring a failure.

As usual the meeting was held in the sports hall where General Melnikov told everybody his offer which was what he had already told me. Even though I had already heard all this I was nervous and I think everyone felt the same. This was perhaps the most important part of the project, the icing on the cake, the finish, our chance to enjoy the culmination of this spectacular intercontinental journey. He mentioned Melissa O'Reilly and there was quite a murmur to allow Elena Guseva some part in the finish. Melissa immediately offered the important American place in the finish to Craig and there was spontaneous applause. The idea was that Oleg Dokuchaev, a Russian would be greeted by an American on the beach. Oleg agreed that Craig could do this job after his exemplary conduct and the human qualities he had shown. I couldn't argue with that as he had been an example and a leader especially in his assistance of James even if he had shown something like summit fever at the end.

Finally the details were thrashed out although there was of course some confusion. Oleg addressed me asking "Jack, will you swim?" I was confused and answered "Of course, I will be a swimming journalist this time", pointing to my Go-pro camera, which brought a few laughs. So there would be a team of 4 Russian swimmers to continue the relay, with Oleg being the last of these 4. When he reached 300m from the shore, Vladimir Chegorin, one of the Amur swimmers would enter the water with the Russian flag, then a large group of us would enter the water with our national flags and regional flags of Russia, making for spectacular and colourful finish. Once on the shore there would be this symbolic greeting between the Russian and American swimmer.

We came out of the meeting and I met Andrew Chin in the corridor who was fuming. He couldn't understand why the final 4 swimmers were Oleg and his son after his son had only swum a little bit. I could see Andrew's point but I had no problem with the format of the finish or the people picked to do it. The final 4 swimmers were as mentioned Oleg Dokuchaev and his son Yevgeny, the youngest swimmer Alexandr Golubkin and Elena Guseva. Elena was trying to do this for the 4th time after first having swum in the Bering Strait when a young girl during the 1991 expedition which made it as far as big Diomede. Oleg was the chief organiser and I had no problem with his son and the young Golubkin being included, as young people need to be encouraged and inspired so that they can go on to bigger, better things.

Elsewhere there was confusion as Alexandr Brylin had been put in charge of the flags, after all swimming with flags was his baby and finally he would realize his dream of a mass finish, swimming with flags to the American shore. I quickly took the Union Jack, guilty of my own summit fever I said there was no way I wouldn't carry our flag onto the American shore. I did try to find Jackie to explain the situation to her but in the end it was fine as everybody who wanted to participate in the mass finish was able to with me and Jackie sharing our flag. I was clear and direct in wanting to reach America just like at the start when I went on the first reccy mission to Cape Dezhnev.

At 3.30pm, we were all to be ready and the first zodiac ferried the journalists to the shore. Then the rest of us piled onto the other 2 zodiacs. We were overloaded with about 12 people plus flags on each one. We made it to the GPS mark and the swim restarted. First the Golubkin boy and then Elena. As I looked across to the south east at Elena swimming beautifully I saw the edge of the Cape Prince of Wales and it was great sight, we had made it past the headland and we were into the calmer waters of the bay where the native village of Wales was situated.

We were all getting excited and soon Oleg Dokuchaev was in the water heading for land. The culmination of many years of work and the end was in sight. I had stood on that frozen beach 2 years ago, staring out at the nothingness in front of me and at the big hulk of the islands trying to make out the coast and wondering how and when we would get across. I saw the place where I had fallen thorough the ice and I chuckled to myself. It looked so different now, of course it was summer but also approaching from the sea made everything look totally different. Summer it may have been and the previous day had been sunny with air temperatures over 10c but today we were blessed with the more usual, typical weather which meant air temperature of 4c, combined with wind and rain.

The water looked inviting and we were all eager to get in. Soon our time came. I put my Go-pro on my head in an effort to make a personal document of the historic finish. I had also decided to keep my neoprene socks on. The reason for this was that the final swim with flags was not counted as part of the relay and I decided that having these socks would make for a more comfortable stay on Alaskan soil and also allow me to stay there for a longer time and perhaps do some exploring.

I jumped off the boat with the Union Jack and almost immediately ran into trouble. The neoprene socks slow you down which wasn't an issue for me. However, the 2 zodiacs started to converge as I went for a gap between them. I nearly got clobbered and had to frantically back pedal and come round the first zodiac, leaving me some way off the rest of the swimmers. Luckily it wasn't a problem as people were still jumping in.

I found Jackie and we shared the flag before I took it alone for the final 50 metres or so. Swimming with a flag is a unique skill that needs some practice, swapping hands isn't easy, but does help, depending on where the wind is. You also have to be very careful to keep the flag in an upright position. Crawl is possible but of course only with 1 arm. This swim wasn't easy and was a good metaphor for the expedition and the final 300m took some 8 minutes for us to reach the shore where euphoria took over. As we walked in Alexandr Yurkov came to me and as I saw his beaming face all the memories came flooding back to me. He doesn't speak much English but his favourite phrase is "Maybe, maybe..." and it had become something of a joke between us. Maybe we said and I tried to teach him the word definitely without success. It didn't matter we had finally succeeded and there would be no more doubts and maybe, we had arrived in America, 6 days and nights after we left the Russian coast exactly. We had faced all manner of conditions and the format of the swim changed from non-stop to staged but the important thing was that together we had covered the distance and therefore linked the 2 great continents by swimming.

There were many hugs and embraces as we met the local people. I saw Stacey Mueller, one of the school teachers we had met here in 2011, but I wasn't capable of stringing more than 1 or 2 sentences together. It was strange feeling which I guess is the feeling of success and at the same time the feeling of "OK we've done it, now what!?" Then I started to get really confused. I met Alexei, the record man and he was almost completely dry and fully clothed but wearing a life jacket. I asked him "How did you get here" and he said "I swum" I also saw Vladimir Nefatov who had his clothes on and then he changed into swim suit which was bizarre. Viktor Godlevsky was also wearing clothes and had even found time to visit the village shop and was munching on Doritos and a small salami sausage.

It was very strange, and the adrenaline was making it stranger. I couldn't get my head round how these people were dry and fully clothed when the zodiacs wouldn't land. Then I recognised some of the locals whom I had met before. We chatted for a few minutes and I asked one guy if he would take a boat out in this weather. Sipping from a thermos he said simply "No." Then he told me how they'd had their 3 days of summer already. Another added that the weather had been terrible lately even by western Alaska standards. The confusion and euphoria continued for some time. I was talking to some of the locals with Zděněkek and Craig. Suddenly everyone was running back to the sea and swimming for the boats, just as the locals were inviting us into the warmth of the school. I started to get very confused. I wanted to stay but how would I get back? The others such as Viktor looked like they even had their luggage with them.

Suddenly there was only Craig and me left. I opted to swim back to the zodiacs. At this point Viktor handed me his flag which was strange and even stranger perhaps was that I took it and was now faced with a near impossible task – swim back to the zodiacs with 2 flags in my neoprene socks! I would be exaggerating if I said this was the most difficult swim but it really was a test of endurance if only for another 8 minutes. Swimming with 2 flags is basically about not drowning while trying to go forward and somehow I managed this although just in the nick of time as the rest of the swimmers had long since safely boarded the zodiacs which were just about to head for the Irtysh when they saw me.

As I came towards the zodiac an arm stretched out to me but the problem was I couldn't grab it due to the 2 flags. Finally I got back on the zodiac with the help of Alexei Golubkin, the biggest drinker but perhaps the biggest heart and a fine and fearless swimmer. He saw my plight and helped to pluck me from the water. Now we set sail for Irtysh still in good spirits but desperate for the sauna. We had now been exposed to the elements for over 1 hour and the wind was blowing.

When we got back I was still looking for some of my things and this meant I was last off which in turn meant that I had to help James to disembark. I eventually reached the safe haven of the sauna and crammed in with everyone else, around 25 of us. We were pretty happy and it reminded me of the finish of the marathon swim at the world championships in Bled when we were all crammed into a tiny sauna. After my difficult swim and subsequent delay I was unable to go back with the gifts we had brought for the villagers but Zdeněk had quickly got dressed and he did that job, boarding a zodiac with Alexandr Brylin for a final brief visit to the native village of Wales. Meanwhile, the madness subsided and we went to the canteen for dinner. By this time the media and the last group had come back and the mission was accomplished, or at least the American shore had been reached, our official entrance to the USA would have to wait for Nome and the next day…

That day the only thing left for us to do was have a small celebration on the ship. At 20.30 we gathered in the sports hall and the medal ceremony took place. I didn't hear my name and almost missed my medal. General Melnikov embraced me and I gratefully took my medal. I am not much into these kinds of things so I hung around for just a few minutes before heading back to the peacefulness of my cabin.

A little later I ventured out to find that there was a small party going on, mostly with the guys from Blagoveshchensk. Andrey Mihailov toasted me which was nice and I stayed with them for a while. It was funny to watch Semyon Petrovich from Yakutsk dancing with Anne Marie Ward, a woman twice his size. It looked like maybe he wanted to take her back to Yakutsk with him.

My old friend Sergey Popov gave me a small gift and soon I left them all to it and went back to my cabin for what I thought was a well-earned rest. I contemplated our success and my mind drifted to the old explorers and particularly the naturalist Georg Steller who felt aggrieved that on the discovery of Alaska back in 1741 "10 years of planning had led to but 10 hours of exploration." Nevertheless Steller succeeded in recognizing and describing various new species of flora and fauna. We, on the other hand had prepared for a few years and finally the swim took 6 days and 6 nights, it was enough, we couldn't be disappointed and what's more the medical and scientific team had carried out many experiments on us to ascertain the effect of multiple cold water immersion on the human body. Soon I fell asleep, content that we had done it, even if we were now back at anchor in international waters just off the coast of Alaska.

Arrival in Nome

After finishing the relay we travelled to Nome, some 100 nautical miles. We dropped anchor 3 miles offshore in the Norton Sound. Our large 150m vessel the Irtysh was simply too big to make a port at Nome. Not that something small like that would stop us from entering the USA especially when many of our Russian friends had many dollars burning holes in their pockets and just as many friends and family waiting for authentic US souvenirs back home.

It soon became apparent that there was an issue with customs. Christian Vergara got on the phone to none other than Dane Robinson the lone ranger in sole charge of the US border at Nome and from where he used as a base to cover the Alaskan wilderness of the Seward Peninsula, primarily its coastline along the Bering Strait across to Russia. Outside the Nome Nugget hotel in downtown Nome there is a signpost pointing in various directions with the distances. Here you begin to realize the actual geography of Nome and its remoteness. LA 1900miles, London 4500miles, etc, and then Siberia 164miles is the closest place!

Anyway, Christian dealt with Dane and soon I was in on the conversation and helping to ensure the safe passage of everyone across the border. Christian told me that Dane was surprised by our arrival and that he didn't normally work on Sundays, although I have to say that I think it may have actually been Saturday in the USA. By this time everybody was completely confused by time although I knew what time it was in Vladivostok by our mealtimes even if my watch was confusing or wrongly set! On the bridge it was decided that the foreign swimmers go first. I went with them and as Christian rightly said "You better get the lowdown on the procedure for the Russians." Ira also confirmed this and I began to feel like some kind of spy or double agent...again I was acting out one of my James Bond fantasies! Actually the customs and border control for the foreign swimmers passed without incident. Dane came in his car and a queue formed just off one of the jetties in the small port. One by one we were stamped into the USA, after stepping off a zodiac and having previously swum across the Bering Strait from Russia. This was unprecedented even in the terms of Nome, a city which gets its fair share of crazy adventurers passing through. I felt reasonably comfortable about the procedures. Dane was a professional and had no problems with our unique entrance. There was one small problem in that we didn't have the list of those people who were coming. We asked for it to be brought and soon a zodiac appeared with the paperwork. My Russian had been working pretty well but I am not sure what happened at this point as Yevgeny the chief zodiac driver (and Russian Special Forces) told me that no more people were coming today. I agreed with Dane that we would probably be coming at 10am the next day and soon we were heading back to Irtysh. That was when I saw a mass of "Russia" tracksuits crammed into the other 2 zodiacs apparently heading for Nome. Then another load including Oleg and the kite surfers appeared on mine. I quickly got on the phone and told Dane that we were coming back. At this point I really began to feel like James Bond and I was constantly humming my favourite theme "*The man with the golden gun.*" This continued for several days.

30 minutes later and Dane Robinson was inundated with Russians and I was working as a translator, Rafael and Ira coming later. This was when a small problem started. The captain appeared in his full navy uniform. It turned out that he wanted to enter the USA. The problem was that they had not obtained a courtesy letter which is a simple document allowing the crew of ships onto land for 24 hours without a visa. This meant that the crew including the captain couldn't enter the USA. Despite being told by Leonid Kokaurov about this, it was dismissed as "under control" by the organisers. I am not sure exactly what went on but it is true that there was communication between the Russian and American military at a high level. Dane agreed to call his superiors to see if he could find a way around this problem. He mentioned the Renda tanker which was a Russian oil tanker that brought fuel to Nome from Russia when fuel ran out in winter 2011/12, effectively saving Nome and how nobody from even that vessel was allowed into the USA due to not having the correct documents. I tried my best to push him in a completely unpressured way. All I did was simply mention how we all knew including him that higher authorities in the USA were aware of our project and our potential arrival. Around this time, Sergey, one of the kite surfers and a Muscovite said to me "Tell him to call now." Then I took the bull by the horns and discreetly motioned for Sergey and our navigator, the kite surfer Yevgeny to come with me a few metres away for a quiet talk. I told them in a low and serious tone and they listened to me thankfully, that basically they wouldn't get anywhere with this low level guy and that he would not bend the rules but equally if somebody slipped off unseen into the city for a few hours it was unlikely to raise eyebrows, after all this was Nome and travelling any further would require a passport and valid visa. It might seem like I advocating breaking laws which I was but at the same time I was taking a common sense approach and I did the best thing I could given the situation. I am sure nobody

in Nome complained after the amount of cash that was spent. Admittedly there was a problem in the Bering Sea Bar but that was forgotten when the bill was paid. As for the Nome Nugget hotel, well perhaps they were a little put out by the Russians behaviour although at least our arrival ensured that their hotel was full.

I soon left them all at the border control when the translators Irina and Rafael arrived. I had done all I could and more. My next surprise was to see our Chinese swimmer Zhoung hanging around the main square in Nome. He sat down with 3 native Alaskans who turned out to be from St Lawrence Island. They were friendly and we talked for a few minutes. Zhoung seemed to fit in amongst them and I asked if I could take a photograph. It is one of my favourite photos from the trip. The 3 Alaskan natives, and our Chinese swimmer, sitting in Nome with the church in the background. If you look at that photo it says a lot about recent – and by that I mean late Holocene – history of the region. The 4 people look similar. We know that the Americas were populated by migrants crossing the Bering land bridge during the Pleistocene but we don't know exactly when. We also know that it is fairly certain that these migrants had originally moved up the East Asian coast from China. As for the church looming in the background, it was Europeans, missionaries that had played a big role in shaping the region in the last few hundred years. What it meant for our expedition I didn't really know but it seemed fitting to me that we should end here in Nome, a ragtag band of extreme swimmers, from different walks of life, different countries and continents. Here in Nome, this was a place representing a crossroads, and a journey in the history of human life. The great land Alaska, the new world, the United States of America was still the place where dreams could come true and broken hearts could be mended, like the lyrics from the song in west side story.

"I like to be in America, okay by me in America, everything free in America…"

Telling the story

On arriving back home or where ever it is that you might call home after a project like this a couple of inevitable things happen.

The first is that you suffer from some ups and downs as you struggle to adjust back to your normal routine. I had already negated this to some extent by making my short 'warm down' trip in Alaska. Then when I got back luckily I got a call from a friend who asked me to join a group to climb Wildespitze the next weekend, at 3776m the second highest mountain in Austria. I hesitated little in agreeing to this, so within 4 days of my arrival I was back on the adventure trail, and by the start of the next week I was really ready for my (semi) normal life. I knew that some of the other swim team members were having trouble with the transition but in my opinion they did themselves no favours in running back home immediately. I know it is easier said than done when there are families and jobs to think about but likewise you must also consider your own wellbeing.

Still one month on and Facebook was alive with Bering stories and I wondered how long it would be before this all died down – not that I was complaining as I was also a part of it and I was contributing my share. However, I did wish that rather than just posting huge amounts of photos people could at least choose a shorter and more meaningful slideshow for public display. My own preferred method was a maximum of 1 decent photograph per day. Naturally there were other members of the team who were posting and sharing nothing. I worked feverishly with my writing and also with choosing photographs, I had some quality in there but I was very much overwhelmed by quantity. It seemed that many people had enormous amounts of photos aboard the Irtysh but little of the action. I just got on with it the best I could and was extremely grateful when a short – 23 second – clip of the swim finish was shared on Dropbox. This clip was worth more than 1GB of samey "ship life" photos. As much as I sound grumpy I was also a romantic and looking at the photos was sometimes emotional and I longed to be back in the thick of the action in the Bering Strait.

The second problem that was faced by us on returning was the explanation of this incredible and unusual event to people, friends, family and strangers alike. There were so many complex aspects to this project that it would take several days to explain it in the spoken form and that was one of the reasons that I chose to write this book. I knew then that I could happily type away without being interrupted, pausing only for simple human reasons or as and when I pleased. Hopefully now the complexities of the project are far clearer and I have answered all those questions …

It is necessary when one has completed such a project to make reports in whatever form is appropriate and tell people about it, therefore hopefully negating the need for endless questions that are always forthcoming. For the asker it seems completely reasonable to ask a question such as "Why is it difficult to take a boat from Russia to the USA across the Bering Strait?" Asked like that it does seem like a simple matter, but far from it. Maritime law, customs and border procedure and international shipping are topics with myriad nooks and crannies waiting to invite you in when you attempt something slightly out of the ordinary and as such the simple answer doesn't suffice. I also remember the phrase "Don't make a mountain out of a molehill", usually heard when I was forced into doing something I didn't want to do or if I was trying to fake an illness to get out of school. Now this phrase is valid, it is all well and good but not when it comes to bureaucracy and bureaucrats. They are experts at turning the smallest bumps into summits of Himalayan proportions. Annoying, but at the same time these rules are what make our society function and it is right that you obey them or be prepared to face the consequences of non-compliance and I think we can apply this internationally across the board whether it be our own country's laws, neighbouring country's or another country on the other side of the world.

Cooperation is a word that means working together and this is what should be done. Negotiations are always possible to a certain extent but sometimes there is no room for manoeuvre and you simply have to accept that you can't do things exactly as you want to do them. An example of this would be when we unfortunately didn't have our permits to make port in Provideniya. Never mind, customs and border control came on board Irtysh and conducted the exit procedures there and so we proceeded after an unorthodox exit from Russia.

The only other option is to rebel against the system to change it which is not the smartest idea in the world and probably won't get you anywhere. In short, respect the rules.

We had finally achieved our goal and swam from Russia to America, across the icy Bering Strait. I breathed a huge sigh of relief for it had been a difficult journey, far more difficult than I could ever have imagined back in 2011. Make no mistake, forgetting the planning, the failures and the build-up, the swim itself took 6 days and 6 nights, far longer than we expected and we faced huge winds waves and currents, extremely cold water down to 2c, ambient air temperature of around 5c, and thick fog, but through it all our international team stayed united and together we reached our goal.

I hope I have managed to convey in the previous pages the reality of this undertaking and the ups and downs we faced during this time. It was a difficult period for me personally and perhaps it was time for a rest but in truth I was looking North again for a new challenge. I felt confident as I remembered the words of the great British sailor Captain James Cook who said:

"Do just once what others say you can't do, and you will never pay attention to their limitations again."